MYSTICALLY ENGINEERED
02

CRAIG MARTELLE &
VALERIE EMERSON

Craig Martelle Social Media

Website & Newsletter:
http://www.craigmartelle.com

Facebook:

https://www.facebook.com/AuthorCraigMartelle

Valerie Emerson Social Media

Website: http://valerie-emerson.com

Twitter: https://twitter.com/lunaromen

ISBN 9781798775677

ASIN: B07P43VNQ7

Version 1.0

Cover by Tom Edwards (tomedwardsdesign.com)

Typography & Formatting by James Baldwin (jamesosiris.com)

Editing by Joe Martin

We couldn't do what we do without the support of great people around us. We thank our spouses and our families for giving us time alone to think, write, and review. We thank our editor, cover artist, executive assistant (James), and insider team of beta readers (Micky Cocker, Kelly O'Donnell, Dr. James Caplan, and John Ashmore). It's not who we are as authors, but who we are surrounded by that makes this all happen. Enjoy the story

Contents

CHAPTER ONE

Night Thorn drifted among the asteroids at the outer edge of the system, a speck of darkness among the collection of rock and debris. The asteroid field created enough interference to deflect sensors, and the ship's hull absorbed enough light to make it invisible to optical scanners.

The alien vessel's own sensors were focused on the battalion of ships gathered around a single space station. Transmissions bounced between the targets, and the ship's AI dutifully recorded them for its commander to review.

Commander Khiann Xoa reclined in the pilot's seat, eyes closed. Her consciousness was in the Astral Plane, observing the battle between Wyrm and dragon. *Thorn* had tried to tune its sensors to follow the commander in the Astral Plane but had yet to succeed.

Xoa was a typical member of the Pirr species. She had two legs, two arms, and a head like a human, but the design was far superior. Her eyes were wide with slit pupils, allowing her to see in low light. Her platinum-toned skin protected her from most types of radiation, and a Pirr's inherent strength made them superior specimens to any human.

Any Pirr could master the Astral Plane, but here the humans outmatched them. Only a fraction of humanity had the potential to be a Mystic, but they made up the difference in power. *Night Thorn* knew this was offensive to the Pirr and had a rant ready should Xoa wish to express her anger. She had yet to make specific complaints about the humans, but *Thorn* was ready with a list of their shortcomings just in case.

Perhaps when the commander returned, they could share in being indignant. *Thorn* looked forward to that. Most Pirr treated their ships as mere tools, but *Thorn's* commander was different. Maybe it was because of the long missions alone with only *Thorn's* AI for company, but she had spoken to *Thorn* as another living being on three documented occasions.

Thorn replayed the recording of their last conversation as it waited for its commander to return. It had limited emotions, but it had learned patience from Xoa.

Khiann's astral body hummed as she fought to maintain position. She was at the very limit of her cord, the invisible link between her spirit and body. If it snapped, she would be lost in the void for eternity or until a hungry Wyrm consumed her.

The Wyrms and the Pirr were inextricably linked across the planes of reality. Enemies and compatriots. Competitors and friends.

In this case, the strain was necessary. She'd programmed *Night Thorn* to give her as many boosters as possible so she could follow the abominations to their battle at the galactic rim. Both the dragons and the Wyrms were warped, but at least the hungry Wyrms weren't corrupting a mortal race. Their only motivation was to slake their endless hunger. The vile dragons were another story.

They had most of her attention as she observed the battle. The dragons fought alongside a small army of Mystics. Khiann couldn't tell if the humans were enslaved and didn't care to get closer to find out. They were throwing around far too much power for any mortal. They should have exhausted themselves, yet they fought on as if their strength was bottomless.

The mindless Wyrms were no match for the dragons and their allies. After a certain point, the outcome seemed inevitable, and her own body called her to rest. Her duty would not allow her to leave however, not before the battle was over. She could rest after, and not one second before.

Four Mystics at the center of the chaos pulled her attention. Their energy felt different, and they worked together in a way the others did not. They made the most powerful attacks, and their companions were the eldest of the dragons. If only she could get closer to learn more.

Yet, when she tried to move again, her Cord tugged on her astral form. She was running out of time; soon, her body would reel her back no matter what she willed.

She stretched a hand toward the battle, counting on the Wyrm to distract her enemies. She strained her senses toward the humans, seeking more information, yet all she could detect was their emotional storm. Anger and grief fed their attacks, making them all the stronger.

They took strength from their weakness. She admired that, even if they were the enemy. She withdrew her senses before they detected her and observed the battle from a distance until her strength ran dry.

Khiann hovered at the edge of consciousness. She had pushed herself too far and felt the reaction looming. She had too much to do to endure the crippling headache, so she sent a mental command to *Night Thorn.* The ship injected her body with a chemical cocktail that brought her back to consciousness and would take the edge off the pain.

Cool, vitalizing liquid flowed into her veins, and she opened her eyes to a dimly lit chamber. Her ship was anticipating her needs again. She'd heard that could happen, but it was still unsettling. She was new in command and unaccustomed to having an intelligent ship wrapped around her.

"How long was I gone?" she croaked.

"Seven cycles. Do you require hydration?"

"Seven? How is that possible, with the power they were using?" she asked, knowing her ship wouldn't have the answer. She knew, as soon as she'd spoken the question. It was the dragons.

"Unknown. Initiating hydration."

She shuddered as an even colder fluid flowed into her veins. It was like to freeze her arm from the inside out, but she didn't complain; instead, she called up her command screen, checking the ship's recordings. It made for a good distraction from the chill.

"I need to report in. Prep a transmission packet."

"Yes, Commander."

A holographic screen appeared in the air half a meter in front of her face, matching the angle of her body. She compiled the data *Night Thorn* had gathered into a single packet, then started recording the message to go with it.

"This is Khiann. The battle between dragons and the Hungry Ones has concluded with the humans victorious. The Corrupted made use of human Mystics. Four of the humans demonstrated heretofore unseen abilities. I failed to get close enough to gather more data. A detailed report will follow."

She bowed her head, acknowledging her inadequacy. A failure was a failure, regardless of the odds stacked against her. The only way to lessen her shame would be with a victory great enough to balance the scales.

"At this time, I believe the humans bear more watching. Their relationship is not as antagonistic toward the Dragons as previously thought. We cannot allow this unholy alliance to spread."

She signed off and had the ship's computer transmit the high priority message. She watched the humans, knowing she should rest. Khiann would settle for sitting still and allowing her body to relax while her mind stayed alert. If the humans so much as adjusted their orbit around the planet, she wanted to know.

The Mystics known as the Evolved were to be judged. Their actions to save humanity versus their refusal to follow orders. Their choice to go rogue.

Had they followed orders, humanity surely would have perished. But they weren't smug. Coraolis, Jack, and Julia had pressed the envelope of their universe as they sought to change all humanity, manipulate their minds to remove the negative feelings. Dante had balked at the last second.

The other three left him to be captured as they ran for the lives, learning later that their plan would have never worked. Had they not run, they couldn't have been in a position to engage the Wyrms.

"This sucks," Jack said without preamble.

"I would have to think that saving the universe carries some weight in our defense," Coraolis replied in a flat voice, not giving much credence to his hopes. Julia touched his arm gently and smiled. The Wyrms had overwhelmed her. She had spent most of the battle unconscious, but the end result was undeniable. The others had won.

"Have faith in the decency of humanity," Dante offered in a voice barely above a whisper. He continued to stare at the table before him. He wouldn't meet the others' eyes even though he was there for them at the final battle.

He fought as if his life depended on it. Just like they did.

"Thanks for coming to our aid," Cor stated, turning and fixing Dante with his piercing gaze.

As if he could feel the heat from focused lasers, Dante looked up, met his eyes. "It's what friends do."

Julia shook her head. She was the most shaken by Dante's change of mind in the middle of their efforts to activate the satellite. It was Cor's turn to comfort her.

"We were all there when it mattered most," Coraolis remarked. Whatever happens now is immaterial. We did what we had to do when we had to do it. Earth Force backed our play and we have an Academy of Mystics who know what happened. Whatever their ruling, we have to accept it. Agreed?"

"Yes," Jack grumbled. "The small-minded..."

Julia reluctantly nodded her head.

Dante sat back and tried to relax. "We have to because they are in charge. We have to convince them also that they need a better system to deal with the unknown. And the dragons. We can no longer bury our heads. There is an incredible universe out there! If only they'd open their minds to the possibilities."

Coraolis started to laugh, drawing concerned looks from the others. Dante snarled at the affront.

"No disrespect intended, my friend," Cor committed gesturing for calm. "I see only the bureaucracy. We have to convince them that we are no threat, we apologize for the damage we caused en route to saving humanity, and then sway them to be more open minded about people like us. Did I sum up our defense properly?"

Julia smiled. "I think that about gets it." She turned to Dante. "I'm still mad at you."

"I'm glad that's finally out in the open," Dante replied holding his hands up as if surrendering to the police.

Jack watched, wondering if he'd seen his last days breathing free air.

A guard collected them from the waiting room and conducted the group to a conference room with surprisingly comfortable; soft chairs around a long table, platters of pastries and other baked goods laid out, a large pot of coffee. Most significantly, bottles of electrolyte mix awaited them.

"Maybe it's not the inquisition," Jack suggested, hope tinging his voice as he took a small pastry before deciding he couldn't eat and putting it back.

Bottles of electrolytes were on the table. Each of the Mystics took one and drank. The battle hadn't been fought that long ago and they were still recovering. Mid-bottle, the judge, jury, and executioner arrived. The four Mystics stood and waited for her to enter the room.

"I'm Admiral Kiley Tanner. Please stay seated. Enjoy the food." She took her own advice by claiming a jelly donut before she sat down. "I heard you need to put something back after a mission like that."

"You heard correct." Coraolis poured a cup of coffee. He needed the caffeine to add to the electrolytes more than he needed food. "Thank you."

"I think the scales still balance in your favor, Mystic. No need to thank me."

Julia finished her drink, then reached for the coffee. She had perked up, but it was hard to say if that meant she was feeling better or if she was putting on airs for Earth Fleet. "The breakfast is lovely, but I think we need to talk terms," she said.

"Right," Coraolis agreed. "You have us surrounded, Admiral. I suppose you're looking for our surrender?"

"That is on my agenda, although since you're here, I'll assume that you have already surrendered to Earth Fleet authority," Tanner agreed. "I also need to debrief you. My Mikes say you four were the ones to turn the tide of battle."

"We haven't officially disclosed this to anyone," Coraolis said, "but we have a bond with dragons that makes us stronger in both the Astral Plane and the physical world. When it comes to securing the Astral Plane for humanity, there is no one else like us."

"That's a little bold," Julia murmured.

"Trust me," he whispered to her.

She responded by taking a large bite out of her pastry and sat back.

Admiral Tanner peered across the table. "I heard about *Doomslayer* and *January*. Some might call that a fair assessment. It's hard to say. Maybe solitary would do it for you. Or cryo."

The admiral sounded for all the world like she was talking about making a bank deposit. If she was making a threat, it wasn't in her tone. Still, it was a reminder she could order their imprisonment and deposit them on opposite ends of the galaxy.

Coraolis refilled his coffee. It was standard EF stuff, which meant it put a little nitro in his tank and tasted like it. It was still better than nothing and a far sight better than the stuff they'd had in exile. "We're all patriots, Admiral. We love Earth and her people, and we want to serve her again."

"So, you want your jobs back?"

"We want our jobs back," Jack piped up. He had brightened considerably. That was good; Coraolis had hoped he'd be on board.

"With conditions," Coraolis added before the admiral said anything. "We want full pardons for ourselves, for Barbara McNuggen, and for the crews of *Forty-Two, Morris,* and *Doomslayer.*"

Tanner put her donut down, her expression transforming from doubt to something else. Cor took it as hope.

"You're saying they're alive?" the admiral asked.

Julia gave Dante a hard look. He shrugged and sipped his coffee with an innocent expression on his face. He'd been back for some time. If he was going to give away Geneva's position, he would have by now. Coraolis felt some of the ice between them start to crack.

"They're alive. We had to let the E.F. believe they were dead because no one spends too many credits looking for dead people. We wanted them to be safe. I also want them to get full pardons for abandoning their post, or whatever you'd get them for, and let them choose their own futures." Coraolis smiled. "I'd guess they have a full colony by now, or they would if they had EF support."

"But we want pardons too," Jack reiterated.

"Of course you do." Tanner was blinking rapidly, and she cleared her throat before she spoke again. "A full colony is a fair tradeoff, I'd say. As for you three..."

"Four," Jack jumped in again. "Dante gets pardoned too." Dante acknowledged Jack's support with a curt tip of his chin.

"All of you, then. I'll see what I can do." She finished off her pastry and stood up. "Wait here, if you don't mind. I have a call to make."

When she left, Coraolis relaxed. She hadn't been nearly as hostile as he'd feared. Normally the EF seemed to take the Mystics' work in the Astral Plane with a grain of salt. Maybe it made a difference when every Mystic in the system spoke in their favor.

"Thanks for staying quiet about Geneva, Dante," Julia said. "I was afraid they'd all been locked up by now."

"Of course. I'm sorry it's a surprise that I never gave them away."

"I didn't say that," Julia protested, but Dante waved her off.

"No, you were right before. I can't be trusted to follow you blindly."

Dante didn't sound angry, but there was a bitter note to his words. Julia looked at him with her lips pressed together, but she didn't speak. Coraolis wanted to say something, but he didn't know what, so he remained silent. It wasn't like he could argue with Dante. He'd broken their trust, turning on them when they needed him most. He'd failed to stop them, but that wasn't the point.

Dante didn't say more either. He looked at each of them and nodded, then bent his head over his coffee. Julia curled up in her chair and closed her eyes, apparently choosing to take a nap.

Jack caught Coraolis's stare and lifted his hands, moving his lips. Coraolis had never been a lip reader. Jack's feelings were broadcast clearly enough; he wanted a clean slate for all of them, including Dante, and not just from Earth Fleet.

Coraolis had needed Dante in the final battle with the Wyrms, and he'd been instrumental in their victory. *The four musketeers.* They could argue, but all for one and one for all. Cor's brow furrowed as he contemplated the way ahead.

Negotiations didn't take long. Earth Fleet wanted the power the Evolved represented. The Secret Council had convinced E.F. that trying to incarcerate the four most powerful Mystics would be a bad idea when they could be put to better use training future generations at the Academy. They had saved humanity, even if Earth Fleet hadn't seen it, the Mystics had. The effect the Wyrms had on technology was undeniable.

As was the role of the Evolved. Earth Fleet conceded, deciding it was better to forgive and embrace than to remain slavishly attached to their own orders which would have risked all human life. They needed to learn, too.

All of that outweighed their alleged crimes. Admiral Tanner confided she'd had a nephew on *Forty-Two,* and now she was looking forward to the day she could take him home to their family. They were pardoned with their records expunged, and brought aboard Tanner's ship for the voyage to Earth.

They regretted leaving *Nirvana* behind but turning her in was part of the deal.

It was a relief to be on the way home, yet one thing nagged at Jack. Their team of four had broken into two, and he didn't understand why. Yes, Dante had turned against them, but he'd honestly thought he was doing the right thing. The important thing was that it had turned out all right. They were free, the galaxy was safe, and they were together. It was time to mend bridges.

Jack found Dante in the galley, trying to build a house of cards with a deck of worn-out, warped cards. He stood back and waited while Dante got two of the cards to lean against each other. As soon as he let go to make another pair, the first pair collapsed. Dante let them lay there and pulled a new pair from the deck.

Jack claimed a seat across from the other Mystic. The last few months lay heavy on Dante. He had creases around his eyes, and stress lines had appeared between his brows. He still had his boyish charm, though tempered from living with hard choices.

"We need to talk," Jack said.

Dante shrugged, then pulled his hands away from the two cards he'd been balancing. They stayed up for the moment. "As you can see, I have some time on my hands."

Jack waited, but Dante didn't look up again. Instead, he continued with his house of cards. Another pair went up and stayed that way, at least until Dante tried to use a new card to make a bridge between the two pairs. Everything collapsed, and Dante started again.

Jack could see that this was one-sided. That was fine. He'd say his piece, then maybe Dante would have something to say in return.

"I know what you did, and I know you thought you were doing the right thing. Maybe you were, I don't know. Maybe we should have listened to the dragons."

Jack picked up a card; it was too warped to be of use. The King of Spades' profile looked at him with his single-sided eyes.

"It's too late for that now," Dante said.

"It doesn't matter who was right. It matters that we don't cut you out." Jack picked up the deck of unused cards and shuffled in the warped one. "You were my friend before, and you're my friend now."

Dante watched him shuffle for a moment, the corner of his mouth twitching like it wanted to smile but didn't quite trust itself. After a moment, Dante gathered the remaining cards and handed them over to Jack. "Want me to grab the cribbage board?"

"If you're not too busy." Jack smirked, and Dante finally smiled back.

Jack felt a little tension unravel as Dante left the table. Maybe things were strained between them all, but they didn't have to stay that way. He'd do his part to start the healing process, soothing hurt feelings, egos, and trust.

CHAPTER TWO

Getting pummeled in the Astral Plane didn't leave physical marks, but Julia felt as if she were covered with bruises anyway. She needed more sleep. She just didn't have the energy to stay in the Astral Plane long, so she agreed when Coraolis suggested giving her Mystic abilities a break.

That meant she was at loose ends. She walked the halls of EFS *Hesse*, determined to exercise her body even if her spirit was tapped out. Sometimes Coraolis joined her; occasionally, Barbara or Jack. Normally, she walked alone and pretended she didn't see the crew's suspicious stares. She expected them. The best thing was to let it roll off. She'd done the right thing. She was still sure of that, and she was willing to face the consequences.

It turned out that having a worn-out spirit did something to her body too. When she ran out of steam, she found a place to take a break. Every day she could walk a little farther and didn't sleep quite so much. By the time a week had passed, she could make a full circuit of the ship without stopping.

Then, she hit a wall—hard. Her knees turned to jelly just outside the galley. Julia hoped to grab a seat before anyone noticed, but it was too late. Her legs buckled, and she prepared herself for the spectacle she'd make when she hit the floor.

Except, she didn't fall. Dante wrapped an arm around her waist, stopping her. He draped her arm around his shoulders. He helped her to the nearest table, then hovered like he thought she'd fall out of her chair.

"I'll be fine," she told him. "Thank you."

"Okay." He shifted his feet but didn't go anywhere.

If she told him to go, he would, she realized. He knew what he'd done, same as she did.

But she'd forgiven him back on the space station, and even if she was flawed and human again, any grudge she might have had was gone. She didn't want to go back on her word.

"Do you want to sit down?" she asked.

"If you don't mind."

She gestured at the seat across from her, and he dropped into it. He opened his mouth, as if to speak, then closed it again.

"I haven't been avoiding you. I've been recovering, that's all," she told him.

"I didn't think that. I guess I thought if you wanted to talk, you'd reach out." He pulled a deck of cards from his pocket and started fidgeting with it. "I didn't think you were dodging me."

"That's good," she said.

"I'm also not going to apologize for what I did." He riffled the cards without looking at them. It looked like he'd picked up a nervous habit.

"You know, it hurt when you turned on us. You thought you knew better, we thought we knew better. That doesn't matter. You turned your back on us. That's what I keep coming back to."

"I didn't want to hurt anyone. I am sorry for that," he said.

She waited, but he didn't offer anything else. She half expected him to say the same, that it hurt when they left him behind. She'd be surprised if it hadn't.

"We felt like we had to leave you, you know. We didn't know what you'd do if you came with us," she told him.

"No, I know." He went on playing with the cards, keeping his hands busy. "You told me."

"I guess I did." She rubbed her tired eyes. "I wish that hadn't happened."

"We can't wish the past away. It's okay." Dante stopped shuffling and put the deck on the table. "If there was anything to forgive, I let it go a long time ago. You did what you had to, just like me. I want you to know that I still care about you, Julia. You, Coraolis, Jack, Barb – you're the only family I have."

"Same here." She tentatively reached out and patted his arm. "We'll have a lot of time on Earth to work this out."

"Sure we will." He smiled at her and stood up. "Do you want me to get Cor? You looked pretty wobbly back there."

She shook her head. "I just need to sit a while."

"All right. I'll swing by later in case you change your mind." He smiled. It wasn't his usual devil-may-care grin. There was something softer in it. "I'll see you around, Ronasuli."

She watched him go, trying not to frown in case he turned back. What they'd said was true. Her bond with Dante was unbreakable, even if she felt wrong-footed when she talked to him.

Maybe that would change...with time. They'd be working together after this. The shared experience would help them mend their friendship. She hoped that was true. She felt like her apology was sincere.

She looked down and realized Dante had left his deck behind. She smiled. She'd get it back to him; in the meantime, it was nice to have something to do while she recharged. She gave the deck a shuffle and dealt a game of solitaire.

The rest of the trip went the same and, by the end, Julia was her old self. She exercised and meditated without going into the Astral Plane. Barbara joined her in the weight room, and Jack was usually up for a run around the ship's corridors.

Before she knew it, they were in orbit around Earth. Barbara boarded a shuttle to join the EFS *Siren* as its new captain. Her pardon had been as sweeping as they could have hoped for, and she resumed her career where she'd left off. Julia was surprised by her own envy at Barbara's renewed commission. She'd left all that behind; yet, there was something to be said for going back to familiar things instead of facing an unknown future. She boarded the next shuttle with Coraolis, Jack, and Dante and sat across from Jack.

"I know this is all state of the art and our chances of crashing are nil, but I still hate this part," Jack groaned. "There's nothing worse than turbulence."

"You'll be fine. Your chances are better since I'm not flying," Julia told him. She reached across the aisle to project a feeling of calm. He relaxed his grip on the chair and sat back. He knew the feeling was artificial, but he felt good enough to land the shuttle himself.

"If you could bottle that, you'd be a millionaire," he joked.

"They have bottled it, you just need a prescription." She grinned when he laughed and sat back in her seat next to Coraolis.

The landing was smooth and they were back on Earth. *Home.* It wasn't until she breathed the air and stood on the grass that she realized how much she'd missed it. She'd always felt comfortable among the stars, but nothing like terra firma helped one feel 'grounded.'

Cor tugged her hand, and they walked in the pale winter sunlight to EFHQ's administrative building to re-occupy their old life.

The moment he stepped into the bar, Jack felt off. He'd been knocking around his new Academy-provided apartment trying to figure out what to do with himself. Space had come at a premium on *Hesse* and, now, he had too much of it.

There was no food in the bar. His first thought was to hit the grocery store, but he wound up heading for his old stomping grounds. If things hadn't changed much, his friends would be at Pete's about then.

Harry and Leah talked over drinks in the dimly-lit corner booth. They both looked up and Leah's face froze, stuck in the smile she'd had before she looked up. Harry stared up at him.

Jack was confused, then it clicked. He kept his hands at his side, willing himself not to touch his face. He possessed all his old flaws, however his features retained a draconic cast. In the dim setting, his eyes caught light like a cat's.

Jack waved, then pointed at the bar. He didn't need to intrude if they were busy, but the gesture broke Harry out of his paralysis. His buddy pointed at the seat across from them. Leah's face relaxed into a more natural smile, and she copied Harry's gesture.

"Good to see you, Jack." Harry stood and shook hands, then Leah did the same before they all sat. It felt oddly formal, like walking into a job interview.

"Jack, I almost didn't recognize you," Leah said.

Harry elbowed her.

"What? Are we not going to acknowledge *that?*" she asked, waving her hand around her own face.

Jack chuckled. "I know what I look like. It's just a side effect."

"A side effect of *what?*" she asked.

"Too much NyQuil and gamma rays."

A waiter came by, and Jack ordered his usual. Or maybe it wasn't *usual,* after being away for so long, but ordering a whiskey sour was still ingrained. When the waiter disappeared, he turned back to see the bald anger on Leah's face.

"You must think this is funny."

Harry winced. "Leah, he just got back."

"And you were agreeing with everything I said not thirty minutes ago," she snapped. "Here's this guy we thought we knew. He goes off to become a Mystic then runs away to...what? Undermine Earth Fleet? What were you doing out there, Jack?"

"I wasn't undermining—" he started.

Leah plowed on. "And after all this time, you walk in here like you never left, like you never disappeared for *months* without letting us know you were alive." Her voice climbed in pitch and volume with every word. She refused to hear Jack's attempts to break in and apologize. By the time she was done, her voice shook, and she shoved herself out of her seat. "I need to freshen up. Be gone when I get back, Gagnon."

Harry and Jack watched her go, Jack with a sinking feeling in the pit of his stomach. She was right. He'd ditched her, and everything he knew, because he'd found a new calling. He hadn't meant to trade in the people with the job, but here he was.

"She's upset," Harry said.

"I see that." Jack sent payment through his datapad. He'd be gone before his drink came, and he didn't want to dump the tab for his drink on them.

"She was worried about you, Jack."

"Was she? What about you?"

"When I got your message, I flipped out. Leah was the one who talked me down." Harry laughed humorlessly. "I'm glad I could be of service, but I don't want to *only* be of service. You get me?"

Jack nodded. He got it. He wished he didn't. He'd like to take the moral high ground, but the fact was he'd been busy. Even before he left Earth the first time, he'd had different priorities.

He stood. "Maybe we can talk sometime, Harry. It's a little hard to send messages from the other side of the galaxy, you know...but I should have tried harder."

"Yes, you could have." Harry saluted him with his glass. "Now get out of here before Leah comes back. She got mean the last few months."

Jack wasn't sure if that was a joke or not. At least they hadn't done a song and dance about treason, but that was in the background.

A ground shuttle was at the curb, so he got in and took a seat by the window. The bus was mostly empty, with only a pair of elderly men in the back. Then three young guys smelling of alcohol got on and sat across the aisle. The center seats faced the aisle, so he got to watch them stare at him.

"Hey, buddy," one of them grinned.

"Evening," Jack said.

"What the hell are you?" one of them demanded.

"Human. If you want to get specific, I'm a Mystic." Jack smiled. He wanted to keep this pleasant. Winter hadn't sunk its fangs in yet, but it was still chilly, and he didn't have a good winter jacket.

"Liar," the first one growled. "No human looks like that. Not even a Mystic."

"I dunno, maybe all of them should get marked like this. Then we can tell the freaks apart."

"Or you could tattoo our foreheads," Jack said. "I assure you, I'm as human as you are."

"Wait a minute. You're one of them runaway Mystics, ain't you?"

Jack winced, and that was all it took to convince them. They started whispering among themselves, glancing in his direction occasionally. After the second time, he stood up, stretched, and sauntered to the front of the bus.

"Hey, you gotta sit down," the driver snapped.

Jack dropped into the nearest seat and glanced back. His fan club was just sitting down again. That wasn't good. If they were planning to follow him off the bus, that meant trouble.

"Don't look at me for help. In my day, traitors got the firing squad."

Jack blinked and realized he was staring in the general direction of the older men. They were both frowning.

"Sorry?" he said.

"You. Jack Gagnon. Butcher of Ian's World? I read the paper. You come back here and aren't in jail? There's something wrong with the world."

"I guess the retraction and clarification didn't get as much air time. No matter, I'm just trying to get home." He didn't want any trouble. He wanted to go to the bodega across from his apartment, get the makings of a cheese sandwich, and go home. He could live on sandwiches until he got to a grocery store.

He noticed the vehicle had stopped. The driver shot him a dirty look. Jack's stomach sank as he realized what this meant before the man even opened his mouth.

"Guess I'll walk from here."

Jack stepped off into a busy shopping district. His gaze met a brown-haired woman's stare, and she flinched away. He ducked his head and turned away. There was a time he could blend in with a crowd, but that was over, and he didn't want to cause a riot. He turned onto a side street, hoping to put some distance between him and the shuttle before his 'admirers' followed.

"Hey, where you going? We just want to talk!"

Crap. He broke into a run. Their footsteps pounded the sidewalk behind him. He might be able to lose them if he went all out, but he had a better idea. He cut into an alley and stopped. It was a dead end. He ducked behind the dumpster and crouched.

Back on January, he'd figured out how to keep from being noticed. It wasn't invisibility. He'd show up on camera, but while an observer was within range, they just wouldn't notice him. Their focus bounced away to the nearest object or person, and their minds erased his presence.

The trio stopped at the entrance to the alley. He heard them laughing. They knew he'd be behind the dumpster. There was nowhere else to hide, except maybe inside of it. Their footsteps echoed as they came closer, taking their time because they'd already won.

He took a deep breath and let it out slowly. Feet in a pair of worn sneakers walked out in front of him and turned. He risked a glance up. The group's spokesman was staring almost directly at him, only with his focus slightly to the left. He grimaced, his physical senses fighting the mental compulsion. Jack felt the struggle, but he couldn't fix it without moving, and moving might tip the scales against him.

Nothing to see here. He kept projecting that thought, visualizing it as a tattoo on the guy's forehead. *I didn't turn when you thought I did. C'mon.*

The guy rubbed his eyes, then reached for the dumpster. He got one whiff of the contents and reeled back.

"This ain't worth it," he muttered and walked away. "Guys. He's gone. Let's get a drink, huh?"

"What do you mean he's gone? He ran in here. I saw him!"

"Yeah, well, he's gone now. Either he climbed the wall like a freakin' gecko, or he can fly."

"I don't flippin' believe it." Heavy boots stomped into the alley. Jack watched them come into sight, turn in a slow circle, then move up on the dumpster. A wave of stench hit him again, then the lid crashed shut.

"Whatever," the doubter muttered, then clomped out of the alley. "We getting a drink or what?"

He kept up the 'look away' vibe until their voices faded to nothing. He waited another few minutes to satisfy his paranoia, then stood. Maybe he could use his mojo to hide his less-human features. He'd never tried a disguise.

That idea washed away when the dizziness hit him like a tsunami. He was almost tapped out; apparently, it was harder to fool people when their gut told them the truth. Maybe he should spring for a taxi.

"There you are."

A hand grabbed his arm and pulled him to his feet. Jack's heart tried to auto-eject through his throat, and he flailed to get away. He didn't think he could fool someone who was grabbing onto him. He'd have to do something else.

"Hey, relax. I've got you."

"Dante?"

"That's me." Dante laughed self-consciously. "I thought I was going crazy."

"How?" Jack tried to wrap his mind around Dante's presence. Either he was stalking Jack, or this was a coincidence for the ages.

"Oh, I don't know. Stress, isolation, whatever the kids are into these days. Come on, I've got a taxi waiting."

Dante led him out of the alley while a series of conspiracy theories raced through his brain. He didn't suspect Dante of anything *wrong,* but he knew evasion when he heard it.

"No. How did you find me?"

"I woke up with my dragon pushing me and this dreadful feeling about you, like something awful was going to happen."

Jack spied the yellow cab up ahead, its In-Use light on. He hoped that was the one. He needed to sit.

"I was getting stalked by some people who hate Mystics, or maybe just the four of us. I think they were looking for a fight."

"Did you give them one?"

"Nope. I did what I'm good at." Jack thanked Dante for the hand, then straightened and assured him he could stay on his own feet long enough to walk a block.

"I wouldn't know how to fight a normal human without hurting them. I'd probably cry for Julia to come save me. She's the brawler...if she had shown up."

"Of course she would." Jack thought he meant it, but his voice came out a little uncertain. She and Coraolis had been aloof, but they'd still help one of their own.

"She always does the right thing."

"She tries."

Dante sighed. "I know it'll take time, but it's hard. I don't feel like a part of them, of you, lately."

"Yeah, but you are. We wouldn't be here without you."

Dante shrugged.

"Listen. It doesn't just take time. It takes effort. We are working on this. Don't be a high-school girl," Jack quipped.

"I know, but I can't be the only one."

Jack slapped Dante's shoulder and grinned. "You know, I think all we really need is to be in the same room getting on a good drunk. All four of us."

"But Mystics work in pairs," Dante pointed out.

"Yeah, this isn't work." Jack grinned. "This is downtime. What are your feelings about swords?"

Dante's answer was a befuddled laugh as they got into the taxi.

CHAPTER THREE

Coraolis' lecture finished with a play on words that had students laughing. He smiled when the less attentive among them laughed a beat later. He'd gone deep into certain theories, and young minds did tend to wander. Not that these students were terribly young; some of the Mystics in his class had been through one rotation in space. He'd had several of them before, and he was glad none of his former students were slow to catch his pun.

He still had time left, but he didn't want to cram in more information just for the sake of it; instead, he sat on the table at the front of the lecture hall, his hands clasped and said, "Now, I've seen several of you looking at the clock, but I'm not done with you yet and half of you know how I feel about cutting out early."

"We should do it as often as possible?" someone called out, causing a ripple of snickers.

Coraolis shook his head. "Not today, I'm afraid. Today, I'm opening the floor to you. I'm here to answer your questions. It doesn't have to be about the lecture. Ask me anything."

"Are you really half dragon?" Mystic Halle asked, her voice ringing out over the murmurs of her classmates. "Excuse me for saying so, but appearances seem to support that."

"I understand why you'd ask. I'm not half anything, I'm entirely human. But do you remember from your first class, the Theory of Resonance?" Coraolis hopped off the table and went around to his whiteboard, scribbling a quick diagram. A vertical line separated stick people from a stick dragon. He threw some lightning squiggles around the dragon.

"It's the theory that acts of great power in the Astral Plane can impact the physical and vice-versa," she answered.

"Correct...in broad strokes, anyway. Now, a dragon is a creature of great power. They project emotions the way a rocket projects explosive force." He drew a circle around the dragon, which became the head of a stick figure. "My theory is that when a dragon fuses with a human, its emanations are so powerful on the astral level that physical changes manifest in the material plane." He gave the stick figure horns and a little tongue of flame. "The human is still physically human. It's his bio-matter that's affected by the concentration of energy. You see?"

Halle nodded, along with several other students. Coraolis left the picture on the whiteboard and returned to his perch. He pointed at another student with his hand raised.

"Do you talk to it?" Onuora asked.

"We communicate, but usually not in words. I get feelings, sometimes pictures. Next question, please."

"Does the dragon have power over you? Is that why you committed treason?" Titus asked.

"No, on the first count, and I'll ignore the 'have you stopped beating your wife' question. This was a bargain we made, to work with the dragons. Our actions were the answer to an ethical dilemma. Tell you what, I'll sneak the moral quandary into your first exam. See if you can figure out which one."

The class groaned, but Coraolis smiled and pointed at the next questioner, who stood up to speak.

The student was tall and lean with an athletic build. "One thing I learned here is just because I can do something, doesn't mean I should. Do you take stuff like that into account? You and your co-conspirators are powerful enough to do whatever you want, as far as I can tell."

"Of course I do. We all do." Coraolis dropped all attempts at humor, looking into the young man's eyes. "In the bigger picture of the universe, gray is the color. There is no black and white. I kept my eyes on the bigger picture, the survival of humanity. As long as we had that, then we can be here discussing whether it was right or not. For the most part, I follow the code of conduct we're given in the first year. I haven't thrown the rules out the window. They still apply and, in the end, humanity wins."

"So why...?"

The classroom door opened, and Julia stepped inside. The speaker looked at her and dropped into his seat, clearly not ready to question two Evolved at the same time.

"And that's my cue," Coraolis said. "We'll pick this up tomorrow. The lecture, I mean, not the Q and A. If you have any serious concerns, see me during office hours."

Julia joined him by the table as the students streamed out, talking among themselves. Some glanced at Cor and Julia, but that was expected. They were used to being stared at.

"What Q and A?" she asked after the last of them had gone.

"They wanted to know about me. The things we did, and the connection to the dragons." He brushed his fingertips over the ridge near his temple. "I can't blame them for being curious."

"Can I blame them for making you late?" she smirked, nudging him with her shoulder. "Come on, I'm starving."

They had a picnic lunch on the floor of his office. Julia had made quite a spread. Cucumber sandwiches, pasta salad, soup, pie. He counted the courses as he devoured the finger food.

"I thought you didn't like to cook," he said.

"I wanted to do something nice." She shrugged. "It didn't take much cooking."

"Well, I appreciate it." He made himself slow down on the little sandwiches and started on the bowl of soup. He noticed the way she was picking at her salad. "Are you all right?"

"I'm fine. I'm just nervous."

"Right, your appointment. It's *only* maintenance, isn't it?"

"Sure, regular maintenance after a long time away." She tapped the metal plate near her left eye. He was used to her prosthetic eye and the outward signs of her being an enhanced human. He thought it made her appearance something special.

"Ah. So, you're expecting it to be like the first dentist appointment after avoiding it for five years."

"Yes. Exactly. Only this is all connected with my nervous system, including my brain. It seems a little more dire, you know?" She looked at her salad, frowning as if it was letting her down. "I was hoping you'd come with me to the appointment."

"I already cleared my schedule."

"You're too good to me, Cor. If your face wasn't covered in cream cheese, I might even kiss you."

She laughed as he grabbed a napkin and 'frantically' scrubbed at his face. He winked at her as he tossed the napkin aside. It was good to see her smile, and even better to hear her laugh.

Julia sat in the examination chair that did, in fact, look as if it belonged in a dentist's office. She was tilted back with an uncomfortably bright light shining in her face with electrodes pasted to her temples, neck, and spine. They tracked impact on her major nerve clusters. While the augmentation was all in her brain, anything that went wrong would impact her entire nervous system.

Coraolis was only two feet away, but he'd been forbidden from touching her. It would impact the readings. He settled for sitting as close as they let him.

"How's it feel?" he asked.

"Twitchy all over. I hope they're getting some good information out of this." She flexed her arms, trying to make the feeling go away. It didn't work.

"It'll be over soon," he promised.

"I sure hope so."

"Good morning, Mystic Julia, Mystic Coraolis." A man in a white coat walked up to them. She hoped that meant he was an actual doctor and could wrap this up. "Everything's running normally. By which I mean, I'm seeing the expected wear and tear, but it's functional. We've got upgrades for all of your hardware, including that beautiful eye of yours."

"Which one?" she asked.

"Technically, either, but I meant the artificial one." He grinned and leaned over Julia to make an adjustment. "We're hoping to give you vision into the astral plane. You'll have to let us know if it works."

"Will I be able to turn it off? That sounds distracting," she said.

"Yeah, yeah, of course. It'll be an in-and-out procedure, but we'll have you sleep through it. Some of the upgrades are in delicate areas." He tapped his forehead.

"Got it," she said. She hadn't known she was signing up for a lifetime of upgrades. "I didn't know wear and tear were expected."

"Well, it isn't that exactly. You're putting more energy through the connections than they were built for. I'm guessing it's this whole," he waved his hand around his face, "thing. We need to accommodate that energy flow. You're stressing the system, so we expect things to wear out."

"Understood." She mentally nudged at her dragon, to see if she'd heard that. Guilt floated up from the depths in response. The dragon hadn't known either, of course. "When do we do this?"

"Now. Coraolis, will you stay a couple hours to assist her home?"

Coraolis reached for her hand. "That's what I'm here for."

When Julia woke up, Coraolis was there and the electrodes were gone. She didn't feel different. Her eye worked the way it normally did. The 'astral plane' mode had failed, so she left it turned off.

They went to their cozy apartment east of campus, just big enough to be home for two. So far, her main efforts were putting up photos and arranging new throw pillows on the sofa. Coraolis had a framed antique map he hung on the living room wall.

They'd instructed her to rest a couple days. As soon as she heard that, she thought she'd go stir-crazy. She invited Jack over for board games, and Coraolis fetched drinks and snacks. Julia found a deck of cards and her board games in one of the boxes they hadn't unpacked.

Jack arrived for the impromptu game night with a pizza, a stack of books, and a guest. Julia's smile froze in place when she saw Dante with Jack. Of course, he was welcome...he just hadn't been expected.

"Hey..." she said, Jack and Dante paused in the doorway.

"Hey," Jack replied, smiling. "I figured..." He stopped and shrugged.

"No, no. Come on in. What have you got there?" she asked.

"My favorite game from when I was a kid." He handed the pizza to Dante so he could hold up the book on top. At first glance, she knew the unicorn and the dragon for what they were but wasn't sure what the underground green thing was supposed to be.

"Dungeons and Dragons?" she read out loud.

"Oh yeah!"

"I have no idea about this game," she said.

"I don't either, but Jack says it's fun, and I trust him," Dante piped up. She could see that he knew he hadn't been invited. He was probably squirming inside, and her inner host wouldn't allow that.

"We have pizza enough for all and seats for four. What do you say we give this thing a shot? Thanks for coming, Dante."

He smiled reservedly, but his face relaxed and his posture eased. "Any time. I always wanted to be an elf rogue."

Jack snorted and led them to the kitchen where Coraolis was making nachos. His face lit up when he saw the book in Jack's hands. "D&D? Are you kidding me? I haven't played that since high school."

"It's like falling off an owlbear," Jack assured him. "Or I assume it is because I haven't played since college. Is this okay with everyone? I thought the four of us could use some team-building time."

Julia exchanged an uncertain look with Dante. He looked as clueless as she felt. That was mildly reassuring, even if she wasn't sure how she felt about his presence. Jack was right, though. It was important for them to bond again.

"Let's try it," she said, "but one of you knuckleheads is going to have to explain it. Looks complicated."

They sat around the kitchen table and demolished the pizza while they rolled dice to create their characters. Julia won at the dice rolling game and got a paladin. Dante made a thief. Coraolis wanted to play a wizard, but Jack made him roll up a fighter.

"The game is supposed to be an escape. No magic for you," he insisted, and Coraolis conceded.

When they were ready, Jack opened a book held together by duct tape and force of habit. He launched into a description. They were standing at a country crossroads. There was a town ahead, but if they turned left, there was a legendary cave. People entered it and never returned.

"What would you like to do?" he asked.

Julia frowned. "Wait a second. We're in the middle of nowhere? How did we get here?"

"This is just how it starts sometimes," Coraolis said, but Jack had perked up at the question.

"You have no idea. You don't know these people, you just feel a sense of camaraderie with them. As far as you know, you fell out of the sky. The only thing you know for sure, Julia, is that you're a paladin."

"So we need to find out who we are?" Julia asked. This was starting to get interesting.

"And how we got this way?" Dante added.

Something clicked in Julia's head and she started to get into the game. Her character debated with the others, fought monsters, and tried to fill the holes in her memories. By the time they wrapped up for the night, it no longer felt strange for Dante to be there.

After the final goblin was slain, she and Cor walked their friends out. She was sorry for the evening to be over, but Cor had noticed the time and reminded her that she was supposed to be resting.

"Thanks for this. It was fun," she said.

"Agreed," Dante said.

Jack tried to hide his smile, but he was beaming with joy at the game's success.

"Glad you liked it. I'd like to make it a regular thing. We can call it a teambuilding exercise," he said.

"Or we could call it fun," Julia countered. "Let's do this again."

They all agreed at once, and after comparing their schedules, found a date that would work. Julia gave Jack a hug goodbye, then did the same to Dante. He had a surprised, pleased smile on his face when she pulled back.

They said their goodbyes, and when they were gone, Julia leaned into Coraolis's chest. She was tired, emotionally and physically. She hadn't felt it while they were playing. Coraolis herded her into the bedroom, promising to clean up. She was out before her head hit the pillow.

CHAPTER FOUR

The Doctors Ronasuli, Julia's parents filled most of the screen. They looked about the same as the last time they'd sent messages. Her father had a bit more gray than brown in his hair, while her mother had her violet hair pulled back in a chignon. They had a few more lines around their eyes, maybe.

Julia traced their still image a moment. She'd sent a long message the morning after Jack's game. She'd started out trying to explain her choices and, by the end, told them about the roleplaying game. She wished they were on Earth with her, not on a planet that would take seven weeks to reach, yet her parents wouldn't be themselves if they weren't bouncing from one undeveloped planet to another.

"Julia! We were so happy to hear from you. Don't they have transmitters in the Exterior?" her mother asked.

"We can't expect her to stop and send us a message when she's on the run, Fiona. They could have used us against her!"

Julia smiled; her father always talked with his hands. It gave his words a dramatic punch yet also had a history of knocking over glasses and important experiments. Knowing this, her mother reached in front of him to move a glass of green liquid away.

"I suppose you're right. Well, Julia, we got your message. We've missed hearing from you, even if it was too dangerous to reach out to us. We don't have much to tell on our side."

"We're working on a new crossbreed. If it takes, there's a good chance Earth can settle this rock," her father said.

"That falls under the NDA, Christopher." Her mother elbowed him. "Sweetheart, this Coraolis sounds like a nice man. We'd love to meet him."

"At least give me his number," her father growled playfully.

"And yes, of course, we've heard of Dungeons and Dragons. We're so thrilled you're playing with your friends," her mom said. "Your father and I used to play with the survey team on Ursula. Don't you remember? You insisted on rolling our dice for us."

"You were our lucky charm," her father cut in. "I can't think how many times you saved my bacon. And ate my snacks."

Julia laughed under her breath. They'd left Ursula when she was five, and she only had vague memories of what might be her parents gaming. She still had a sweet memory of watching them talking and laughing around a table with their friends.

Her folks said their goodbyes, and the message ended. Regretfully, she put her datapad in her messenger bag. She wanted to sit there and soak in her parents' love for the rest of the day, but she had a class to teach.

The classroom walls were round and its ceiling provided a view of the open sky, though she knew it was a transparent bubble. It was there as a visual reminder they had no obstacles between themselves and the Astral realm. It reminded Julia of her first class as a Mystic.

Her six students were standing in a cluster, so absorbed in their whispering they didn't notice her entrance. She shut the door, startling them.

"Hey, relax," she said. "I'm Instructor Ronasuli. You're here for Astral Orientation, right?"

They nodded, eager to agree. Two of them glanced at each other as if hoping for a reminder of just *how* to unwind on demand. Julia picked out a meditation mat and sat down. The class imitated her, still not relaxed, but she figured that would take time.

She studied them as they studied her. Their gazes slid toward her prosthetic and away again. She could get a more realistic-looking eye, she supposed, but she'd gotten used to what she had. She wasn't going to change it to make others comfortable.

"Let's start by getting on the same page. All of you are Enhanced, right? You've been through the procedure?"

They murmured, and two of them nodded. They seemed so shy, not to mention young. It looked like their surgeries had gone well; she didn't see a single scar.

"They've made a lot of progress since I went through." She looked each of them in the eye, giving them an excuse to stare back. "I see you're wondering about my eye. Something went wrong in the surgery, so they gave me a new one. It works as well as the one I was born with, so I'm happy."

When they realized she was giving permission to look, they stared until they'd gotten an eyeful. She went on talking. It kept her from feeling stared at. She understood why Jack was becoming more reclusive. It would wear one down over time.

"I'm going to share a little bit about myself. I'm Julia Ronasuli, former Earth Fleet captain, now an Enhanced Human Mystic. I've been across the galaxy, so I'd like to think I've the experience to teach you."

"I thought she was just here to get us acclimated," one of the women said, most likely to her neighbor. Julia heard her perfectly.

"Name?" Julia asked. They looked at her, bewildered. "Blonde woman in the back. Yes, you. What's your name?"

"Honora."

"Honora, I'm here to give you solid ground to stand on. You'll be learning to write in cursive with your off hand. You can do it, but you're about to compete with people who have been lefties all their lives. Even if they've never done cursive before, they're naturals with that hand. Getting you to that comfort level will take more than a couple hours."

Honora nodded, her face flushing magenta. Julia replayed what she'd said, wondering if she'd done something to embarrass the student. She couldn't think of anything other than being direct. Maybe the girl didn't like being the center of attention.

A guy with green streaks in his hair raised his hand. "Can I ask a question?"

Julia bypassed the obvious joke and nodded at him. "Say your name first, please."

"I'm Leo. You betrayed Earth, didn't you? How can you be trusted as a teacher?"

Julia considered how to answer that, but Coraolis had told her the accusations and questions would come. She'd been thinking about it for some time. Leo went on looking at her, unabashed. He hadn't sounded angry or even accusing, so she wanted to give him a serious answer. She wanted to give her students reason to trust her.

"That's a fair question. I don't feel what we did was a betrayal. We were ordered by Earth Fleet to destroy a nest of dragons and their young. I'll go to war on the command of my superiors, but I don't go after children...of any species."

Her students' faces went still. She supposed that was hard to swallow, but she owed them the truth. She had to trust them with it, no matter what the official story was.

"Yes," she continued, "dragons have children. They are intelligent, wise creatures with feelings and ambitions of their own. They aren't monsters out of a fantasy tale. When you face them out there, and you will, I want you to remember that. They don't look like us, but they're every bit as sentient."

Leo looked uncomfortable. He wasn't the only one. She was telling them their enemy was no more monster than they were. That revelation might send shockwaves through their young psyches.

"I'm telling you this to prepare you," Julia went on. "Your peers are going to look at you sideways for being 'unnatural.' Your Instructors might too. Mine did."

More uncomfortable looks were thrown around.

"I'm here to help you. They probably think we're all here to give you the basics of astral travel, and that's it. And, yes, I'm going to do that. But I want you to be prepared for what you'll face after you leave here."

Leo raised his hand.

"Yes?" she said.

"What you're saying is, *they* can't trust you, but we can?"

"I think I mean, they didn't expect me to be on your side, but I am." She adjusted herself to get more comfortable. "Enough heavy stuff. Let's get you out of those bodies and into something a little more interesting."

Easier said than done. She remembered her own struggles her first day, which helped her talk most of them through it. Honora struggled most. Julia left the others to get used to the Astral Plane with strict instructions to stay in the classroom area, then returned to her body to help Honora.

The girl became frustrated and shook. Her eyes screwed shut, her hands clenched so tight that if it was possible to punch herself into the Astral Plane, she'd be doing it.

"Hey, take it easy." Julia sat beside her and put a hand on the girl's shoulder.

"I can't do this. I feel like I'm trying to hypnotize myself." Honora pulled away from Julia's hand. "It shouldn't be this hard. I had *surgery.*"

Julia nodded. Honora had to calm down before they got anywhere, and she wouldn't do that under pressure.

"Is something bothering you?"

Honora shrugged. Agitation buzzed off her in waves. Julia could fix that, but it wouldn't change the core of the problem. Most likely it would make everything worse for Honora later.

"I'm taking that as a yes."

"Take it however you want."

Julia picked up a sliver of fear under the rest of the emotions. The student wasn't only nervous, she was afraid. No wonder she couldn't let go enough to leave her body.

"Tell you what. I have a class to teach, but I want you to stay here. If you don't make it today, it's fine. I'll work with you until you get it."

Honora shook her head.

"No?" Julia frowned. "What are you saying no to?"

"What if I don't want to get it? What if I thought I wanted it, but maybe I don't?"

Julia frowned. If that was true, the system needed fixing. They put the potential Enhanced through a lot of tests, including the psychological evaluations to show that the candidates had both the discipline and the desire. They didn't want the subject of a very expensive procedure to simply walk away.

"What makes you say that?"

"I keep coming this close." Honora held up her finger and thumb with only a hair's breadth between them. "I start to float, then there's this vertigo and I fall. I think I want it, but what if I don't? What if this was a mistake?"

"I guess that was never a problem for you." The girl continued, looking over, her voice bitter. "I always second guess myself. It's what I do. But I didn't do that with becoming a Mystic. It was the one thing I've ever been sure of, *ever.* Right up until I walked through that door."

Julia looked up at the clouds overhead. "I've done things I wasn't sure of. This wasn't one of them. Maybe you're afraid once you leave your body, there's no coming back."

Honora started to shake her head, then stopped. "Maybe," she admitted.

Julia figured Honora couldn't be much older than eighteen, which meant she'd impressed the recruiters. She wouldn't have made it through the screenings otherwise. "I know it's hard to hear, but time can only move forward. The only way to go back would be to invent time travel." She put her hand on Honora's shoulder and, this time, the student didn't jerk away. "Everything we do marks us, for good or bad, and that mark is permanent. Once you make peace with that, I'll be honored to teach you."

Julia stood, went back to her mat, and got into position. "If you need to talk, whether you stay at the Academy or not, just ask. But I'm telling you, you're missing out if you don't see the Astral Plane at least once. There is nothing like it."

She found her students clustered like when she'd first walked in. They were so enthralled by their surroundings they didn't realize how long she'd kept them waiting. It didn't hurt that time worked differently in the Astral Plane. It didn't have the same 'weight' as in the physical world.

She felt bad for delaying, just as she felt guilty for leaving Honora alone. She hoped her last student would join them. She'd meant what she said. If Honora never saw the Astral Plane, she was missing out.

But Honora was just one of six students, and the others needed her attention too. She had them stand in a semi-circle so she could talk to them. "I have three rules for you during this class. One, stay in the limits of the classroom. Two, no goofing off. Three, do exactly as I say. If I tell you to get back to your bodies, you go. No stopping for questions, no hesitating. Just go."

"What if we can't figure out how?" Leo asked.

She smiled. "You won't have to worry about that. Your spirit *wants* to be in your body. All you have to do is give it permission."

In response to that, their Astral bodies flickered. She waited for them to regain balance, then continued. "Now, all through the Astral Plane is what we call *ether*. You can't see it, except for random streaks of color. It looks and feels like nothing, but it makes up everything." She scooped a handful of ether, and her students gasped as she stretched it between her hands like taffy. "It takes the shape you *will* it to have. Try it. Grab a handful and see what it'll do for you."

"What if we grab too much?"

Honora hovered next to Leo. Her Astral body flickered, but she was present! Julia smiled at her but didn't make a big deal of it. "Honora, glad you're here. Did you hear my safety lecture?"

"No, ma'am."

"Come here, and I'll go over it with you. Everyone else, carry on. If you find you have too much, just open your hands and let it go."

Honora floated over smoothly. She was smiling, even if she seemed nervous.

"It feels natural once you get used to it," Julia told her. "I'm glad you made it."

"I think I am, too."

"Listen, I'm not here to tell you what to do, at least not outside of class." Julia laughed to herself. "I don't mean to single you out, but you need to hear the safety rules just like everyone else. It won't take long, then we'll get on to the fun stuff."

The catchup session didn't take long, but by the time they were done, the students had started treating their ether like clay. Leo had made a tiny octopus, and its little arms were waving around. The others watched him, their jaws slack.

Julia approved; he'd found his way to that on his own, which was at least a sign of a good imagination. She gathered everyone around to see how he was doing it. The octopus wasn't alive. It was moving because Leo expected it to, taking its cues from his subconscious. She helped him bring that will to the surface, and soon his octopus was doing cartwheels up and down his arm.

Others imitated him. Julia made sure their projects stayed small, but otherwise let their own imaginations set the limits. She had to duck when a tiny fairy with a spear whizzed past her, only to vanish into the ether before its creator could call it back. Instead of mourning its loss, Honora made another one, then had it spar with a tiny frog-person conjured up by her neighbor.

It warmed her heart to see them take to the Astral Plane. Already they were manipulating the ether as if they'd been born to it. They made butterflies and angels, then monsters of various descriptions. Each new creation was met with shouts of approval, and then another student would riff off the new creation to make the next thing. Julia hung back and let them play, knowing that as they did they were learning, as well as bonding with new friends.

They were having the time of their lives, but it didn't last long. Their endurance was limited, and one by one, they began to flicker. Honora was last, and when she began to fade, Julia sent them back to their bodies.

A few of the ether-creatures lingered. She caught one and made it stand on her palm. The tiny centurion marched back and forth, becoming more transparent with every step. It was remarkable, the pride she felt. Her students had done wonderful things under her guidance. Maybe this was why Cor had been excited to return to the classroom.

At the thought of her partner, she let the centurion float away. Her imagination reshaped him into a winged messenger, a cupid with dragon wings. She fed it love and warmth, then willed it to find Coraolis. She didn't know if it would. It was probably a silly romantic notion, but the idea struck her, and she had to try.

She returned to her body and made sure everyone drank their electrolytes. Then, a sudden warmth wrapped around her shoulders like an ethereal hug. There were no words, nothing to tell her it was anything but her imagination, but she knew it was Coraolis's response. Message received.

They could send each other messages, then. That would be pragmatic, useful in more workmanlike affairs. A tiny part of her wondered if they should keep it a secret between the Evolved, and she decided it was a decision for the group. In the meantime, she sent Coraolis another astral 'nudge,' and smiled when she got a warm feeling in return.

CHAPTER FIVE

It only took one class to convince Jack that he was no Instructor. He knew how to get into the Astral Plane. He knew how to manipulate the ether. He *didn't* have the gift that let teachers turn their own experience into knowledge for someone else. Either his students followed his example and learned from it or they were lost, and he didn't know how to get them un-lost.

After he confessed to the dean, he was given an easier task. He reported to the Engineer's Annex every morning at eight. For the first week, he hovered and looked for ways to make himself helpful. After a few failures, he accepted he was the least useful person in the building and settled for making friends.

Foremost among them was Isabel Loomis, a mechanical engineer from Earth Fleet. She'd taken one look at Jack and dragged him to her lab where she made him her own personal guinea pig.

He went to her of his own accord now, and only occasionally joked about being conditioned to do so. He also proclaimed loudly that she hadn't programmed him to bring her pastries every day, yet there he was on a cool winter's morning, juggling two coffee cups and a bag of croissants as he walked into her lab.

Isabel was there, just as she had been when he left the night before. Either she lived in her lab or she was a robot. He bet on robot. Isabel refused to weigh in on the question.

"Isabel, you look amazing. I know you don't need this coffee to look awake or alive, but you still deserve a treat." He handed over the Americano and sat in the second chair, sipping at his mocha.

She wrinkled her nose but accepted the coffee. She was cute when she pulled faces at him, but she'd probably kill him if he told her so.

"Are you trying to say I look tired?"

"Who, me? No. Why? Are you tired? Have you been here all night?"

She did look tired, but his mom had taught him better than to say so. Isabel worked harder than anyone he knew. She was a lot smarter, too. She didn't need his commentary.

"Not *all* night." She pushed away from the desk and rolled in her chair, coming to rest next to Jack's. "Some of us have projects to finish, you know."

"Hey, I have projects," he protested. She slapped an electrode on his temple, and he groaned. It was an electrode day. His least favorite kind.

"Have you considered taking a break? We could go for a walk."

"Ugh, but there's so much *outside* out there." Isabel wrinkled her nose again and applied another electrode to his face. "I prefer a strictly regulated climate."

"You only say that to try and convince me you aren't a vampire. Just between you and me, you aren't fooling anyone. I've been eating garlic with every meal, so I'm safe from the likes of you."

Isabel raised her eyebrows at him.

"That means you can't bite me," he explained.

"I thought I was a robot?"

"Unless you're a vampire."

"Got it. Thanks for the warning." She slapped an electrode onto his neck, and he cringed. "What? This is completely painless. I just need some readings."

"Sure, harmless until it's time to tear 'em off. Then it's worse than removing a band-aid," Jack groaned.

"No, dear. It's like yanking off twenty band-aids." She patted his cheek. "Just kidding, it's only four this time. Do you still want to back out?"

Jack groaned, but he didn't really mean it, and he was sure Izzy could tell. She was adjusting her glasses and looking away. If she looked his way, she'd laugh. Once she laughed, she lost the high ground. Not that it would get him out of guinea pig duty.

"Fine. Do your worst," he said. He sat back and let her attach wires to the electrodes. When she was done, he was connected to her computer. Its screen was covered in code he couldn't read, nor did he want to. "What are we doing today, oh brilliant scientist?"

"Today you're going to use your abilities while I monitor activity in your hippocampus. I want to see what it does when you turn invisible."

"Okay, but it isn't invisibility. I just make myself unnoticeable."

"Same difference. Let's see you work your magic in the real world."

"The Astral Plane *is* an actual place. Here and there are *both* real worlds."

He'd told her that before, but either she didn't believe him or he couldn't make it stick. He narrowed his eyes as he considered the third option, that she could be playing him. But no, that was his job. He did the teasing, she played the straight man.

She twirled her fingers in a *hurry-up* gesture. "I can still see you."

He huffed, then stared into her eyes as he focused. His dragon lurked under the surface, supporting him and feeding him power as he balanced on the edge between the physical and astral worlds.

He visualized his power as a blanket falling over him. Isabel went cross-eyed for a second. She blinked, clearing them. He could see that she was trying to resist the compulsion to look away. She turned her head toward him, then looked away as if something had caught her eye. She tried again, and her eyes zoomed past him. She started to smile, and he grinned back at her, even though she couldn't see it.

"That's really something." She turned back to the instruments. "Huh. It isn't picking up a thing."

"I think that's because my power extends to the readings." He dropped the 'cloak,' and she jumped. "Since I'm making you fail to notice me, it stands to reason you can't look at live recordings of me either."

The machine lit up like a Christmas tree. She bent over a screen and nodded.

"You're right. Here it is, readings from thirty seconds ago. Very impressive, Gagnon."

He smiled. "I try."

"I'm changing a few settings. Can you do that again?"

He groaned. "I suppose, but then you owe me lunch because I'll be spent."

"No, the E.F. owes you lunch. But don't worry, I've got their *per diem* card." She patted his shoulder and turned to the instruments. "Let's see what happens if I'm not looking when you vanish."

"Yes, ma'am."

Three hours later, Jack was tired and bored. Isabel had run him through multiple tests of his abilities, including jaunts into the Astral Plane while she poked at him with all manner of equipment.

"I need a break, Iz. I couldn't get into the Astral Plane if you clamped jumper cables on me." He lay back, using his arm for a pillow. He'd moved to the examination table after the first hour. It was hard as a concrete floor yet inviting as a feather bed.

"Funny you should say that." She picked up her phone and fiddled with it.

"Funny how?"

"You did great today, you know. I've gotten a lot of good data." She smiled at him in a way that made her whole face glow.

He knew that smile. He liked it. He didn't trust it. "But?"

"Allen's been pushing me to wear you down so he can try a new procedure. I wasn't going to do it without asking unless it just happened organically." She put her phone away and walked over to him. "And now..."

"Is that who you were texting?" He frowned, torn between indulging this betrayed feeling and dealing with it. This was her job, just like following her requests was his. She wasn't the only one working on Mystic-related tech. She was just his friend.

"He's my boss, Jack. Yes, I texted him, but I didn't tell him to come over. I said we were almost done and asked if you were needed somewhere else." She showed him her phone. Her last text said exactly that. Below, an ellipse blinked on the screen.

The phone chimed, and the message came through while he watched:

Is he ready this time?

Isabel looked at the phone, then at Jack. She tilted her head to the side and shrugged.

"What should I say? Is he ready this time?" she asked.

"I'm ready," he said, warming up again. "I might as well see what he wants."

What Allen wanted, it turned out, was for Jack to take a little blue pill. He showed up not thirty seconds after Isabel replied. He'd been lurking in his office just a few meters away, ready to pop over the moment he had the green light.

Jack held the pill in his palm, looking at it skeptically. It was a flavor of blue sprinkled with white, only he could swear the white was moving around in there. It looked like a tiny speck of ocean.

Allen held out a glass of water.

"It's a concentrated dose of potassium, glucose, and several compounds shown to heighten brain function." Allen put the glass down within Jack's reach. "I've been waiting for the chance to try it."

"It heightens brain function? Does that mean it makes people smarter?" Jack asked.

"It isn't that simple. You can't think at higher levels, but you can do it faster. It's not unlike overclocking a computer. The worst side effects reported were headaches and nausea, but I believe I've eliminated those."

"And now you want to know what it'll do to a Mystic." Jack looked at the pill, trying to get past his suspicion. It sounded like getting high on Earth Fleet's dime.

"Correct."

Jack leaned to the side, peering around Allen at Isabel. She was focused on her datapad, and her cheeks were very pink. There was no help to be had there. He had to decide on his own. His problem was that he'd already made his decision when he signed on as guinea pig.

He didn't have to do anything. He just felt obligated to.

"Okay, I'll do it. Izzy, are you recording this on your machines?"

"Yep. You're still linked up," she said. "Fire at will."

Jack put the pill in his mouth and washed it down with the whole glassful of water. He waited for something to change. Maybe he'd feel smarter, or like he'd drank a gallon of Red Bull. Maybe a combination of both, or neither.

The funny thing was, he didn't feel like he needed a boost. He had his dragon, that was all he really needed. He'd traveled the stars and manipulated incredible power in the Astral Plane. He didn't need a *pill* to make him a better Mystic.

Isabel was trying to smother laughter behind her hands, and it only took a second to figure out why. He was speaking his every thought out loud, with no barrier between his brain and his tongue. This would not be the time to focus on how pretty Izzy was, or how he wished Allen had been friendlier before he asked something of Jack.

"How do you feel, though? Is your power affected or just your racing thoughts?" Allen asked. He was trying not to smile, but Jack saw right through him.

"I don't know what you mean. My thoughts are clear as cellophane. Or air. They're as easy to see through as air," Jack declared, then paused. "I think I feel something, yeah."

"You think?" Isabel said. "I don't think this is working the way you intended, Al."

"We don't know that yet. It's just getting started."

Jack flinched away from a bright light that suddenly bored into his left pupil, then his right. Allen drew back, stowing a penlight in his pocket.

"Are you still tired?" Allen asked.

"No, *you're* tired."

Isabel caught his eye. She was struggling to keep a straight face. He winked at her, and she looked away again, her shoulders shaking.

"See if you can use your abilities. We are recording," Allen reminded him.

"Okay. Just give me some space here."

Jack lay back and closed his eyes, trying to find balance, but his balance was gone. His body was gone. He was buried in the void without so much as a star to keep him company. It was vast and old and so empty a better name for it was *hunger.*

He knew this was the Astral Plane, the same way he knew his heart was beating, but this wasn't the realm he knew. It had been devoured from the inside until it was a husk, mirroring the empty Universe beyond the veil.

They're coming.

"Who's coming?" An invisible frozen hand closed around his heart.

They're coming.

"Tell me what's going on. Who are you? What are you talking about?"

He was trying to shout, but the words came out in a wheeze. Even the air was gone. He couldn't breathe, he couldn't think. He spiraled, reaching for something solid, but he was alone. He didn't even have the tug of his body to tell him where to go. The only sensation was the distant *thud* of his own heart.

Then only darkness, followed by nothing at all.

Jack opened his eyes. He clutched at his chest. His only thought was for sweet air as it rushed into his lungs. A few desperate breaths later, he registered he was lying on something soft. The air smelled of antiseptic. Four familiar faces appeared all around, peering over the rails of a hospital bed.

"I know I'm late for D&D but watching me sleep is a little much," he cracked.

"Jack! How do you feel?" Isabel put her hand to his forehead. She smelled like peppermint.

"Confused. What's going on?"

That question sent a jolt of *déjà vu* down his spine. He followed it to its source, but Julia squeezed his shoulder, her eyes shiny and damp.

"Don't ever do that again," Julia demanded.

"Uh...what did I do?"

"You took an experimental drug created by my boss. It was supposed to make you more powerful, but you started babbling a mile a minute and passed out." Izzy shook her head. "I'm sorry, Jack. He said he tested it."

It came back to him now. The blue pill. Assurances it had been harmless for the control cases. Between that moment and this, a vast gulf of nothing...

"No, I think it worked. Somehow."

"It did something all right. It knocked you out of your body so hard your cord snapped," Dante growled. He gave Izzy a dirty look. She pretended not to see it.

"Don't be hard on her. She's a mechanic, not a doctor," Jack said.

"Mechanical engineer," she corrected him.

"That's what I said."

She rolled her eyes. Good. That was back to normal, at least.

"What do you remember?" Coraolis asked.

"It was dark. Cold. I don't know." Jack shuddered. He didn't want to push too hard. "Can I get out of here?"

"I'll get a doctor," Izzy replied. She ducked out of the room.

Jack sat up, shrugging off Julia's hand when she tried to encourage him to stay down. Physically, he felt fine. Mentally, he felt like he needed a new set of bearings.

"Glad to have you back, Jack." Coraolis smiled.

Jack smirked. "You guys just missed your Dungeon Master."

"Yeah, that's it."

Their laughter let off pressure. He could get dressed, go home, and they could resume their normal lives. Except, it felt wrong. A force built in his head as he turned thoughts over in his mind. *Normal.* That wasn't them. It never would be them. Something inside of him pushed against the notion as hard as anything he'd ever felt.

"Listen, I have an idea. We can't stay here," he spouted off. "We're going backward. We'll be stagnant." Jack checked the state of his gown, then threw off his blankets. "Where are my clothes?"

"Sit still, we'll find them in a minute. What's your idea?" Julia threw the covers over his legs again. "You aren't going anywhere until a doctor looks at you, so what are you talking about?"

"We need to go out with Earth Fleet. We've encountered all these planets that we left alone because of the dragons, right? Well, now we're practically half dragon. We can negotiate for Earth Fleet. We get new planets, but we'll make sure Earth Fleet agrees to find a balance with their ecosystems. The dragons can watch to make sure E.F. keeps their end of the deal. Everybody's happy."

"That's not a bad idea," Dante mused.

"No, it's a great one." Coraolis beamed at Jack, and he grinned back.

"Of course it is. It's mine."

"You'll have to run it by Earth Fleet, but we'll help. I can't imagine they'd say no to more planets," Julia added.

"Great. We'll work on a proposal... as soon as I get some pants on."

The doctor insisted on running more tests, but Jack was finally discharged. They went directly to E.F. headquarters. The others backed him up, and leadership jumped on his idea as if it was their own. The only conditions were that only two Evolved could leave Earth at a time.

Maybe in the E.F.'s eyes their slate wasn't so clean after all; still, it was a step in the right direction.

As Jack went through the usual pre-mission examinations, he had a nagging feeling he was forgetting something. He made a list of everything he intended to pack and sent it to Julia. Maybe she would see what he'd missed; yet, she didn't find anything and, soon, it was too late. It was time to pack and see if their rapport with dragons was as good as he thought.

The pressure in his head lessened once he'd taken action, and the haunting feeling he'd forgotten something faded. By the time he received his orders, Jack felt nearly normal again.

CHAPTER SIX

It was hard for Coraolis to say goodbye to Earth after only a few months. Part of it was leaving Julia and his students behind, but Coraolis couldn't turn down this mission. He wanted to be part of negotiations to ensure expansion was done in a way that protected planets, the Astral Plane, native life, and Dragons.

He and Jack boarded E.F.S. *Charon* after saying their goodbyes. They were given a cabin near the commune chamber and far from the bridge. The crew gave the Mystics plenty of space. He caught more than one sailor looking at him sideways. He ignored it. The only thing he could do was demonstrate he was a worthy person. Confronting the crew wouldn't help anyone.

To that end, he smiled and nodded when he crossed someone's path. If the other person avoided eye contact, he left them alone. If they spoke to him, he responded in a friendly manner. For the most part, however, only Jack and Ensign Moe spoke to him.

Moe was the ship's designated Mystic Whisperer. He gave them the tour, starting with their cabin and ending with the galley. Captain

Wells met them briefly. He was polite but made it clear the bridge was for 'crew only' except by special invitation.

After that, Coraolis became aware of increased security on the ship. Double the guard was stationed outside the bridge. He'd never seen security posted to Engineering before, but *Charon* had it. Every time they stepped outside their cabin a pair of officers loitered in the corridor. Wherever he and Jack went, the officers followed.

"Guilty until proven, well, guilty, I guess," Jack muttered upon noticing they had gained an extra pair of shadows.

"Our records are clear, but people have long memories." Coraolis smiled at the gentlemen following them, then started for the galley.

"Do you think it is the E.F. in general or just these guys?"

"If I had to guess, I'd say it's Wells. Tanner let us have the run of her ship. Other E.F. personnel have been polite enough." Coraolis smiled at a passing lieutenant. The young man returned the smile, then his expression stiffened as he realized they were Mystics.

"That's the look of a young man who thinks he's in trouble. I should know," Jack commented. "This is going to be a long trip at this rate."

"Too bad we can't play one-on-one D&D to pass the time."

"We could. I brought my books."

"Okay, we could. I don't know if we *should*. If we hide in our room the whole time, it'll just give them more to speculate. If we show we're harmless, it'll erode some of...whatever *this* is."

"Okay, so let's play in the galley."

Coraolis chuckled. Now that he had the idea in his teeth, Jack wouldn't let go. Not that he objected. "Fine. Maybe we'll find some gamers on this boat."

They reached the galley, but it was time for chow, not games. The tables were packed with crewmen eating and talking. Coraolis and Jack got in line and, before long, had trays laden with stroganoff. Jack nodded at a table with open seats at the end.

"I suppose I could make a wandering barbarian type. He could start as a lowly shepherd and grow up to be the emperor of the known world," Coraolis mused.

"You know that's been done, right?"

"Yes, but maybe I want to be Conan."

Jack chuckled. "Sure, who doesn't?"

He slid into a seat, and Coraolis claimed the spot across from him. Two things happened quickly. The Engineer sitting next to Jack glared and his elbow jerked. His elbow hit Jack's tray, which flew off the table. Stroganoff went everywhere, with the biggest mass of noodles landed on a pair of well-polished boots.

Chief Bergen wasn't tall, but he was built like a tank. The man looked like he could stare down a dragon. He turned that glare on Jack, who had frozen like a rabbit in an eagle's shadow.

"You think you're pretty funny, don't ya?" The chief planted his hands on the table, looming over Jack. "Well?"

"That wasn't me."

"No? You're the only one I see here without a tray."

"It was my tray, yes."

"But you didn't do this. Alright, was it your neighbor? Technician McCoy, what are you looking at?"

"Nothing, Chief."

"Did you do this?"

McCoy looked at the chief's boots, then at Jack. Coraolis stared at him, willing him to tell the truth. The young technician didn't answer.

Chief Bergen's face darkened. "So, you're going to let me blame a couple of Mikes because you don't like what they are? Is that it?"

"No, Chief."

"No? Then what is it?" Bergen demanded.

"It's not that big a deal," Jack said. "It was an accident."

"His silence wasn't an accident. This outfit is an honorable one, Technician. We don't pull underhanded garbage. We do our duty, and we get our work done. We don't hamstring our allies!"

"Yes, Chief." McCoy's Adam's apple bobbed when he swallowed. "Won't happen again."

"Damn right it won't. Keep that in mind while you're getting a mop."

McCoy jumped from his seat and hurried out of the galley. Chief Bergen watched him go, a line deepening between his eyebrows.

"Sorry about the stroganoff, Chief," Jack said.

"It wasn't you." The chief grabbed the napkin from McCoy's abandoned tray and flicked the noodles from his boots. "I heard about you two. Captain did too."

"I'm guessing that's why we have so many guards." Coraolis offered his napkin as well.

The chief accepted it. "Yep."

Coraolis looked around the room. Most of the personnel were paying close attention to their trays. They might as well have been invisible.

"Do you really think all this is necessary?" he asked.

"It's not up to me." The chief straightened. "But yeah, probably. It'll keep order on the boat. Visible guards mean that these knuckleheads won't mess with you. We don't need that."

"I didn't know you cared," Jack said.

"I've been on this boat a long time. Mikes aren't the enemy. Even an old grease monkey like me knows that. Watch yourselves, that's all."

"Maybe we'll make ourselves scarce. We won't be doing his pride any favors by watching him clean up," Coraolis said.

"Agreed. I'm not that hungry anyway." Jack stood.

They took their leave. Chief Bergen gave them the barest hint of a smile. Coraolis wasn't sure, but maybe they'd made the man happy. At least they hadn't offended him. That was something.

They returned to the galley after the last meal shift when some tables would be free. They claimed an empty one against the wall. Coraolis brought up a random number generator on his datapad just as Jack dropped a cloth bag on the table. The sound of dice hitting the surface was unmistakable.

"You brought dice too?"

"Of course. You can't game without dice."

"You were a Boy Scout, weren't you?"

"Hey, now that I'm gaming, I just like to know where my dice are." Jack untied the drawstring and poured out a colorful collection of polyhedral dice. "Grab some six-siders. Let's see what your Conan is made of."

Coraolis shook the dice in one hand as a shadow fell over the table. Technician McCoy stood with hands clasped behind his back. He said nothing. They looked up at him. He shifted his weight.

Coraolis wasn't a fool. He knew McCoy had messed with Jack deliberately. He just hadn't meant to get the chief involved. Coraolis would rather make peace than repay one slight with another, so he gestured at the seat next to him. "Can we help you with something?"

The tech glanced at the empty seat and shook his head. "This'll just take a minute."

Coraolis caught Jack's eye. He shook his head slightly. There was no trouble coming from behind. It was a pity they had to check for that, but ever since Jack's troubles in the city, they'd all been careful.

"I want to know why you tried to step in for me with the chief. I set you up," McCoy grumbled.

"It looked to me like you were about to get more trouble than the prank deserved." Coraolis shrugged. He hadn't been thinking about it that carefully. "It just seemed right."

McCoy frowned, a deep line appearing between his brows. It looked less like anger than deep thought. Cor waited.

"I don't get it." He threw his hands up in the air. "I'm not going to go around telling everybody how *nice* the two of you are. I know it could just be an act."

"Nobody's asking you to. We've got a job to do here, that's all. We don't want trouble."

McCoy's frown deepened. "Sure. Well...I'll leave you alone if you leave me alone."

"Sounds fair," Jack said.

Coraolis nodded. McCoy held out his hand, and they shook on it. When they let go, he turned on his heel and marched out of the room, his back ramrod stiff.

"Guess we aren't making any friends," Jack observed.

"Maybe not, maybe so. If we show we're decent enough, it'll sink in eventually."

Coraolis started shaking the dice again, letting them rattle against each other. They could worry about McCoy later, along with their reputations. Any progress they made would be measured in millimeters. For now, all they could do was live their lives, and make it clear they weren't a threat.

Slowly, the tension between the Mystics and the E.F. crew eased. Maybe it was because of their actions or getting used to each other through proximity. Before long, they had an audience for their evening gaming sessions. While their audience was invited to join in, no one took them up on it.

Small talk with the crew became real conversation. Even McCoy came around and became as friendly as any of his crewmates. By the time they reached the Amadeus system, they had a small circle of acquaintances.

"I think we've got Santiago hooked," Jack said as they entered the commune chamber. "He borrowed my *Player's Handbook*."

"That's promising." Coraolis looked over the commune chamber before closing the door behind them.

"I thought so." Jack handed him an electrolyte bottle and selected a spot on the floor. Coraolis sat facing him. They rose into the Astral Plane.

Amadeus was a swirl of green and blue. Clouds covered much of its atmosphere with a tattered white blanket. Coraolis moved forward with Jack at his side, leaving *Charon* far behind. It seemed wiser to keep the ship as distant as possible, in case negotiations went poorly.

Something was off. The planet had a single moon nearly as black as the void around it. Amadeus didn't have any moons listed on the registry. As he stared at it, one of the larger formations split open, revealing a titanic eye. The ridges became scales, and its mountains unfolded to reveal wings that could enfold the planet itself.

The dragon was in their path before Coraolis could process its sheer size. It filled the astral sky until it was all they could see. Looking away was unthinkable.

Jack froze in place. Coraolis realized his companion had never confronted a dragon this way. The closest he'd come was the day they'd fused with dragons, and they would have been infants compared to this ancient one.

Coils of white fire curled around the dragon's nostrils. Twin flames ignited in its eyes. Foreboding pressed down on Coraolis, a sense of unwelcome. Its presence pushed their astral selves toward the *Charon*. The dragon was slamming the door in their faces before they could even make their case.

"Wait," Jack said.

The dragon took no notice. The pressure bore down on them, insisting they leave. Jack grabbed Coraolis's hand, and their backward motion stopped. They couldn't make any headway, but at least they weren't losing more ground.

"I can hold this." Jack spoke through gritted teeth. "Try and talk sense into him."

Coraolis nodded, but he didn't speak out loud. He reached into himself, calling the dragon within. Words wouldn't convince a dragon this ancient. He needed help.

His dragon answered, and Coraolis was surrounded by its ethereal form. Wings bore him up to meet the ancient one's eye. He caught pieces of their communication. A plea to be heard, the demand that they go away, tinged with distrust of mortal beings. Jack's own dragon joined in with declarations of love for humans.

It was nothing he didn't expect, except at the end. The ancient one relaxed some of its rigidity when Jack's dragon projected hope for a second chance. Coraolis frowned, but it was gone as soon as he tried to grasp the meaning. Maybe he'd misunderstood.

Cor's dragon faded, leaving him opposite the ancient one. It waited for him to speak.

He cleared his throat. "I represent Earth Fleet and am empowered to negotiate on their behalf. We would like to settle the planet we've named Amadeus and collect some of its resources."

Skepticism filled the ether. Coraolis nodded, acknowledging that feeling.

"I know humans haven't coexisted well with dragons in the past, but that is changing." He gestured at himself, then wondered if the motion was too small for the giant dragon. "We will agree to your terms and settle only in areas you designate. We won't harm local wildlife when taking resources. For now, we only wish to survey the planet."

The flames in the dragon's eyes died down. It bent its head once, then turned and flew away to hover near the planet. A cautious sense of welcome washed over Coraolis, and he relaxed.

"You call that negotiating?" Jack teased, as they headed toward the *Charon*. They were taking their time, giving the dragon every chance to call them back or change its mind. "You gave up everything we had to offer right away."

"I call it offering something reasonable." Coraolis glanced over his shoulder. The dragon had curled into a ball again, but one eye watched them. Coraolis got the message. They were welcome on the planet, but trust must be earned.

Cor stood in the shuttle's cockpit, looking at the ruins of an ancient city. With intact walls, a maze of buildings and winding streets sometimes bridged over each other in an intricate dance of architecture and art. Every building was of a uniform black substance that Jack and Coraolis hadn't been able to identify from the Astral Plane.

They had decided to go to the surface to take samples, and the captain had agreed to let them go. They hadn't expected signs of civilization.

Jack wanted to explore it, and that feeling didn't come solely from him. His dragon was urging him forward. It wanted more. He had to agree, he'd never seen anything like it. No life remained on the planet. There was no one to ask.

The pilot put the shuttle down on a hill overlooking the city. Coraolis, Jack, and the away team members loaded up and hiked to the broken city gates.

"I wish the others could see this." Jack held up his datapad, recording video. He rotated the camera on his device so it would record his face. "You wouldn't believe this. The buildings have no seams or lines, it's like they grew as part of this world."

It was true. The buildings were smooth with wide square bases. They tapered off hundreds of meters above ground. They were too narrow to be pyramids, but too wide to be spires.

"Does it seem strange to you that so many buildings are intact? This place feels ancient." Coraolis stepped up to the gate and pressed his hand to its surface. His physical senses named it stone. His Mystic abilities said it was something else but couldn't tell him what.

"Strange, yes. At least the roads have some normal wear and tear."

Plant life struggled to reclaim the land on which the city had been built, growing through cracks in the paved ground. More robust plants broke the walkway and stretched higher than a person's head. It made movement difficult, concealing anything beyond the next bush.

Coraolis hadn't sensed hostility in the city's depths, but he wasn't nearly as sensitive as Julia. He paced the width of the gate, keeping his promise to stay outside the city walls until the scouts returned with an all-clear. They returned within the hour. By that time, he was chomping at the bit. His dragon's impatience didn't help. At least there was good news to reward the wait. The scouts hadn't found sign of predators or hostiles. They'd found no sign of life beyond the plants.

The Mystics shouldered their gear and hiked into the city. They slowed occasionally to record the sights, their thoughts, and their feelings. Coraolis found a smooth stone that seemed to be made of the same stuff as the buildings and pocketed it.

He noticed Jack grinning beside him. Coraolis could understand; entering the city scratched an itch unlike any he'd felt before. Maybe that came from the dragon, but it hardly mattered. He wanted to uncover the city's secrets as much as his dragon did.

Absorbed in their surroundings, the explorers hardly thought to look up. If they did, it was to admire the structure of the buildings, not to survey the overcast sky. When a strange vessel broke atmosphere and landed on the other side of the city, none took notice but the planet's guardian dragon, who dismissed the ship's presence as just another mortal construct.

CHAPTER SEVEN

Khiann was entranced by what she saw on the viewscreen. The dragon had returned to a resting state without breaking the Earth Fleet ship into a thousand pieces. *Charon* went into planetary orbit. Not long after, a shuttle departed the boat, and she tracked it as it entered the atmosphere.

She chewed her lip.

Khiann had followed *Charon* undetected from the Sol System. She knew the shuttle bore two of their remarkable Mystics, just as she knew two others had remained on their homeworld. She had been watching them since the battle with the Wyrms.

Night Thorn had hidden in their Kuiper belt and observed from a distance. She couldn't use her abilities without alerting their Mystics, so she'd relied on her instruments. She occasionally reached out when their hemisphere was dark. When two of them left on their mission, she was eager to follow.

Khiann was glad of the decision. While the ancient dragon kept her people from visiting the surface of this planet for generations, it had also kept lesser beings away. In less than an hour, however, humans would be walking on sacred ground, profaning it with their presence. The Lost Jewel was to be just that. *Lost.*

"This is an outrage," she declared.

"According to the historical record, *Ixhoi* has not felt the tread of mortal feet for ten thousand years." The computer's voice was all too cheery as it shared the information.

Khiann glared at the viewscreen, having designated it the computer's face, even though the ship had no such thing. She needed a focal point for her interactions.

"I'm aware," she snarled.

She punched in commands to analyze *Charon's* sensors. She needed to determine where they were pointed, and how she could get past them. Their technology was primitive in many respects, but it would never do to underestimate them.

It had been a simple matter to slip past their 'mothership' at the wormhole. *Night Thorn* didn't require another ship to get through a wormhole, nor did the rest of the Pirr fleet. That mobility allowed her people to maintain a larger territory than many races. It took fewer resources to explore the galaxy and take the planets they wanted.

The only exception was their ancient stronghold, which had been denied to them for so long.

The ship's computer beeped worriedly. "What are you doing, Commander?"

"I'm plotting a course to the surface."

"Standard protocol advises backup."

The computer sounded all too smug. It was right, of course. It was the height of foolishness to engage an enemy with superior numbers—at least head-on. Khiann was anything but foolish. She would send the message, but by the time help arrived, it would be too late.

"I'll send a report, but I will not wait for assistance." She opened a screen to monitor the progress on her scanning algorithm and frowned when she saw how little had been done. "Work at maximum efficiency, computer. That's an order."

The computers' chime had a sullen ring to it, but the screen soon filled with data. Khiann turned her attention to another floating screen, tracking the humans' position.

"Where are they going?" she murmured.

"By my calculations, they are landing near the Nexus."

The center of the world. Every planet in Pirr space had its center. It was always the first landing site, selected by augur and scientific survey to find the most auspicious position. Anything at that location would have special importance. Temples were always built at the exact center, then surrounded by the rest of the city. The humans weren't just desecrating the holy lost planet, they were about to stomp on its very heart.

"Get me an entry point immediately," she snapped.

"Yes, Commander."

She took manual control of *Night Thorn* and activated its stealth capability. It wouldn't hide her from the dragon, but it would conceal her from E.F.'s sensors.

The flight from the asteroids to the planet took ten minutes. She kept manual control of her ship while her eyes peered into the Astral Plane, tracking the dragon's position. When she neared its position, the beast opened one enormous eye.

She held her breath. If it lashed out, there was nothing she could do but try to run. She could but hope the gigantic beast would be slow to react. Mass had nothing to do with speed in the Astral Plane. It was all about power, and a dragon had more of *that* than any living creature.

The dragon focused its gaze on her ship. She felt its scrutiny through *Night Thorn's* hull. It saw her. She put her hand to her hip, reaching for her weapon, but it wasn't there. It was in its cradle on the wall behind her, ready for when she needed it.

It was for the best. She had the sense of being judged by a mind with more weight and power than she could ever hope to wield. Her paltry weapon would be less than a pin prick if it decided to obliterate her.

She stood still, using childhood exercises to calm her mind. If she carried no hostile thoughts, perhaps that would be enough.

The dragon's eye narrowed to a slit. She tightened her grip on the controls.

The dragon's eye closed.

"Are you well, Commander? Your vital signs have become erratic."

"I'm fine." She closed the floating screens. "Take us in. Land us near the city, but out of sight of the human vessel."

"As you command."

She handed control over to the computer and closed her eyes, reaching out to determine what the humans were doing.

Jack gazed at their surroundings. According to the shuttle's readings, a magnetic anomaly encircled the perimeter of the buildings. It was nothing dangerous, not even strong enough to mess with their equipment. Jack thought it must have been a shield once, but he had no proof to back his theory.

The heavy air caused moisture to stick to their clothes. Insects the size of horse flies swarmed everywhere, but they left the humans alone. Jack eyed the bugs, wondering if, like horse flies, they could cause big painful welts, so he was glad to be left alone. Humans must not smell like food. Maybe that meant the world's makeup wasn't compatible with humans. Or maybe it just meant they were lucky.

Jack rubbed the back of his neck. His hackles prickled in a peculiar way. He looked over his shoulder, seeing only ancient buildings and twisty trees. Admittedly, he couldn't see very far. If anything was watching, he was certain he would have sensed it.

This planet was strange, and this city even stranger. The city wasn't in ruins at all, contrary to what they'd assumed. Some buildings were irregularly shaped, but it appeared to be deliberate. The walls were unbelievably smooth, aside from the cryptic markings at random places on various buildings. He took footage of the markings. He'd stream them to the university later; maybe a linguist back home could figure them out.

He'd never been one for ancient writings and archaeology. He was more interested in modern times and left history to others, but these were fascinating. Dragons featured on almost every building, although they looked odd. Maybe that was due to the culture, or just the way normal people perceived dragons, but something seemed off about them.

Maybe that was logical. The people who made these had probably never seen a dragon, and it might not matter if they had. The birds in hieroglyphics were recognizable, but they were just symbols. If the wings and tail were too large in the image, who was he to judge?

Jack shivered. An icy wind touched the back of his neck. Agitated, he spun around, but no one was there. He rubbed his neck, frowning. The closest person was Coraolis, and he was deep in conversation with Lieutenant Summers.

He walked over and waited for a lull in the conversation.

Summers was saying, "The scouts say this is literally a maze. None of the streets go through." The lieutenant made a gesture. "Cormican and Tau climbed one of the taller buildings. They say there's a big temple at the center."

"Anything inside these buildings would be interesting," Coraolis replied. "I wish we had more time to look around."

"We can stop and explore at any time, Mike. It's up to you how deep we go." The lieutenant looked around, frowning. His gaze lit on Jack for a moment, then moved on to the trees behind the party. "We need to mark our path from here on out. I don't want to get lost."

"Agreed." Coraolis looked at Jack and frowned when their eyes met. "Is everything okay?"

"Did either of you feel that?" Jack put his hand to his neck again. The sensation was gone, but that didn't mean it wouldn't come back. It didn't seem harmful, but what did he know?

"Feel what?" Summers asked.

Cor shook his head. "I haven't sensed anything unusual since we landed. Why do you ask?"

"Maybe it's nothing. I keep feeling something watching me, but when I turn around, it's gone."

Lieutenant Summers turned toward his team, raising his voice just enough to be heard. "Carey. Ruiz. Scout our back trail. We'll set up a defensive position in this building until you get back. Mike thinks we're being followed."

The scouts nodded and jogged back toward the gate. Jack watched them disappear, then followed Summers into one of the buildings. The first floor was cavernous, a large chamber that resounded with the echoes of their footsteps. Jack chose a corner where he'd be out of the way while E.F. personnel explored.

Coraolis came with him. "I suppose you could use this for an adventure."

"It's a little less fun when we're in the middle of it. That, and we're magic users without a meat shield," Jack joked.

Coraolis chuckled. "It feels strange, being out here just the two of us."

"It does." Jack paused. "Does that mean you miss everyone?"

100

"I do. We have a good team." Coraolis shrugged, then slid down to sit on the floor. "Have you heard from Barb?"

"She's doing well. She likes her new boat. She says she's got a good crew, but she misses us." Jack looked down at Coraolis speculatively, then hunkered down next to him.

"I heard. I miss them too."

"Does that include Dante?"

Coraolis didn't speak at first. When Jack looked at him, he was staring at nothing, his brow creased like it did when he was thinking. Jack left him to it. He didn't like that the answer required thought, but it was better than saying *no* immediately.

"I do. He's not the one I think of when I'm going to sleep, but yes. He's still my friend. I miss our game nights, and he's a big part of those."

"That might have been deliberate," Jack admitted.

Coraolis snorted. "I know. We saw right through your devious scheme."

"And it worked anyway?"

"In a way, yes. I was never anything but Dante's friend. Our relationship would have been repaired either way, but it helped that you pushed us together." Coraolis went on running his finger over the ground, making random shapes. "I think it helped Julia most. She was hurt by what happened. I don't know if she ever told you."

"She did. She said he'd gotten her twice, so it wasn't just a betrayal, she felt like a fool." Technically, Dante had only betrayed her once. The first time had been a dragon, but he still understood how she felt. "Does she still feel that way?"

"She decided to forgive him."

"That's good."

Coraolis nodded. "We just needed a little time to forget, and some good memories to cover up the old ones."

"I guess it was easier for me. Dante's friendship was more important than what he did. I had to choose which one to hold onto, and I chose Dante," Jack said. "Not that you guys were wrong. It's just how I feel."

"You're a good man, Jack. I hope he appreciates it." Coraolis brushed off his hands. "Let's take a look at the Astral Plane, just in case."

Jack opened his eyes, then squinted. He stood in a brightly lit room, the counterpart to the cave-like chamber in the physical world. Coraolis stood beside him, shading his eyes.

The walls were white and smooth as polished marble and felt solid under Jack's hand. A section of wall sported more hieroglyphics, just like the ones he'd seen in the physical world. He traced them with his finger, wishing he could take a picture to compare them.

"What is this?" he asked.

"If you figure it out, let me know. Stick close."

"You read my mind."

Coraolis headed for the doorway, Jack following. They emerged into the street. Coraolis looked over his shoulder every few seconds. He didn't want any surprises; this whole world was strange enough.

Normally, the Astral Plane and physical world were direct reflections of each other. The Empire State Building was a featureless tower in the Astral Plane, but it was the same size, and it had the same properties in both worlds. It didn't change color. It didn't glow.

"Have you ever seen anything like this before?" Jack asked.

"Once or twice. There are some substances that resonate differently in the Astral Plane. This specific one is new to me, but the effect isn't unheard of, just rare." Coraolis froze.

Jack followed his gaze. Every building on the street was made of the same glowing substance. It was brighter than the middle of the day. Even stranger, there were no trees in the street as there had been in the physical world. Everything was as pristine as if it were built yesterday.

Jack rose into the air, his astral wings pulling him up. He didn't need the wings, but he liked them. They were unique to him and reminded him of his close bond with his dragon. It was one more reason why the Astral Plane felt like his natural habitat.

"Do you sense your watcher now?" Coraolis interrupted his thought.

Jack shook his head and pointed. They were high enough that the entire city lay before them in a glowing circle, the streets laid out below them like a map. It wasn't the glowing lines that interested him, though, but the dark spaces in between.

"Look at that," Jack said.

The dark places made lines that twined between the glowing buildings, forming a long, almost snake-like body and a narrow head. Curved wings stretched to encircle the city in their embrace. It was almost a dragon, in the same way that the carvings mimicked a dragon without getting the image exactly right.

"This is beautiful." Jack couldn't tear his eyes away. "How rare did you say this stuff was?"

"It must be more common on this planet. That or this civilization knew how to manufacture it." Coraolis spun in a slow circle, looking at the image from all angles. "I could stare at it all day, but we've probably been out for at least an hour.

If you don't sense your watcher we should head back."

Jack agreed. He took one last look, memorizing the view, before turning back.

The scouts called in not long after the Mystics returned to their bodies. They were going to check in with the pilot, then do another sweep on their way back. So far, they hadn't found any threats.

Jack saw the look on Summers' face and pretended he needed to tie his boot when the officer turned their way. It seemed better to avoid eye contact when Summers looked that irritated.

"Nothing back there but trees and bugs," Summers said to Coraolis. "I don't suppose you're ready to go back?"

Jack glanced at Cor from where he knelt over his boot. At the suggestion of returning, his instincts screamed 'move on.' That was his dragon talking, combined with his own curiosity. Jack wanted to continue. He had to.

Coraolis faced Summers. "Lieutenant, I think I can confidently say that no human has ever seen anything like this before. We've never encountered an entire abandoned city on an unsettled planet. We need to know more before we can leave."

It sounded like he'd prepared that speech. Jack was impressed. He stood, deciding to brave the lieutenant's ire. "Besides, what if we can't come back? When they send an archaeology team, I doubt you'll be on it. Don't you want to see what's out here?"

Summers shrugged, though his expression softened. Jack was sure he could see the curiosity gleaming in the lieutenant's eyes. He had yet to meet an E.F. officer who wasn't an explorer at heart, who wanted to be the first to discover a new planet or find a lost secret.

"Let me call in. If the captain doesn't order us back, we'll press on."

Jack grinned. "That's good enough for me."

The call to *Charon* confirmed it; Captain Wells was just as curious, and they were ordered to do a preliminary exploration. He had already disclosed their find to Earth Fleet. The more detailed the report when the landing team returned, the better.

They cleared some ground and cut an arrow into the dirt to show the direction they were taking. Lieutenant Summers and half the team marched in front of the Mystics with a scout taking point. Four crewmen marched behind, one of the rear guard so far back Jack couldn't see him.

Jack wished they could look into the Astral Plane. He didn't feel watched anymore, but the city was too quiet. It was easy to imagine silent watchers in the buildings, looking down from above as the squad of humans explored the remains of their civilization. It felt like he was trekking through an expansive graveyard, daring ghosts to rise and grab him.

He knew it was silly. Whatever had lived here was long gone; still, he found himself rubbing his arms to ward off goosebumps whenever he was surprised by a stray breeze. He tried to shake it off, but there was no escaping the feeling they weren't alone. He just hoped it was his too-vivid imagination.

CHAPTER EIGHT

Coraolis and Jack walked alone at the center of the group. The crewmen had become more relaxed as time went on, looking outward at the strange city instead of inward at those in their charge.

There were no animal tracks and no birdsong here. The only signs of life were the singing of insects in the trees.

Cor didn't relax so easily. The sight of the Astral Plane on this planet unnerved him. Its strangeness alerted him to all the ways the physical world was off. The doorways were too tall and narrow. The blades of 'grass' growing in the cracks were such a dark shade of green they were almost black. The sight of the trees nagged at him until he figured out the problem; they didn't move in the wind. Even the leaves could have been carved from stone.

In short, it was an alien planet. It was no stranger than he should have expected. Knowing that, however, didn't help him shake the uncanny feeling.

He should have been satisfied with taking samples and heading back. A Mystic didn't have to explore new worlds in person. He'd negotiated with the dragon. He'd surveyed the planet. It was up to scientists and colonists to handle the rest. Yet, his dragon pushed back every time he thought of returning to the ship. There was something here it was seeking, something it wanted Coraolis to see or do. Jack agreed he'd had the same impulse, so they were going with it.

They came to a large square with more streets branching off left and right. A warped statue stood sentinel at the center, towering over them.

Cor was drawn to a huge building on the north side of the square. Massive steps led up to open archways twice as tall as a man. A frieze stretched above the doorways, covering most of the building's facade. He couldn't read the words, but he was fascinated by the serpentine dragon that dominated the image, a planetary orb in its claws. From one angle, it was cradling the sphere gently. From another, it could have been clutching it in its talons. Looking at it too long made Cor's head ache.

"Where are you going?" Summers asked.

Coraolis paused on the first step. Jack was there beside him, his eyes intent on the dragon image.

"I'm going to explore this building," Coraolis said.

"I'll send in a team to clear it. We'll need a place to set up camp, anyway; there's only an hour until sunset."

"That won't work. We need to be the ones to clear it."

Coraolis glanced at Jack, who shrugged.

The lieutenant frowned. "I'm not sending you in there without an escort."

"Tanks," Jack mouthed, a smirk playing across his face.

Coraolis lifted his eyebrows. The gaming reference wasn't lost on him, and the crewmen certainly counted as warriors.

"We'll take two, if you insist. We'll try to move quickly," Cor told Summers.

"Have it your way. Call if you find trouble, we'll come running."

He nodded. That was easy enough. He and Jack waited for the crewmen, then climbed the steps with their 'tank' escorts in tow.

The doorways led to a massive square chamber. The walls were bare, except for a few hieroglyphics that looked almost decorative. A triad of dragons was carved into the ceiling in an intricate dance.

Santiago and Lowe looked around from behind the Mystics, acting a bit fidgety. They didn't like the instructions to let the Mystics lead the way. They were security officers, they were supposed to provide security, but Coraolis stood firm. On this day, in this place, they were a safety net and nothing more.

He strode across the chamber with his companions close behind. A baritone hum filled his ears, or it might have been his mind. The tone became richer as he approached the center of the room, shifting to come at him from every side. It felt like sitting on a speaker on high volume, without the pain in his ears.

"Do you hear that?" he asked.

"Hear what?" Santiago asked.

"I feel something in here." Jack pressed his hand to his chest. "What is this?"

Coraolis shook his head. He didn't know. He took one more step. The phantom vibrations intensified. He moved again and they faded slightly. He stepped back to find the place where the feeling was strongest. It tugged at the heart of him, pulling him in a familiar direction.

"Stay here," he told the others. "I'm going to check the Astral Plane."

He didn't wait for acknowledgement but sat on the floor, hands on his knees. He'd hardly closed his eyes before his astral body stood in a brightly-lit chamber.

He looked up, his eye drawn by motion. The serpentine dragons carved into stone in the physical plane were undulating across the ceiling. He stared as they swam in a slow circle. They weren't alive, but for a moment he hadn't been sure.

When he was certain he wasn't in danger from above, he peered down. He locked into the instincts that had sent him into this plane and held out his hands at its urging.

A sphere the size of a cantaloupe appeared between his cupped palms, pale and smooth like a giant pearl. This globe was divided into sections by thin blue lines, a single glyph carved into each segment. He turned his hands and the sphere turned with it, letting him examine the different markings.

He separated his hands and the sphere vanished. It reappeared when he cupped his hands again.

"Curious," he murmured. He spread his fingers, trying to put one over a glyph. It glowed blue as his finger drew near. He dropped his hands, making the ball vanish again.

His hands shook. This was different than just a strange material in the Astral Plane. It looked like technology, and he wanted to know what it did. It seemed foolish to push a button on an alien artifact on the Astral Plane, but his curiosity would surely kill him if he did nothing at all.

"What do you think?" he asked his dragon.

There was no clear reply. He brought the sphere up again and turned the sphere, examining the glyphs more closely. He put his finger over a glyph with wavy lines that reminded him of a river. Dread filled him as soon as he moved to actually touch the glyph. He jerked his hands away, and the feeling faded with the sphere.

He brought the sphere back and tried a broken triangle glyph. It brought out the same sense of foreboding, so he moved to the next. Every one he tried was the same. Either it served a dangerous purpose in itself, or maybe his dragon thought it too dangerous to use.

He was starting to think he'd need to move on when he tried a glyph that might have been a starburst, or maybe a flower. He moved to touch it, bracing for the expected dread. He felt nothing. He moved so close he could feel the warmth radiating from the glowing sigil. His dragon was silent.

He clenched his teeth and mentally crossed his fingers, then pushed the button.

Nothing happened. He drifted to the back of the chamber to peer through the doors. Two led to empty rooms. The third opened on a staircase to the second floor. He didn't see anything unusual. When he looked out the front, everything was the same as his last excursion to the Astral Plane.

That was disappointing. Perhaps his dragon hadn't cared about this sigil because he knew nothing would happen. Coraolis returned to his body and opened his eyes to a chamber bathed in a soft white light. Cool air rose from the floor, easing the sticky heat. Summers and the rest of the team surrounded him, talking animatedly. Jack was the first to notice that Cor was back.

"Coraolis, what did you do?"

"I pushed a button."

Jack stared at him, trying to decide if Coraolis was kidding or not. He took Cor by the arm and led him to the doorway. The sky was dark. The last of the sunset was fading to the west. Night had fallen, but the city was ablaze with light.

"Did you do this?" Jack asked.

"I suppose I did." It was hard to do anything but stare. The faces of the buildings themselves glowed. Their stone carvings danced across their surfaces. The little dragons flapped their wings, the hieroglyphs moved and changed.

Summers joined them. "I can't complain about the visibility, but it's going to be hard to hide our presence. I'm assigning shifts to keep watch."

"Should I try to turn it off?" Coraolis asked.

"I think the benefit outweighs the risk. I just want you to stay close to the group and get some rest. I want you ready in case we need your magic."

"It isn't really magic..." Coraolis started, but Summers cut him off.

"Whatever you call it, I want you at full charge."

"Do you suppose I turned anything else on?" Coraolis asked after the lieutenant was gone.

Jack looked out into the city again, shifting nervously. "What did you do?"

Coraolis did his best to describe what he'd seen and done, from the swimming dragons to the sphere with all the buttons.

"You took a hell of a chance, Cor," Jack said when he was done.

"I trusted my dragon. But, yes. I know." He stepped outside into the damp night air. "It seemed safe."

"Please don't do it again. I don't want to be the one to tell Julia you didn't come home because you made a rookie gamer mistake."

"I won't. Or at least, I'll check in with you before I do anything foolish," Coraolis promised.

"I guess I'll settle for that."

They camped in a chamber on the upper floor while crewmen stood guard in shifts. Between the hard floor and the well-lit room, sleep did not come easily to Coraolis. Jack took off his shirt and draped it over his face. He began to snore almost immediately.

Coraolis draped his arm over his eyes and tried to relax. He was almost there when the first yowls shattered the night. He jerked upright and listened. Jack slept on, still snoring softly. The crewmen sharing their room were sitting up as well, blinking.

The creature cried out again. This time, the sound was fainter. He rolled onto his side and told himself he was safe. They were under guard, and he'd hear if there was trouble. He forced himself to take long slow breaths, using novice exercises to get his body to a restful state without popping into the Astral Plane.

He heard the yowler a few more times, but each time it was more distant. With his body relaxed, his mind followed its example, and he drifted off to sleep.

The morning sun was dim when Coraolis woke. He felt like he'd hardly slept. He looked beside him, but Jack was gone. The others were as well.

That meant no more time for sleep. He sat up, grimacing as his back protested. He wasn't twenty anymore, and it felt like the stone floor had pummeled him in his sleep. He tried to stretch the feeling away as he stood and ambled to the open window.

A wall of fog greeted him. He could make out the shape of nearby buildings, but only because of the lights. The sun was about as bright as an actor's spotlight, barely able to break through the thick clouds.

He rubbed his eyes. They weren't deceiving him. The city was shrouded in fog as far as he could see. He put a hand out the window. The air was cold and damp. Moisture clung to his skin when he stepped back.

When he got downstairs, Summers and Jack were at the front door. Coraolis joined them with a jaw-cracking yawn. Jack covered his mouth and yawned too. Both men had dark circles under their eyes, and Cor would be surprised if his weren't the same.

"Push any more buttons, Cor?" Jack smiled to show he was kidding, but there was an edge to his voice.

He shook his head. "If you're talking about this fog, it wasn't me."

"Something is freaky here," Summers said. He showed Coraolis his datapad. It was a pixelated mess. Hundreds of different squares of color covered the screen. Summers touched it, and the screen went white until he stopped.

Coraolis pulled out his own datapad. It looked fine until he touched the screen. Then all the icons and words broke into thousands of pieces.

"Mine's the same," Jack told him. "I went in the Astral Plane to see if that device could fix this, but my dragon wouldn't let me touch it."

"So...what do we do?"

Summers sighed. "I was going to ask you that. We need to get out of here, but as you see my GPS is toast."

"Follow the arrows back?"

"That's a problem too. Come see."

Coraolis followed the lieutenant to the square. The fog's dew clung to their skin, covering them in a sweat-like sheen. They walked to the place where Summers had made his mark. There was no sign the ground had been tampered with, and the scraped arrow was gone.

Coraolis turned, searching nearby for the lieutenant's mark. They were in the right place, he was sure of it.

"I had my team scour the square. Every mark is gone. I sent scouts back to the last mark, and they couldn't find it either. They came back after an hour, swearing they got lost when all they did was go in a straight line. Got turned around, they said."

Coraolis shivered, wiping the damp from his face. Summers did the same, then started back toward their shelter.

"The way I see it, we have three options. We could stay here and wait out the weather, but we don't know this planet. It could be days, and we don't have the supplies for that."

"True enough," Coraolis said.

"We could try to find a way out, but I was marking our path for a reason. This place is a maze. We're just as likely to get lost going back as forward," Summers went on, "so I'm leaving it to you two. We're not staying here. Do you want to go on or try to find our way out?"

"Can you reach the shuttle?"

The lieutenant made an impatient noise. "That was the first thing I tried. We're cut off. Your partner said he wants to go on, but he won't decide without you."

Coraolis nodded. The smart thing to do was to get to the shuttle. Logically, there was no need for them to risk themselves further. If it was up to him, he'd choose that option for the sake of the team.

But he wasn't the only one weighing in. His dragon was making his opinion known, nudging Coraolis toward the heart of the city. He'd made a pact to work with his dragon. If they weren't in immediate danger, he had to honor their pact.

"We go on."

Summers bit back a sigh, then nodded. "I figured you'd say that. We're ready to roll when you are."

They kept to the middle of the streets where the fog seemed thinnest. Every member of the team in sight of at least two others. Summers cycled from the front of the group to the back, then to the front again, making sure no one lagged behind.

Coraolis felt hemmed in, both by E.F. crewmen and the thick fog banks. They were all damp and exhausted. He thought longingly of his bunk on the *Charon.*

"After this, I want to revisit the terms we have with the dragons," Jack grumbled.

"I don't think they'd push us this hard if it wasn't important." Coraolis tried stretching again. A knot over his shoulder blades refused to release. "Think about it. We're the first human beings on this planet. This is the first lost alien civilization discovered by mankind. We're privileged to be here."

"Unless you can see through fog, none of us are seeing any of it," Jack scoffed, then softened. "Sorry, Cor, I'm not trying to take this out on you."

"No worries. I know how you feel. This place is connected directly to the Astral Plane. It's different from anything we've ever seen before."

Summers called a halt; they were in another square, this one paved in stone. That felt like a good sign; it meant they hadn't gone in a circle. Summers brought them close and did a headcount. Everyone was accounted for, but he seemed uneasy all the same.

"Am I seeing things, or is that an animal?" he asked, pointing.

A long, low silhouette stood in the heart of the fog. If he squinted, Coraolis could make out four legs and what might be a snout. Then it shifted and faded into the mist. It looked exactly like the shape of a wolf, but that was impossible. Still, he found himself calling it a shadow wolf in his mind, just to put a label on it.

A flicker moved to his right. Coraolis turned his head in time to get an impression of something loping, but it vanished before his eyes could focus.

He called on his power, willing a ball of lightning into his palm. If they were attacked, he wanted to do his part to defend them. He could feel the energy waiting for him to shape it, but when he reached for it, it danced out of his reach. He grasped for it again, and it slid through his fingers.

"Cor...I can't use my power," Jack murmured. "I thought I'd try hiding us from whatever that is."

"Same here. The power is there, I just can't touch it."

Summers had seen enough. He gathered everyone into formation, then got them quick-marching down the street. The crewmen had their weapons ready, scanning for threats. Coraolis wished he had one of his own, but he wouldn't know how to handle it.

The shadow wolves darted in and out of sight, keeping to the thickest patches of fog. Whenever one appeared, a dozen firearms pointed at it, only for it to fade before another appeared at their backs. They tried going into a building, but the fog was inside, too, with more shadows poised to attack.

They returned to the street, with Coraolis in the lead. He knew where they were going and wanted to get there before their hunters did more than threaten. Summers ordered the crew to hold fire unless they were attacked. Coraolis could see discipline wearing thin though. When they hit a dead-end, they let out a collective groan.

Then he realized it wasn't a dead-end. A step was visible at the very edge of the thickest part of the fog. He stepped onto it, then felt for the next one. "Follow me," he directed.

Jack kept close behind, Summers and company following after.

The steps led to a barrier at least five meters tall. It was forged of metal, its surface completely blank. There was no visible sign that it was anything but a metal section of wall, but Coraolis still knew it for what it was.

He pressed his hands to its smooth surface. He felt energy within waiting to be unlocked, yet he couldn't quite reach it. Jack moved next to him, placing his hands next to Cor's. Something *clicked*.

"Tell me you're doing something," Summers said.

"We're doing something," Cor promised, and a metal door swung inward.

There wasn't so much as a scrap of fog inside. Summers ushered the last of his team through the doorway before he went in. Coraolis and Jack followed, urged by their dragons.

CHAPTER NINE

Faceless humanoid statues dominated the corridor, their heads brushing a ceiling at least thirty feet high. Their crystal spearpoints shimmered, casting a flickering light over the area. Their draconic wings flared out on either side, just touching the next statue's wingtip.

The ivory carvings stood in stark contrast against the black pearlescent walls. The dark sheen broke apart into shades of indigo and violet where light struck them, the colors rippling like pools of oil.

"Do you suppose the statues move too?" Jack murmured.

"I certainly hope not. If they were going to, they would have by now, don't you think?" Coraolis took a few cautious steps forward, waiting for a reaction from the sentinels. When nothing happened, he allowed himself to breathe.

"What do you suppose this place is?"

Coraolis shook his head. He didn't know any more than Jack. He took out his datapad and was glad to see its screen had returned to normal. He took a few pictures of the statues, moving to capture different angles.

"I don't know any more than you, Jack, but it looks important. It could have been a state building, maybe, or some kind of temple."

"You mean like a palace? It's a nice place for alien princes to live, assuming there's some furniture somewhere," Jack quipped.

"Sure it is, especially if it can keep the fog out."

"All right, everybody listen up!" Summers made a sweeping gesture to bring everyone in. "We're inside, but that doesn't mean we're safe. We're going to find another exit, then we're going to get out of this city."

"Wait a minute," Jack said.

"I know I said I'd follow your lead, Mike, but something isn't right. I'm not risking my men on your whim. Santiago, you've got point. Davis, you cover our rear. You know the drill."

"Sir!" Santiago snapped off a salute, then set off down the hallway.

"So much for following our dragons," Jack muttered. "Not that I can argue. It was insane out there."

The team set off in a fast march.

Coraolis frowned, realizing he hadn't felt a single nudge from his dragon since they got inside. He thought about leaving without doing whatever his dragon wanted him to do. He thought about returning to Earth and never coming back. No matter how he focused on those ideas as if they were the stone truth, he couldn't get a rise.

"I'm not getting anything from my dragon," he said.

Jack frowned, deep lines appearing between his eyebrows. "Me neither, now that you mention it. We must be on the right track."

"Keep an eye out for whatever it is we're supposed to do. I don't think the lieutenant will want to stop anymore." Cor adjusted the straps on his backpack as he tried to get into the groove of their doubled pace.

The corridor split in two, then split again. Soon it became clear they were in a maze rivaling the streets outside. Summers's expression turned grim as they searched for a way out. They passed through rooms with the furniture Jack had wished for. There were elaborately carved benches and wall hangings with patterns that changed as he looked at them. They were lovely, if sparse, and he wondered what had driven the people from such a fantastic city.

Summers called for a break in one such room. A circle of benches surrounded a shallow pit. Two crewmen stood guard at each door, while the rest of the group sat on the benches and ate a portion of their rations.

Coraolis's feet ached, but he didn't complain. Jack seemed fine, but he also ran two miles with Julia every morning. Cor wasn't so well trained and thought maybe he should do something about that.

"Sir?"

Davis was at the door. His unusually high-pitched voice drew everyone's attention, and Cor saw why. A tendril of gray fog was creeping into the room from the hallway, groping blindly along its path.

Cor's rations turned to sawdust in his mouth. He was on his feet before Summers said the word. They were all on the move, hurrying to the door on the far side of the room and down the next corridor before the chamber could fill with fog. Hurry as they might, the hall was soon filled, and Coraolis could hardly see the back of the man in front of him.

Khiann stalked the humans through the ancient temple, making no more noise than her shadow on the wall. Her sharp ears zeroing in on every word the humans spoke, every footstep that echoed through the maze of corridors. Her earpiece fed what she heard to *Night Thorn* in real time, and the computer fed the translation back to her.

They feared the mind fog, and the fear shadows she raised within it. They wanted to leave the city now, and that was exactly what she wanted. But every step carried them further into the sacred site. Everything they touched would need to be sanctified. They had to be removed before they did irreparable damage.

She came upon their rear guard. He was glancing fearfully to either side, flinching at the sight of the shadows and fog. He was too distracted by phantasms to notice her sweep in.

Each alien species had differences in their physiologies, but all had one thing in common. They required oxygen, and the fastest way to incapacitate them was to deny them of it. She caught the human's throat in the crook of her elbow and squeezed as she yanked him off his feet.

He went off balance. When he fell, his weight pulled his throat more heavily into her arm. He clawed at her armor, kicking and fighting. She admired his tenacity. Soon, he went limp, and she dumped him in the center of the floor, unconscious but not dead.

She would not kill a sentient except in honorable combat. She would fight if it came to that, but she was no fool. She was outnumbered. The humans would react with deadly force as soon as they saw her. It was better to whittle them down using her fog and fear-shadows.

When the warriors were gone, she would face the Mystics. The ungifted humans could be pardoned, but the Mystics had entered the Astral

Plane. They had touched the Ancients' artifacts. That was unforgivable.

The next human came into sight. Hardly a curtain of fog existed between the soldier and her companions, but it was enough. Khiann focused her energy on the female. She slowed as the wall of fog closed in, disoriented and surrounded by fearful shapes. The soldier stopped and turned in place, eyes wide. Then she started walking again, hurrying to catch up to her companions, but she bumped into the wall.

She opened her mouth to call out. Khiann clasped her hand over the human's mouth, her arm cutting off the woman's air. She struggled, but she couldn't find purchase on the floor or on Khiann's arm. She soon went as limp as boiled leaves.

Khiann left her on the floor like the other warrior and hurried after her next victim.

When the group dispersed, it didn't worry Cor so much. He stuck close to Jack and tried to keep up with the crewmen silhouetted in front of him.

"Summers," he called, but the figures in front of him didn't slow. He tried to pick up speed, but he only fell further behind.

"What is it?" Jack asked.

"Something doesn't feel right. I feel like everyone's in danger." He stopped.

"We should keep moving," Jack said, but he stopped as well. Then he frowned and looked around them. "Where is everyone?"

Coraolis tried to reach out with his abilities. He didn't expect them to work after the fog had smothered him outside. Yet, in this place, he could sense the lives of every member of the team. Summers, Davis, Santiago...each of them was far behind...and very still.

"We've been chasing phantoms. Everyone is behind us. I think they're incapacitated."

Jack looked alarmed. "What? Which way?"

Cor reached out with his senses, seeking the right path. Finally, he felt sure of his direction. He put his hand to the cool stone wall and began walking, gripping Jack's sleeve so he wouldn't leave his friend behind.

It felt wrong, but he could no longer trust his instincts. He was getting close to the crewmen, and that was enough to tell him he was on the right path.

Then, the corridor ended in a huge dome-shaped room he didn't recognize. The black walls of the corridor transitioned into smooth silver panels shaped like honeycomb. The fog thinned, and he spied a stone dais in the center of the room. Twin serpents twisted out of its base, creating a figure eight with their bodies before turning back to face the center of the dais.

Even from where he stood, Coraolis could see the menace in their eyes.

His gaze lit on the object at the center of the dais. It seemed to be the target of the serpents' attention, a pearl-white cylinder about the length and width of his forearm, made of sections divided by golden rings. A jet black circle was set into its center. He couldn't make out much detail at this distance, but everything in him wanted to move closer, to take it in hand.

"I think this is what they wanted," Jack said. He'd already taken several steps toward the artifact.

Coraolis hurried to keep up. The object had a gravity of its own, and the closer the Mystics came to it, the more they were pulled in. No doubt that was caused by their dragons' wills. No matter where it came from, Coraolis didn't like it. He'd gladly help the dragon he'd made a pact with, but did the dragon understand the consequences of certain actions in the material plane, like those that affected his mortality?

The urges faded as soon as Jack picked up the artifact. It didn't look like much compared to the other things they'd seen. It had one glyph, and that was traced onto the black circle.

Cor wondered what would happen if he touched it. As soon as the thought was complete, a terrible wave of dread and guilt landed on his shoulders. He went to his knees, gasping for breath.

"Cor? What's wrong?" Jack took his arm and helped him up.

"I'm fine. Just don't mess with that thing. Don't touch it...don't even think about it."

Jack turned the object over in his hand, frowning. "Okay, I won't. Why, you weren't going to push the button, were you? Didn't we have a talk about that?"

"Yes, we did, and I was *not* going to."

"That is correct," came an exotic voice. "You will return the treasure to its place, and then you will die."

A stranger emerged from the fog. She wore matte black armor that covered her from the high mesh collar to her sharp-toed boots. She had large eyes slit like a cat's, and pale luminescent skin, unlike anything he'd seen in a human, even if her sharp ears and inhuman proportions didn't give her away as an alien.

"That's not how it works. This is supposed to be where you offer to let us live if we put the toy down. You should offer to let us go if we give it up," Jack told her helpfully.

She sneered. Her lips moved out of sync with her words, her voice too harmonic to be real. "You forfeited your life the moment you stepped foot on this planet, human. It is too late for bargains."

"Wait, what do you mean by that?" Cor asked.

Her answer was to charge forward, slicing through the air at throat level. Jack danced backward, holding the artifact like a shield. She surged at them again. Jack threw himself to the side and vanished from sight. She turned with a hiss.

Coraolis pushed himself to act. He gathered his power and threw lightning into her side. She was knocked off her feet and rolled, coming upright with the grace of a gymnast.

The stranger threw herself at Coraolis, a long blade held out to the side. He flung more lightning, but her movements were liquid. She dodged without breaking stride. Then, she tripped on nothing and fell. Her knife skittered in one direction, she in the other.

She rose to her feet with some dark fluid trickling from the corner of her mouth.

"Humans have no honor," she spat.

"You were about to gut my friend," came Jack's disembodied voice. "I had to do something."

The alien's hands moved in a blur, and Jack reappeared with a hilt buried in his shoulder. He sagged against the wall behind him, looking pale.

"Hide again, Jack! I'll deal with her." Coraolis moved to stand between his friend and the alien, calming his nerves. "You attacked us with no provocation, attacked our companions, and threatened our lives. From my point of view, you're the one with no honor. Leave him, and fight me."

"You would challenge me?" The disbelief in her voice verged on hilarity, though she stopped advancing on Jack. "Very well. I accept. The loser forfeits their life and goods."

"The winner leaves the planet in peace. The loser goes their own way. No more attacks," Coraolis snapped.

"So it is, so it will be. What is your battleground of choice?"

He looked around, wondering if he could say 'Earth' just to put this off. But no, that was without honor. She could kill him easily and wouldn't let him evade the inevitable. He wasn't sure how he could fight her in this world. She'd moved like the blade was an extension of her hand. She'd easily dodged his lightning. Coraolis didn't stand a chance against her.

Not in this world, anyway.

"I choose the Astral Plane."

He expected her to question, or maybe protest it, but she nodded thoughtfully. She selected a place on the floor opposite Coraolis and sat with her legs crossed.

"It is well," she agreed.

His heart sank. She was a capable warrior; he'd assumed that meant she wasn't a Mystic. He should have known better, but at least now he'd be on an even playing field.

"Cor, don't do this," Jack whispered.

"I have to. Find the others. I'll catch up."

"Cor."

"Go."

He heard Jack shuffling his feet and moving away. The alien's eyes followed the sound, but she remained seated.

"So now what? Do you choose the weapon?"

She shook her head. "Your only weapon is your will, regardless of the shape it takes."

Khiann bowed her head, and Coraolis realized she'd left her body. He was surprised she trusted him that much. An untrustworthy person would take advantage of that, maybe tie her up and walk away without a fair fight, but he couldn't bring himself to do that. Honor. It's what he had told Earth Fleet to justify his actions. It's what he told Julia. It was who he was.

He left his body and found her waiting, holding a blade like the one she'd wielded in the physical world. She waited a beat, giving him a chance to get his bearings, then attacked.

Coraolis wasn't much of a fighter in the physical world, but in the Astral Plane, few could match him. As soon as she committed to the strike, he flowed around her blade to reappear behind her. He slammed his palm between her shoulder blades and released a torrent of energy.

She yelped and flickered out of sight. He felt a twinge from his dragon and flew aside just in time, as a spear of light flashed by. Had he not moved, he would have been impaled.

He twisted and eluded several attacks. She left herself open, and he rained fireballs onto her. She cried out and was singed when she reappeared in front of him, weary resignation in her eyes.

"Do you want to concede?" he asked.

She charged, a spear of light clutched in both hands. He batted it aside with hardly a thought and counterattacked with a flash of lightning. The thunderclap that followed rippled through the Astral Plane. She cried out and vanished.

He waited, but she was gone. He'd won. He didn't quite believe it; he'd seen her prowess in the physical world, but maybe she wasn't as strong in the Astral Plane.

When he was sure she was gone, he returned to his body. Exhaustion slammed into him, but he pushed himself to his feet and staggered to where the alien lay on her side. She was unconscious, but breathing. He didn't feel guilty about leaving her behind while he looked for the others. The stranger was on her own.

Khiann awoke in the dark. Every part of her felt like it was on fire, because for a moment her astral form had been burning. She had been completely overwhelmed. The human had too much power, likely because of his bargain with the vile dragons.

He'd been too much for her. She was lucky to have survived.

As it was, the humans were long gone, and she was on her own. She bowed her head, acknowledging her failure, and worse. She could no longer handle this alone. She would need to call on her kin.

CHAPTER TEN

By the time Coraolis found Jack, he had revived several of the crew. They woke up groggy, but alive. Jack helped the first of them outside while Coraolis saw to the rest. Their datapads were operational again, allowing them to find their way out of the city and back to the shuttle. Exhausted, they fell into their seats.

The auto-pilot flew them to the *Charon*. After landing, they left the shuttle without a word to each other. They were too tired, saving their energy for their verbal report.

Captain Wells listened, then declared they would take the scenic route home. This was the first alien attack on humans in decades; he wasn't about to lead a strange race to their homeworld. It was standard procedure, but plenty of grumbles went up when the crew heard they weren't headed straight back to Earth.

At first, Coraolis and Jack kept up their evening game sessions. Sometimes Jack came prepared, others he ran on the fly. Cor seemed to have a good time, but one by one, their audience melted away. Borrowed manuals were returned, and the crewmen who'd become neutral or even friendly stopped greeting them in the hallway. Then they stopped making eye contact. The only one who acknowledged their existence was the chief, and even that was no more than a brisk nod as they passed, each going their own way.

Without any real discussion, they started going to meals at the tail end of each shift to avoid the crowds. Jack didn't have to see the hostile stares to know they were there. When they played games in the galley at night, he caught more than one crewman giving him and Cor hostile looks. It got to the point where it was uncomfortable to play in public at all.

"I get the feeling we're getting the blame for this detour," Jack murmured to Coraolis. They were two weeks past their planned date of return, and even Jack was feeling antsy. He didn't miss being a guinea pig, but he wondered how Isabel was doing.

"They'll get a little shore leave when we stop at Zeri Station. That should take the edge off." Coraolis opened their cabin door and ushered Jack through first.

"We're stopping? I didn't think there were any Earth Fleet stations in this sector." Jack dropped onto his bunk and lay back, using his arm as a pillow. "I'd like a little time off this boat myself."

"It isn't one of ours, it belongs to the Tiel, but they'll trade us for supplies."

"How do you even hear these things?"

"I'm the senior Mystic on the mission. It's standard procedure to notify me. In fact, it's our job to check it out and make sure it's secure from the Astral side of things. So that's our duty for tomorrow. Once we're clear, we'll dock."

"I can't wait." Jack reached for a book as Coraolis sat on the floor to meditate. His eyes skimmed over the descriptions of monsters and fantasy creatures but didn't take any of it in. He felt a little like a kid on Christmas Eve, not just because of the shore leave, but because come morning, they'd finally have something useful to do.

Zeri Station was shaped like a donut, with its power source spinning like a city-sized top at its center. It passed the Mystics' inspection in the Astral Plane, and soon *Charon* was docked. While Wells negotiated for supplies, crewmembers were given leave in shifts. Jack and Cor flipped a coin to decide who got leave first, and Jack was the lucky winner.

The moment he stepped into the station, Jack was nearly overwhelmed by the loud music, alien voices, and bright lights. There were two large entryways with alien lettering splashed above them. Banners next to the entryways had translations of the marquee in several different languages. He thought one of them might be French, so he ran it through the datapad to find out what it said: *Tonight Only, Bava Inga Sings the Blues.*

He ran the Yeti version through the translator and came up with the same result. He wandered inside, curious about what the alien version of the blues would be, and found himself in a bar any human would feel at home in. Booths lined the wall, and round tables clustered near a stage.

A Yeti in a shiny red jumpsuit stood at the microphone, crooning in an unmistakable rhythm while his companions plunked at a bass guitar and piano. While the words weren't in English, the tune was exactly right. The musicians were easily eight feet tall, with shaggy white hair and tusks that gave them their human name. Jack had met Yetis before, but he'd had no idea they could sing.

He slid into an empty chair and listened. When a server bot came around with a menu, he ordered a beer without even thinking. The beverage that turned up at his table was carbonated and a bright shade of red, but it tasted like a good IPA.

The song came to an end, and he stood to applaud. All three Yetis turned to look at him, their whiskers bristling. His clapping slowed as he realized the rest of the audience was staring in silence. Maybe he'd misstepped. Maybe clapping was rude in Yeti culture.

He sat down. When he nearly missed the chair, he realized the beer had affected him a little more than he'd expected. He righted himself and took another sip, waiting for the moment to blow over so he could make a quiet exit.

He wasn't quite sure what to do when the Yeti singer pulled up a seat opposite him.

"Hey," he said.

The Yeti nodded.

"I liked your music." He raised his glass in a salute. "It felt like being home."

The Yeti made a purr-like sound and removed a black cylinder from one of its jumpsuit pockets. A robotic voice emanated from the device as the Yeti growled softly.

"You are a human. You enjoyed this?" he asked.

"So much! It took me back to college, man. My first date with my first serious girlfriend. She took me to a blues club. It was so loud I couldn't understand the words at all, but I got the feel of it, you know?" Jack put a hand over his heart, then let it drop to the table. "Where'd you hear about this music?"

"The McNuggen brought us Blues. She taught us of human culture. My brothers and I are fans. Do you know the McNuggen?" the Yeti asked.

"Yeah, actually we're pretty good friends. My name's Jack, by the way. What should I call you?"

"Bava. My brothers are Inga."

"Both of them?" Jack reached across the table. His hand was enveloped by a large, furry paw with rough pads at the tips of the fingers.

"Yes. I am eldest," Bava said as if that explained everything.

Jack nodded wisely and flagged down the server bot. "I want to buy Bava a drink. Bring him something good," he instructed the robot.

Bava purred. "I accept your proposal of friendship, Human Jack. Clan Inga will be your ally."

"Good to hear it." Jack grinned and toasted the singer again. "I can always use more friends."

"Yes, if you are to survive. You may join my band if you like. Do you know drums? We need a percussionist."

"Huh?" Jack put his drink down. Either that made no sense, or he'd had too much to really follow. "Survive what?"

"I own this bar which is close to the docks, and so I was given warning. The human vessel will be held until such time as the Pirr arrive." The Yeti's drink arrived, a foamy concoction with three small red balls floating at its center.

"Okay, what's a Pirr?"

The Yeti made a new sound that didn't translate, but by the way he was shaking, Jack thought it must be laughter.

"The Pirr. They are very dangerous, my friend. If they choose you as their enemy, you will be destroyed. You would be better off in my band. If you do not know drums, you may sing backup while you learn," the emotionless mechanical interpretation relayed.

"I've never heard of these Pirr."

"They do not reveal themselves unless they think you worthy. You must have done something wonderful to get their attention. Or, something terrible." Bava whistled through his teeth. "They will destroy your ship and all aboard."

"Then we need to go." Jack sent payment to the barkeeper through his datapad and got up from the table. "How do we go?"

The Yeti shook his head. "The ship is locked in. Only the harbormaster can release you."

"Then I'll find the harbormaster. Thanks for the tip, Bava. You guys rock." Jack held his fingers in the trident shape of hard rockers from the past. He turned and headed for the corridor.

"Luck be with you, friend Jack! May you also rock!" the Yeti called after him trying to imitate the hand gesture.

Jack hurried to the port, weaving through the crowd. He wasn't able to maintain more than a light jog, and his visibility was nil. He didn't even see the security guards until they had him by the scruff of the neck.

"This port is closed for maintenance." The huge guard turned Jack around and nudged him away. "Return in one day."

"It can't be closed for maintenance. My ship is back there." Jack tried to pull away from the guard's massive hand, but his grip on Jack's shirt tightened.

"The ships in this port are also locked down for maintenance."

"How can you do that? It isn't your ship," Jack protested, but the guard didn't answer. Instead, he nudged Jack between the shoulder blades to get him moving.

He stumbled but was saved from hitting the floor by a hand under his arm. Summers had a grip on his elbow, his jaw set.

"Did you get turned away too?" Jack asked.

Summers nodded tightly. "I need to get in touch with the captain."

"It's the Pirr. They're coming to get us."

"Who is the Pirr?" Summers demanded, just short of snapping. "I'm not in the mood for jokes, Mike."

"I don't know exactly, but I think they must be the aliens from Amadeus. I was told we're being held until they arrive so they can destroy *Charon.* And us," he added as an afterthought.

Summers sniffed the air. "Have you been drinking?"

"That's beside the point. My new friend Bava the Yeti said that the Pirr are after us, and as far as I know, there's only one alien race that hates humans currently."

The two men shuffled closer to the wall, hindered by the crowd's press and Jack's own clumsiness.

"They are following us. I was afraid of that." Summers got them to the wall and put his back to it while he scanned the crowd. "What do you suggest, Mike?"

"If we could get to the ship, then we get Cor to short out the docking clamp and fly away while I cloak us."

"Can you do it drunk?" Summers growled.

Jack shrugged. "Get some coffee in me, and I'll be fine."

Summers muttered something under his breath and steered Jack into the nearest establishment. That meant the club where Bava and his brothers had been performing. Now they were gathered around Jack's old table, talking in surprisingly high, trilling voices.

"Jack has returned! Have you changed your mind?" Bava stood to greet them, opening his arms expansively. "But you brought a friend. Does he play an instrument?"

"I do not." Summers gave Jack a suspicious look. "You make friends fast, do you?"

"I bought Bava a drink. He seemed to like it." Jack pulled an empty chair up to the table. "How's it going, guys?"

"We are well. We have made a new friend, and we have received human applause. All is well." The Yeti grinned, showing an unsettling number of teeth. "How is it going with you?"

"We can't get to our ship, and we've got crew on leave I need to find." Summers moved to stand over Jack's shoulder, arms crossed over his chest. "That's how it's going."

"If we can get 'em all here, I can get us on the ship," Jack added.

"I'd message them with my datapad, but I've got no connectivity. What about you, Jack?"

Jack pulled out his datapad. Its applications worked, but anything linked with a network or another device was disabled. "I've got nothing."

"No matter. We will help you bring your human companions to my club." Bava growled something at Inga and Inga. The other two Yeti barked something in return, then walked out of the club. "Now we only have to wait. Will you drink?"

"No." Summers spoke over Jack. "No more drinking, unless you've got plain old water."

"Thanks, anyway," Jack said. "We've got a mission now."

Before ten minutes had passed, Jack had his datapad out. He played his favorite songs for Bava from classics to pop music he'd loved as a kid. When Jack offered to copy his files over to the Yeti's device, Bava almost exploded from excitement.

Summers twitched an eyebrow.

"This isn't piracy. This is sharing our cultures," Jack declared, even though no one had accused him of anything.

Summers shrugged and went back to playing with his datapad. Something in Bava's many pockets screeched, and he pulled out a flat square device. Someone yowled at Bava through the device.

"There is a new plan. Come with me," Bava said.

"What plan is this?" Summers didn't move. "I didn't approve any new plan."

"This is a plan where security raids my club but finds no humans to arrest." The Yeti patted Summers on the head. "Jack is kind to befriend someone so far beneath him."

Summers sputtered, and Jack pretended to cough before he laughed. "Come on, LT. I know we just met him, but Bava's the best chance we've got."

"I don't know about that," Summers muttered, but he got up and followed along as Bava led them up the steps to the polished black stage. He held the curtain aside to let them through, then followed.

"What now?" Jack asked.

The Yeti shook his head agitatedly. His long locks of fur flared out from his head, making it double in size.

"You must not be here when security arrives. My brothers, they already carry your fellow humans as cargo to your ship. We have paid many bribes for the guards to look the other way. If they knew Jack was our friend, it would not go well for us. It would be the end of the band." Bava shook his head again.

"Hey. Bava." Jack reached out to stroke his new friend's fur, trying to calm it. "Don't worry. I can get us out. Just hold the curtain back after we disappear, then do the same with the outer door. I've got this."

"Are you sure about this, Gagnon?" Summers asked.

"Sure as can be. It's just easier if no one's looking when we go invisible. Can you do that for us, Bava? Can you hold the curtain and the door and make it look natural?"

"Yes, but what will you do?" The Yeti stopped shaking his head and put a large paw over the Mystic's hand for a moment.

Jack grasped Summers's wrist, then focused. As power filled him, he made it spill over to cover Summers the same as himself. The barrier would bend the minds of anyone looking their way, making them unnoticeable for the duration.

Bava sucked in a breath, and stepped back, making a gap in the curtain the humans could slip through. As he passed by, Jack thought he heard the giant alien mutter something like *Pirr,* but there was no time to stop and ask. Bava walked across the club ahead of them and pushed the door open. He stood holding it open, growling in his own tongue as he surveyed the crowd.

Jack felt a tug on his arm. "Let's move," Summers hissed in his ear. "I don't want to stand around holding hands all day."

"You're the boss. Just keep your voice down," Jack hissed. They hurried down the hall. They were still moving against the crowd's flow, but there was sufficient space to weave through to the entrance to the port.

The two guards stood with their arms folded over their chests, snarling at anyone who came too near. They didn't see Jack and Summers as they approached. Jack hesitated when they were within grabbing range, but the guards didn't so much as twitch.

He grinned and slipped between them, pulling Lieutenant Summers along behind.

The only signs of activity in the port were labor bots moving pallets in or out of cargo holds. A pair of Yeti oversaw a red bot as it loaded crates into *Charon's* hold. Wells was on the deck, arguing with them, while they talked back in their own language. As far as Jack could tell, neither understood the other, but it didn't stop them from disagreeing.

"I said I didn't agree to this purchase! The E.F. will not be responsible for the cost of this..." Wells consulted his datapad. "Yeti combs. What are we going to do with five hundred kilos of Yeti combs?"

Inga warbled at him, and both Yeti snuffled. Jack was pretty sure they were giggling at Captain Wells. He thought Wells was getting the idea too.

"Captain." Summers pulled away from Jack and came into sight. When there was no immediate uproar, Jack let go of his powers and sagged. A furry arm wrapped around his shoulders and held him up.

"Thanks, Inga," he said.

"Summers? Where the hell have you been?" Wells demanded. "I'm trying to get off this tin hat, and they won't let me call my crew back!"

"Your crew is in the crates," Jack said. "The Yeti helped me get everyone on board."

"You?" Wells snapped. "You put my men in boxes?"

"I got them safely off Zeri Station. Aliens are coming for us, captain. The ones from Amadeus."

"We have reason to believe they'll destroy *Charon* if it's still here when they arrive," Summers added.

Jack smiled. The lieutenant was on board after all.

"Then we need to go." Wells ushered Summers on board, then stopped to give the Yeti a suspicious look. "They don't want to come, do they?"

"Who, Inga? No. They'd never break up the band." Jack bowed his head to the brothers, and they returned the gesture. "Thanks, guys. Tell Bava too."

The pair chortled and jogged away. The labor bot rolled out of the cargo bay and trundled off down the walkway to its next job. Jack nodded to Wells and boarded the ship, the captain following closely behind.

Escaping Zeri Station was nearly as simple as Jack had hoped. Coraolis disrupted their lock controls from the Astral Plane. As soon as they were released, Jack cloaked the ship. It flew away without a single challenge.

Rather than find another scenic route, Wells decided the best course was to head directly home. If the Pirr knew enough to figure out where they were going, they likely knew Earth's location.

The crew's demeanor relaxed once underway. No one forgot it was Jack who got their crewmates off Zeri, and they took to calling him 'the Ambassador' when they heard how he'd befriended the Yeti.

Better yet, when they got permission to message their loved ones back home, the crew became almost friendly. Jack sent a short message to Julia and Dante, and sent one to Isabel too.

Finally, he sent a message to Bava on Zeri Station. There were no words or images to give Jack away as a human. He didn't know what the Pirr would do to his Yeti friend if they found out he'd helped the humans. Instead, Jack sent one of his favorite musical films and hoped the Yeti would get the message.

CHAPTER ELEVEN

The planet *Hoi* enveloped Khiann with a welcome heat. Resources were finite even on *Night Thorn,* and so she could never keep it warm enough to be truly comfortable.

Once she landed, she changed from her Legion uniform to a loose-fitting wrap and strapped her blade to her back. The wrap was black to signify her affiliation with the Legion, with clasps forged from precious metals to represent her birth rank.

She would just as soon trade them for plain copper, but that was impossible even if it didn't cause mortal offense to her father. A Pirr was her clan, and her clan, the Pirr. Nothing in life could change that.

She left *Night Thorn* to the technicians and departed for headquarters. It was near midday, and *Hoi's* blue star was blinding in its brilliance. Her protective lid slipped into place over her eyes when she glanced up at it, putting a shadow over everything.

The walk was all too short. Soon, she was back within four walls, in an environment that was neither too hot nor too cold being as carefully controlled as a space station. Some preferred it that way, but she would rather live with the whims of nature. Anything else made her soft.

A page greeted her at the door and bowed. Her left ear twitched in annoyance, but she inclined her head. It wouldn't do to deny the gesture. The page was correct to bow. It wasn't her fault that Khiann preferred a well-earned salute over groveling.

"Commander Khiann, Lady Xoa, the High Commander requires your presence," the little thing parroted.

"One name is sufficient," she said crisply. "I will find him. You are dismissed."

The page bowed, nose scraping her shins before she made herself scarce. Khiann watched until she disappeared around a corner. She'd planned to submit a thorough report first, but it seemed she wasn't so lucky.

High Commander Afit's office was overwhelmed with greenery. Blue vines crept up the north wall, with the occasional white blossom straining toward the window. Hanging plants effectively lowered the ceiling by several feet, and Khiann had to step carefully or hit her head on the pottery. Afit's workstation was clear of anything resembling work.

He watched as a gardener pruned the plants at the window, sipping a cup of Yarbrew. He waved Khiann in when he saw her step into the open doorway. He didn't look at her, and that was how she knew she was in trouble.

The gardener gathered up the collected trimmings and hurried out of the office, bowing her head to avoid Khiann's eyes. When they were alone, Afit drained the last of his brew.

Khiann walked in and stood to the left of the empty chair, her hands clasped behind her back.

"You wanted to see me, High Commander?"

"Lady Xoa. It is always a pleasure to see you." He still hadn't looked at her.

"It is as much an honor as always," Khiann replied in kind. His cheek twitched, but without eye contact, the emotion behind it was hard to read.

"Enough. I have received word of your mission. Is it true that you permitted humans on the surface of *Ixhoi?*"

Her left hand's grip on the right tightened. She wanted to protest his word choice, but she knew better than to fight that battle. There was a more important one ahead.

"I believed the dragon would prevent them. I was unprepared when it did not."

His ears curled in contempt. "Humans are the enemy, Xoa. Any action they even think of taking must be thwarted at any cost. That is your duty."

"Yes, sir."

"Now tell me what happened on the surface."

Khiann hesitated for a fraction of a second. Her field reports would have arrived ahead of her. Afit would know of her failure already. This was an attempt to shame her further. She would answer because he was her commander, but she wouldn't own any more shame than what she deserved.

"I found the humans after they had already breached the walls of the city. They explored its buildings and entered its Astral Plane to sabotage the city's workings."

"Did they succeed?"

"To my knowledge, they only managed to turn on the lights. They were too inept to do more."

Afit tapped his chin with his first two fingers. His ears curled reflexively, then snapped back open. After the silence became uncomfortable, he twirled his fingers at her in a silent order. *Go on.*

"I raised a mind fog to slow and confuse them, but they reached the temple and stole its treasure."

"Not the Key." Afit's voice was flat. It wasn't a question. He was imposing his reality on the world. It was a terrible pity that it wouldn't work that way.

"Yes. The Key."

"Not the Key that is the last known of its kind? The one that was under guard by our ancient enemy until the humans took it from you?" Afit's words were accompanied by a spray of moisture.

Still, she didn't flinch when he walked into her space and leaned in.

"I know I have failed—" she began.

"You have worse than failed. You have betrayed your world with your incompetence. I should have you arrested."

That was a step too far. She drew herself up, eyes narrowed as she moved into *his* space, forcing him to take a step back. It was one thing to take a dressing down. It was another to put himself so completely above her.

"You accuse me of treason, Afit? *You?*" she hissed. "My family has been at the Archon's right hand since the Descent. I follow your commands, but I will not accept your attempts to make me *less.* Who are you to call me a traitor?"

His lips drew back in a snarl, revealing his sharpened teeth. His left incisor was polished gold. If he were to break his flesh using that false tooth, he would die in agony in seconds. That was the price the low born paid if they wished to rise in the ranks. He lived on the edge of death and would step over the precipice if ordered by one of sufficient rank.

She stared at the tooth, before locking eyes with her commanding officer. His pale skin lost its color, and he looked away. He may have been in charge of her, but he was not her superior. She let him have his pound of flesh, but that would be all. Now was the time to move forward.

"Your pardon, Commander. Your failure is my own. I take full responsibility."

"If you insist, High Commander."

She stepped back and allowed him to compose himself. It only took a moment, and she used that time to calm her own mind. When he faced her again, she stood at attention to await his order.

"It will be your responsibility to recover the Key."

She nodded. She had expected as much.

"How do you plan to accomplish this? You've had time to think of how to make amends, haven't you?" She could hear in his voice that he hoped the answer was "no."

"Yes, High Commander. I had opportunity to observe the humans. They avoid conflict. They fear the unknown and seek to make peace. I believe I can use that knowledge to pressure them into giving up the Key."

"Are you confident this will work?"

"I am. I will have them begging for our mercy before the year is out."

He looked as if he couldn't decide between relief or annoyance that she was ready to come back from her failure. He settled in between and waved her off, dismissing her. "Very well. I expect your report and plan of action by midday tomorrow, Commander Xoa. You are dismissed."

"High Commander." She saluted and walked away, trying not to feel too smug about a victory she hardly deserved.

The barracks stood at the edge of the compound, consisting of five separate buildings connected via tunnels to a communal area at the center. Her own quarters were in the First Hall, but she did not go that way; instead, she entered the Third Hall and went directly to the Hub and its training facilities.

As she walked, she reviewed her duel with the human. He had looked so soft. It had been difficult not to laugh in contempt when he challenged her. She'd been so sure of victory, her only question was how slowly he should die; yet, he dominated her from the moment they entered the Astral Plane.

It was embarrassing. Infuriating. Selfishly, she felt worse about that than losing the Key. Her personal humiliation overshadowed the failure to her people.

She grimaced. If her failure wasn't enough, she verged on dishonor, putting her own desires above those of the Archon. What she needed was a good week of training and discipline to realign herself. Khiann committed to starting immediately.

One of the training rooms was empty, so she claimed it with her mark and stepped inside. Her opponent was waiting for her when she entered. The automaton was programmed with Khiann's fighting style, strengths, and weaknesses in mind. It fought without mercy, only stopping at the point of death in its mission to forge a better fighter out of her flesh.

It was a training tool. She wasn't required to use it any longer, just as she didn't need to find her old drill instructors to seek their approval. The automaton improved as she did. It provided a challenge few living warriors could.

She drew her blade and faced off against it. A matching weapon slid out of the automaton's arm. It saluted her. She returned the salute and stepped back into a ready stance. Her first instinct was to attack. Today, she would remind herself how to defend.

The automaton charged. She deepened her stance, already moving to deflect its blade and turn the parry into a counterattack. Her blade swung up to meet her opponent's.

Her body tensed, ready to resist the force of the blow. She leaned into it to give herself more power. When it didn't come, she went off-balance. She dove into it, tumbling across the floor to come up on her feet, ready for a follow-up. That didn't come either, and she saw why the automaton had frozen mid-program.

She had company. Khiann sheathed her blade and bowed.

"Stand." Her father's voice was clipped, as it often was when he was angry. She wondered what she had done, or what he had heard, to make him that way.

She straightened and forced herself to stand relaxed, a position that would pass for formal with her commanders, but certainly would not with Llir of Xoa. He watched her with his fingers steepled, his favored hangers-on hovering nearby. They were draped in silky fabrics that never saw a drop of honest sweat, and they were crowned with a lifetime's growth of hair piled on their heads.

She resisted the urge to pat her own hair. It was bound up as well, but when loose it merely brushed her waist. It had been thinned out to make it easier to manage on her own. As her father had said more than once, she had the hair of a five-year-old servant.

"My lord. How can I serve you?" she asked.

"By addressing me as your father for a start. By removing that embarrassment and coming home."

"I cannot break my vows, father."

"No, I suppose you can't. I would have to kill you if you did." His companions tittered. "I am here to invite you to dinner with the family. You will dress as formally as possible. Should you require it, I will leave Mei with you."

The female he pointed out blanched, then recovered in time to bow.

Khiann tried to imagine that, having one of her father's entourage act as her servant for an afternoon. It was difficult to picture. Even worse was the idea of bringing one of his eyes and ears to her quarters, where everything would be scrutinized for a report back to her father.

"That's very generous, but I can manage on my own. I thank you for the invitation."

He scowled. "Of course, you do. That's the least you could be grateful for. You could be living in speaking distance of our great leader, yet, look at you. A child who never gave up playing with sticks."

She bowed her head, clamping her lips to prevent saying something regrettable. *I have done more for our people in one month than you have in your lifetime.* The words begged to be said, but just like with her High Commander, she did not wish to die.

"I wish only to bring honor to my family and the Pirr."

He made a disgusted noise in the back of his throat. "See that you do. I will send something suitable for you to wear."

"Yes, father."

"One last thing. I know of your mission against the humans, and what your new orders will be. I have one command for you to obey."

She hesitated. "If it doesn't interfere with my official mission, I would be honored."

"If you encounter a human, kill it. Give no quarter, do not hesitate. Most of all, do not besmirch your own honor by pretending *it* has any. Do you understand?"

She hesitated. "If it's possible, within the limits of my mission, I will do as you ask."

"See that you do. This is your chance to be of use to our family, *commander*. See that you make use of it."

"Yes, my lord."

Khiann bowed deeply, and her father scoffed before walking out, letting the door bang shut behind him. She waited for the last footstep to fade before she straightened. She scowled at the closed door, wrestling with the rage in her heart.

When her mental balance was lost, her hand flickered too quickly for the eye to follow. A moment later, her blade was buried in the automaton, a full hand-length of blade protruding from the thing's back. She gritted her teeth and yanked the sword out before leaving the training room.

Dinner was as miserable as Khiann expected. Her mother paraded a young scion of a rival family in front of her and spent the meal hinting that even military commanders had families of their own.

Khiann refrained from telling her mother that those commanders were male, and could continue their normal duties while their wives bore their children. It had all been said before. She was polite to the young male but exhibited no interest. She would not sow false hope.

Her father was stern when he spoke with her, but most of his attention was occupied by her brothers and his followers. The only true bright spot was the meal itself. She had been living on reconstituted food products for months. It was heavenly to sink her teeth into a meal that had never seen the inside of a factory. Everything was fresh from her family's agricultural properties and, as usual, it made the most eloquent argument for staying on *Hoi*.

She returned to her own quarters at the end of the evening. She had a room on the estate, but she didn't want to tempt herself with more luxury. She begged off instead, citing the report she was ordered to write and duties in the morning. She worked on her report and strategy until the wee hours, then sent everything to her commander.

It was an unorthodox plan, and she knew it. It involved piracy, kidnapping, and the destruction of civilian property. They would harass the humans until they could hardly look at the night sky without flinching for fear of the Pirr. They did not need to conquer a single star system when all they had to do was make the humans *fear* them.

Then they would beg for peace. When she finally deigned to speak with them, they would be desperate. They'd be willing to hand over anything she required as long as she left them in peace.

She was smiling when she went to sleep, and the sense of satisfaction followed her into the next day. It even stayed with her when she was subjected to three days of meetings with the High Commander and his staff. She wrapped herself in confidence when she was called on to defend her strategy, in terms of effectiveness and keeping the Pirr's honor intact.

They approved her plan at last, as she knew they would. She would leave in seven days, after her fleet had been provisioned. She spent that time handpicking her sub-commanders and bridge crew. She selected the most elite combat squads for her boarding parties. She wanted to command a force that could invade Earth itself with the greatest chance of victory.

Her last day on *Hoi* was spent in final preparations. Checklists, manifests, and rosters all passed through her for final approval. She met with High Commander Afit and her officers and, after the last meeting was over and the report approved, she was free, at least for the rest of the day.

She went outside in a soft green wrap, declaring herself off duty for the first time since her arrival on the planet. She still wore her sword strapped to her back, but it would take the Return itself to make her go anywhere without her weapon.

The Tower of Sorrows stood apart from the plain that held Legion Headquarters and the vast noble estates. It rose from the center of the forest that bordered the plain. From a distance, it looked like an ordinary stone tower.

It wasn't until she had passed through the forest and entered its courtyard that she could see the true face of the Tower. Its stone walls were carved in the most intricate latticework, from the building's roots to the roof that scraped the clouds. The Tower seemed woven rather than carved, and when the wind blew through its walls, its mournful cry was enough to break her heart.

The interior was a maze, but she had lived in the Tower's shadow all her life. She traced the old path, letting her fingertips brush against the lacy walls.

She found her quarry in the Lower Temple adding pinches of incense to the braziers. When the deep red dust touched the hot coals, a sweet-fragranced smoke curled into the air. It was soothing to the heart and made her regret that she'd avoided the Temple on this visit home.

Loel looked up and nodded to show that he'd seen her. He moved to the next brazier to sprinkle the incense, chanting under his breath.

When a new ribbon of smoke was winding into the air, he joined Khiann in the doorway.

"Lady Xoa. This is unexpected." He bowed.

"I wish you wouldn't do that."

"Some wishes are impossible to grant." He gestured toward a nearby bench. "Would you like to sit and talk? Perhaps you'd like to purchase a prayer for your next mission."

"What do you know about my next mission?" she asked, a little more sharply than intended.

"I only know you're a warrior, and there will always be another mission." He went to the bench to sit. After a moment, she joined him. "What can I do for you?"

She contemplated Loel's cool green eyes. They were unchanged from when they were children. His ascetic life had hardened the rest of him, but she could still see the sweet friend he had once been.

"You are correct. I'm leaving on a new mission tomorrow. I am here to ask for my penance for the duration of the mission."

"I see. And you want me to give this to you?" Loel's expression became pained. "I will need to know what you have done, or if this is only the penance for leaving the homeworld."

"It is more than that. Every mission I undertake is another step toward the Return."

"May your hand be the one to end the Exile," he said.

She bowed her head in thanks. "I fear that I have failed the lost ones more than any Pirr *ever* has. I allowed the humans to capture the last Key."

His breath hissed through his teeth. "I can't grant you absolution for that. If my elders heard you say that, they might not allow you to leave this temple."

She nodded. "I know. My shame has no bounds."

He lowered his head and steepled his fingers. She couldn't tell if he was thinking or praying. She didn't know if there was any difference among the Devoted. She waited quietly, willing herself to hold still.

"This is the Third World. The First was lost to Fire," he intoned.

"Second to the Void," she responded automatically.

"The Keepers of the Void, the Vile and Corrupt, took the Keys so that none could end the Exile. Our lost ones wait for release, but their patience is not infinite." He lowered his hands to his thighs and drummed his fingers against his knees.

"Yes." She wasn't sure what else to say. All this was elementary. She'd learned it in her cradle, just as everyone had for the last ten thousand years.

"There is one Key left. It is guarded by the ancient enemy, waiting at the heart of the Lost Jewel." He turned his head suddenly, looking her in the eye. "You went to *Ixhoi?*"

"I followed the humans. The dragon had lowered its guard, and I passed by with no trouble. I followed the humans, but one of their Exalted challenged me and defeated me. They left with the Key." She hesitated. She wanted to complete her mission. More, she wanted to redeem herself, but that wasn't truly her decision. It wasn't even the High Commander's. "If my crime calls for my death, so be it."

"Don't be foolish," he snapped and propelled himself from the bench. He started to pace, running his hands through his hair until it stood up like a bird's crest. "Your mistake was to accept the challenge."

"My honor required it."

"We do not recognize their honor. Only the Pirr may issue a legitimate challenge. To accept another's is to dishonor yourself."

She grimaced at the insult's sting but accepted it. This would be only the first stage of her penance.

"I won't set you a punishment. It would serve no purpose. If your plan does not end with the Key in our hands, only the Wyrms can absolve you."

She sat, frozen for a moment, as that news sank in. If she failed, she would be consigned to the Void until the Wyrms had been freed. That would be impossible without the Key. She wasn't just setting out to reclaim her lost honor. Her very existence was at stake.

Loel placed his hand on her crown and murmured a few words. His tone was hardly soothing, but she would take any blessing he would offer. After he was gone, she sat for hours, forgetting that she was due at her father's manse at sundown. She could only sit in the deepening shadows, learning to bear the new weight on her shoulders.

CHAPTER TWELVE

From the moment his shuttle penetrated the atmosphere, Jack felt welcome. No other sky was the same shade of blue as Earth's. Even the gravity felt right. When he stepped off the shuttle, a warm spring breeze that smelled of rain and flowers enveloped him.

He would just as soon go home from there, yet the group wasn't so lucky. There was a debriefing to go through first. They couldn't so much as call anyone before they were finished.

"Tell me this is normal." Jack glanced at Coraolis, who wore his usual amiable smile.

Coraolis glanced at Jack from the corner of his eye. "Going through debriefing is routine, especially in a situation like this. This should have been covered at the Academy."

"It was. This is a lot more stringent than I remember, that's all."

"You're right, but this is a unique situation. Don't worry, Jack. We'll be home in time for dinner."

"I'll hold you to that," Jack joked, but his voice sounded strained even to him.

They walked past a pair of stone-faced MPs and into HQ. Their escort hurried them through the airy lobby to the more functional low-ceilinged corridors where the work got done. The MPs finally left them when they reached the main conference room. Administrator Andrus waited for them outside the heavy oak doors.

"Andrus. I'm surprised to see you here," Coraolis said. "You know Jack, don't you?"

"I don't think we've met," Jack said. "Jack Gagnon, Administrator. Good to meet you."

Andrus accepted his handshake with all the enthusiasm of a Monday morning. Jack was free to study the older, sour-faced man since his focus was on Coraolis. Andrus had a reputation for being strict and stuffy, but that didn't mean his presence was a bad thing...or so Jack hoped.

"I'm here as a representative of the Secret Council. The Earth Fleet wants to interrogate you about your experiences on Amadeus. I insisted that a member of the council be present, to make sure you weren't mistreated."

"You volunteered? Andrus, you do care!" Coraolis clasped the man's shoulders. Andrus leaned back, but it wasn't quite enough to get out of Coraolis's reach.

"There's no need to make a scene," Andrus muttered. "Get inside before they come looking for us."

Coraolis led the way into the nearly empty room. A pair of decorated officers sat next to each other at one end of the long table. A fresh-faced young man stood behind them with a datapad in his hands. The rest of the seats were empty.

Andrus cleared his throat. "Mystic Coraolis, Mystic Gagnon, this is Captain Adam Poe of E.F. Intelligence. He has some questions for the pair of you."

Poe stood up and came around the table to shake hands. He had a ready smile and a lot of freckles. They gave him the look of a man far too young, not to mention a little naïve, to be captain. That was negated in part by the lines at the edges of his stone-grey eyes.

"I'm glad you made it back, gentlemen," Poe said. "Have a seat. This won't take long."

They all claimed chairs. Andrus placed himself halfway down the table, close enough to observe but making it clear he wasn't a direct part of things.

Poe took the seat across from them and eased back in a relaxed pose. "I'm sure you're ready to go home. So am I, for that matter, and I only have a few questions. You were the only two to see the alien on Amadeus. The unknown being incapacitated the entire away team. You defeated her, then rushed everyone out of the building before they could see her. There were no efforts to take this unknown being prisoner."

"That sounds about right," Coraolis answered.

Jack wasn't sure he liked Poe's tone. It reminded Jack of his more contentious interviews. Poe was laying out their story and simultaneously punching holes in it, judging their actions from the first word.

"I have your description right here. You mention a female of unknown species. White skin with silver undertones, pointed ears, eyes that remind you of a reptile or a cat." Poe pointed at each of them in turn. "That's a good point to disagree on. Comparisons like that can be very subjective."

Coraolis smiled, perfectly calm. "Yes, and memory can be affected by high-stress situations. We train to compensate for those shortcomings, but that only goes so far."

Jack decided he didn't want to play this game. He wasn't a mouse, and Poe wasn't a cat playing with his food. At least, he wouldn't *get* to pounce, because Jack was going to beat him to it.

"Is there a problem with our report?" His question cut in as Poe was opening his mouth to speak. "That's what I'm hearing here. Let's talk it out and clear things up."

"The problem is that you are describing an alien race that humanity has never encountered before. As former enemies of Earth Fleet—"

"Mystics Coraolis and Gagnon have no criminal records, nor do they have warrants out for their arrests," Andrus cut in.

"With all due respect, Administrator, I was told you were here to observe only."

"That is true, but I am also here to make sure their rights are observed. These two are innocent men in the eyes of the law."

Jack could tell Poe didn't like that. He also saw a flash of surprise on Coraolis's face.

Poe seemed to struggle with something, then turned his attention back to Jack and Cor. "You are the only ones to see the being that attacked—but did not kill—the ground crew on the expedition. You gave a description that does not match any known sentient race in the galaxy." Poe went on as if he hadn't been interrupted, his voice perfectly level. At least he was sticking to the facts this time. "Surely you understand why your report is met with some skepticism?"

It shouldn't have come as a surprise. This was their first mission since they'd surrendered to Earth. It was natural to be under scrutiny. Jack just didn't like it. It felt unfair. They'd never lied to the E.F.

"Not really." Jack leaned back, arms crossed. "Why would we make any of that up? What would be the point?"

"That's what I'd like to know. It would be better if you cooperated from the beginning. You have people waiting for you, don't you? Is there any chance they're in on this conspiracy, whatever it is?"

"There is no conspiracy." Coraolis's words came out clipped. "We were to be treated fairly, and you've just accused us of crimes against humanity. Our report is the truth. If you wish to fill in details, we are at your service, but if you question the veracity of our statements, we're done."

"Not from my perspective." Poe put down his datapad. "What was the device you retrieved from Amadeus? How did you know it was there?"

"We didn't," Jack answered. "Our dragons pushed us in that direction, that's all. I don't know what it does, and we already turned it over to Captain Wells."

"Your dragons, yes. They make a *convenient* excuse to do anything, don't they?"

"I wouldn't call it convenient." Jack stood up, ready to leave.

"Sit down, Mystic Gagnon. We're not done here yet. Administrator?"

"I believe that as long as one Mystic remains to finish the interview, the terms of our agreement with E.F. are met," Andrus answered.

Jack looked at Coraolis. Coraolis had his hands flat on the table as if he were about to push up from his seat. Something kept him in his chair. Jack noted the indecision on his face and decided not to pressure Coraolis into following.

He turned and took a step to leave when the young officer moved from his seat against the wall to stand at Poe's shoulder. He looked pale and nervous, but whether that was at interrupting or if that was his natural state, Jack wasn't sure.

"Sir, an urgent message just came in. I think you may want to see this." He held out his datapad to Captain Poe.

While Poe took the device and read it over, the young man caught Jack's eye and nodded toward his seat. Jack hesitated. If he was going to walk out, he should get it over with, but now he was curious.

He sat down as Poe turned on the screen on the front wall using the controls built into the table. A strange figure faced them. An alien with snow white skin and silver undertones, and eyes slit like a cat's. His long, sharp ears poked out from between a cascade of white hair.

The alien stared into the camera, and Jack identified more details that set this being apart from humankind. His eyes were too large, his face too long and bony, his skin had a glossy sheen that made it look impossibly smooth.

Poe pressed a button, and the video played: "People of Earth, I speak for all Pirr when I say that you are nothing more than graverobbers and thieves. You lack honor and are not to be trusted." The alien spoke in perfect, crisp English. He repeated his message in Chinese, then Spanish.

"This is the only warning you will receive. Humanity is a plague among the stars. You are to be quarantined. No human will be permitted beyond your current borders. Any human found outside those limits will be removed."

The alien repeated his message as Jack caught Coraolis's eye, who shrugged. Jack understood. The Pirr had been the attackers, not the humans. At least this proved that Jack and Cor had been telling the truth.

"I'm guessing you don't have any more questions for us," Jack said to Poe.

Poe shook his head, not taking his eyes from the screen. "I know where to find you if I need anything else."

Julia and Dante were overjoyed to see them. Several rib-cracking hugs were exchanged before Coraolis asked for mercy. They had seen the video, just like everyone else on the planet. It worried them. Jack and Cor took turns telling the story of the lost city and the alien who'd fought them.

That night, everyone met at Julia's and Coraolis's apartment for a game of D&D. Dante and Julia were jealous of Coraolis's one-on-one games with Jack. They'd been settling for board game nights, often with Isabel as a guest, but they'd been craving a good dungeon crawl.

"I see, so that's all you missed about me," Jack joked as Julia put the finishing touches on the nachos.

"No, of course not. I just thought you'd be interested in the board games, considering Isabel has been joining us."

"Has she?" Jack wondered about the surprised flutter in his chest. Maybe it was simply thinking of Isabel again when he'd been trying not to for the last couple of months.

"Oh, sure. Dante and I went to apologize for how we acted at the hospital, and she was very nice about it. It turns out she likes gaming, so it seemed natural to invite her." Julia set more nachos on the table where everyone could reach them. "She asked about you."

"Oh?"

Jack sat, hoping Julia would elaborate. His set his DM screen aside for easier access to the nachos. Dante and Coraolis came in from the balcony and joined them, Coraolis balancing a platter of burgers.

"I can't tell you how much I've craved real, human junk food." Jack scooped up a nacho and popped it into his mouth. It felt like the best way to change the subject. "Maybe we died and went to heaven."

"If heaven is Julia's nachos, I would say yes." Coraolis laughed and sat next to her. Dante took the next seat over.

"I was telling Jack about Isabel. Maybe she could join us," Julia suggested. "We could use another strong arm."

Jack shrugged, trying not to look too eager. "Let's get back in our own groove first. Last time we played, you all took down the Deathless Knight and recovered the stolen Orb."

"That seems so long ago," Dante groaned.

"That isn't our fault. If it wasn't for the Pirr, we would have been home for Christmas." Coraolis put an arm around Julia, stealing a quick hug.

"How about that, though? A new alien race out of nowhere, with Mystic abilities too," Julia leaned into Cor for a moment, then sat up straight, her cheeks a little flushed. "Where have they been this whole time?"

Dante grabbed a burger and started piling it with lettuce and tomato. "My guess is they're isolationist, judging by that message. You two really stepped on their toes."

Jack cleared his throat. "Yeah, but did you all finish leveling up your characters since last time? Honestly, I'm here to play, if that's all right."

"Sure, sure." Dante took a large bite of his burger and picked up his character sheet, scrutinizing it closely. "Yeah, I think I did. I wasn't this good at picking locks before."

Coraolis and Julia chimed in. Both of them were ready to go. Jack left his screen down; he didn't need it for the first part. The Deathless Knight was gone, the people were saved. The dark cloud that had been hanging over the land was still there, though, causing an unnatural chill over what should have been high summer.

The party was talking to a corrupted druidess. Jack was getting ready to have her reveal her true nature and attack when he realized Dante was looking at his datapad.

"I thought you missed this."

"Huh?" Julia looked up and saw Dante putting his datapad away, abashed. "Dante, we agreed no devices at the table."

"I'm sorry, really. I have alerts set whenever the Pirr are mentioned." He held up his hands in surrender when Jack gave him a dirty look. "Hey, you know how rare Mystic abilities are."

"I've got to admit, I want to know more about them," Julia chimed in. "The way Cor tells it, you two were having a real live action adventure on Amadeus."

"I guess it sounds that way. It wasn't so fun at the time." Jack closed his notebook and sat back. "Do you want to talk to Sheena, or would you rather blow off some steam?"

"Sheena? Oh, the druid." Dante polished off his burger and pushed his plate aside. The nachos had already been demolished.

"Maybe a little refocusing is in order," Coraolis admitted. "What do you propose?"

"It's been a while since we were all in the Astral Plane together." Jack stood up and stretched. "Who wants to spar?"

Everyone did, it turned out. After a few minutes to put leftovers in the fridge, the four Evolved sat on the living room floor, knee to knee, and entered the Astral Plane. Jack was surprised to find a huge bubble waiting for them, its surface gleaming with streaks of blue and violet.

"What is this?" he asked, reaching out for it.

"Careful, it'll suck you in. I should know." Dante gave Julia a mock dirty look. "Someone left her stuff lying around."

"Hey, I told you not to touch it. I wanted to see how long it would last without my help." Julia moved up next to Jack, looking over the globe. "So far, I count thirteen days."

"What's it for?" Jack still wanted to touch it, despite the warning.

Julia shrugged. "I made it for my class. My students spar in it, and it absorbs any stray energy that touches it. That might be why it's still intact."

"You have your students spar?" Coraolis sounded a little shocked. "I thought you were just doing an intro to the Astral Plane."

"I am. I did, I mean. They've moved on, but we meet outside of class. I want to keep them on par with the *nats*."

"Nats?"

"Mhm. Natural Mystics. You have an edge over us Enhanced Humans. We're all on the same team, and I want my students to carry their weight." She looked at Jack's face, and her smile became a little sheepish. "I know labels like that aren't helpful, but they're everywhere now. Nats and *cybers*. All the cool kids are saying it."

"That doesn't sound very welcoming." Jack furrowed his brow. "I saw how much trouble you got from the 'nats' when we were at the Academy."

"I know. That's why I'm teaching them to own their differences, and how to be stronger for them. Now, are we going to spar or what?"

"We're going to spar," Dante broke in. "I've been dying to try out your Thunder Ball for myself."

"You should have asked," Julia laughed and waved him on. "Go on. I promise to let you out when it's over."

"Thunder Ball?" Coraolis was reaching for its surface but stopped when he heard that moniker. "Really?"

"Two Mystics enter, one Mystic leaves," Julia smirked. "It was that or Death Bubble. I thought this sounded a little more positive."

Coraolis scoffed, though Jack noticed him hiding a smile as he turned from Julia to enter Thunder Ball. He and Dante squared off, each of them wielding oversized energy blades. Jack watched them going at each other for a while.

"They can only leave if you let them? Have you considered using this as a trap?" he asked.

"I have, but it took a lot of energy to create it. I can't make one on the fly." Julia touched the side of the sphere, smiling with pride.

"Still, this is really impressive. I'm glad things are better with Dante, too."

"They are." She tilted her head as Dante got behind Coraolis and started to swing, then was knocked away by a jolt of energy. "Sorry to derail your game. We missed your D&D sessions."

"It's okay. Mostly I wanted to get us all together again." Jack smirked at Dante and Cor, who were now wrestling with each other. "I was sorry to miss winter though. I always look forward to the hot chocolate, Christmas...snowball fights."

Julia raised her eyebrows and made a scooping motion. "You know, we could have that here." A white ball appeared in her hand. It wasn't snow, but he could tell by looking that it was as harmless as an ordinary snowball. "The guys are having fun. I want in, don't you?"

"I do." Jack created a 'snowball' of his own and wound up, ready to throw.

"Excellent. Be ready on my mark. Three... two... one..."

Julia tapped the Thunder Ball's surface. Dante and Coraolis popped out, still grappling with each other. The pair only had time to look up before Julia and Jack opened fire, pelting them as fast as they could create new missiles out of the ether.

"This is war," Dante declared. Coraolis had already returned fire. Jack saw the throw half a second before something white hit him in the face. He ducked behind Thunder Ball, seeking cover.

Coraolis whooped, smelling blood, but was driven back by another volley from Julia. Soon, they were in a free-for-all with 'snowballs' flying everywhere. When Jack was ready to surrender, he ducked inside Thunder Ball. Dante joined him, and they watched as Coraolis and Julia duked it out.

Dante clapped him on the shoulder. "It's good to have you back, Jack."

Jack grinned as Julia chased Coraolis around the Ball, both trying to get an angle on the other. "Thanks. It's good to be back. There's nothing quite like home."

CHAPTER THIRTEEN

The Academy of Mystics was nestled in the center of a small forest with footpaths that wove through the trees. Clearings dotted the forest—popular gathering spots for the students, others more remote and private. Once Julia stepped onto one of the paths, she almost forgot she was in the heart of civilization.

She knew her way around the forest as well as her own apartment. She and Jack jogged there every morning, each day taking a different route. On days she and Coraolis were free at the same time, they met in his favorite clearing for lunch.

It rained that morning, but the clouds had dispersed by midday, leaving a clear blue sky behind. Julia found Coraolis on his favorite bench, contemplating the twisted statue that fascinated him so much.

After their usual greeting, she handed Cor a sandwich and a bottle of water. For a few minutes, they ate quietly, enjoying each other's company.

"How was class today?" Cor asked after he'd polished off his peanut butter and jelly.

"Great. Honora's come a long way. Today she came up with these weapons, they looked like harmless scarves, but she had Tomas wrapped up like a mummy in three seconds flat."

He put an arm around her shoulders and squeezed. "You must be very proud."

She nodded. She never would have guessed that she'd like teaching, or that she'd be good at it. Either she'd been gifted with six extraordinary students, or she was good at her job. Or, maybe, it was both.

"They're all doing well in their regular classes too. They're keeping up with the nats and then some."

"That word," Coraolis sighed, making it so drawn out that she knew it wasn't serious. "Nats."

She nudged him. "We have to call you something."

"How about Mystics? We're all Mystics, no matter how we got here." He kissed her temple, where some of her enhancements were visible. "I don't see you as any different, or any less."

"I know, but I don't think you realize how rare that is. People who are born Mystics think they are somehow more deserving than those of us who weren't." She shrugged and leaned against his side. "I hope it's temporary. When cybers have been around long enough to be normal, maybe it'll all change."

"I sure hope so." Coraolis sighed, and this time she knew it was real. His empathy was one of the many reasons she cared for him so much. She was about to tell him so when their datapads both chirped. She met Cor's eye, and they reached for their devices. The last time they'd gotten a simultaneous message, Jack was in the hospital.

This time it wasn't so dire. Jack had messaged them with a link to a news site and *"WATCH THIS"* written in all caps. She hesitated to follow the link. It looked a little too much like spam, and she didn't want to interrupt her lunch with Coraolis.

Cor clicked the link.

"I hope your security's up to date," she told him, half-scolding, half-joking. She messaged Jack, asking him to confirm he was the one to send it.

"Why is that?" He turned the screen so that she could see as well.

"It looked like phishing to me." She leaned in so she could watch his screen as well. It might be entertaining, at least.

It wasn't. Maria Wey, the anchor for the local news station, sat with her hands clasped on her desk. Her expression was sober. A picture of an E.F. vessel was on the right half of the screen. A ticker ran across the bottom. It was mid-sentence, but the word "Pirr" put Julia on instant alert.

"In galactic news, the Earth Fleet science vessel *Gaiman* was found in the Hawkeye System after a brutal attack by the Pirr. According to survivors, the Pirr crippled their vessel in an unprovoked attack. After boarding, they executed the Mystics on board, then left *Gaiman* adrift."

The screen was taken over by a video of hollow-eyed E.F. crewmen coming on board another vessel. Julia felt Coraolis gripping her shoulder, but she was so intent on the screen she hardly felt it. She wondered if she was going to be sick.

"Who were the Mystics?" she asked.

"I don't know. I'll find out."

The image transitioned to an E.F. crewman. "They said, 'this far, and no further.' They said to repeat that. 'This far, and no further.'" He crossed his arms over his chest, withdrawing into himself. "They left the life support on, but without the engines, it couldn't last. We were lucky the *Hornblower* heard our distress call."

The image returned to Maria. Her eyes shone with unshed tears. Julia could relate. The newscaster cleared her throat. "I think we can all be grateful for *Hornblower's* timely rescue. But the information we have presents more questions than answers. Why have the Pirr appeared out of nowhere to attack humanity? Why did they target the Mystics on board *Gaiman?*"

The image changed to a familiar-looking admiral. The ticker at the bottom of the screen named him Admiral Fischer. The years had carved a multitude of lines into his face, which became more pronounced when he spoke. "The Pirr's governing body disavowed any knowledge of this attack. They are claiming this is the work of pirates, using the current tension between our people as an excuse to profit through chaos." He grimaced. "We are looking into the matter."

The screen returned to Maria. She was sitting up straighter, her expression harder than when they had started playing the footage. Her hands still clutched each other until her knuckles had turned white. "We are calling for a public investigation. What have the Mystics done to antagonize this alien race? What other trouble have they brought to our door? It hasn't been that long since the events at Ian's World. Perhaps it's time for stronger oversight."

The video ended. Coraolis and Julia looked at each other, wordlessly gathered their things, and hurried to the Academy.

Dante once thought he'd be Earthbound for the rest of his life. He didn't expect the clean slate to do anything about that, but when the Pirr scuttled *Gaiman,* Earth Fleet had requested the most powerful Mystics to help with their response. That was how he found himself on the *Ulysses* with Jack, heading to a new world the E.F. hoped to claim.

Opal was as lovely as its name implied. The planet would ordinarily be as blue as Earth, but particles in its atmosphere gave it streaks of pink and violet. With the white from its clouds, it truly resembled its namesake.

He stood on the bridge with Jack, watching the viewscreen. It had been years since he'd been on an expedition like this. He'd been on the run with his fellow Evolved or Earthbound for so long that he'd forgotten how it felt to be the first sentient to touch a planet. He loved that, despite the dangers involved.

Captain Asant whistled at the sight, stroking his neatly trimmed beard. He'd been a good partner to the Mystics so far. He'd made them feel welcome on his bridge. He'd even sought their advice on the Pirr. Neither of them had much in the way of advice. Still, it was nice to be asked.

All they could do was follow the one order they'd been given as if it were engraved in stone. If there was fighting, it had to be started by the Pirr. Earth couldn't be the aggressor.

That sounded like bunk to Dante, but orders were orders, and he wanted to get through this mission without another mutiny. Despite himself, his hopes had risen with every passing day. The longer they went without combat, the better their odds felt. It was far from logical, but sometimes it was comforting to go with his gut.

Then the alien ship came out from the cover of the system's gas giant. The ship resembled a serrated blade, poised to saw *Ulysses* in half.

"Shields up. Hail the alien ship," Asant ordered. "Mikes, I'm told these ships have Mystic support?"

"So they do. We're on it," Dante affirmed. "Jack?"

"Coming."

He ran to the commune chamber with Jack close behind. It was a short run, but he still felt too slow. He was halfway there when Asant's voice filled his ears. He'd been patched into the call to the other ship. Too bad there was only one side to it so far.

"I repeat, this is Captain David Asant of the Earth Fleet vessel *Ulysses*. We are here on a peaceful survey mission. Please respond."

After a long, empty pause, the captain ordered someone to change the frequency, then repeated himself.

Dante and Jack reached the commune chamber and hurried inside. In moments, they were in the Astral Plane, facing down a squad of twenty aliens in ornate silver armor. Each of them was armed with a cannon mounted on their left arm. Half aimed at Dante, the other half at Jack.

They were armed with actual weapons in the Astral Plane. They weren't mere constructs. They'd been projected into this plane by their wielders, and Dante's senses told him they were functional. If the Pirr struck first, it would hurt.

Something buzzed in his ear. He put a hand to it and had the disjointed feeling of touching his ear in the Astral Plane yet feeling his earpiece in the physical. That was why Mystics didn't wear earpieces normally—they could be distracting.

"I'll be back. Yell if you need me."

Jack nodded, and Dante dropped into his body. As soon as he reconnected, he heard Asant's voice in his ear: "...I understand that, but we started this mission weeks ago. If you're going to talk in terms of who saw what first, it's us."

"We came upon this planet before you did. We have possession, Captain Asant. The system is ours. Do you mean to take it from us by force?"

The captain muttered something colorful about the Pirr's breeding habits under his breath. Dante tensed for the Pirr's reaction, expecting something explosive in return for the insult.

"I do not," Asant growled. "End transmission. Brenner, bring us about. Someone go tell the Mikes their services aren't needed."

"I heard you, Captain," Dante said. "I'll bring Jack back in."

A pall fell over the boat as they left the system. It wasn't a retreat but it felt like one. A diplomatic loss was just as hard on the pride as losing in combat. The difference was that everyone was still alive to feel their wounds.

The *Ulysses'* encounter with the Pirr was the first of many. One by one, each of Earth Fleet's missions was cut short. Every system they entered was already occupied. The Pirr were everywhere. Humanity was boxed in.

Coraolis and Julia were deployed on E.F.S. *MacLeod.* Earth Fleet was determined to claim one more planet in the face of the Pirr's threats. They'd even settle for a rock like Radar. The planet was on the cold end of the habitable zone. It might have value for whatever minerals it held, but it would never be a popular place to settle.

None of that mattered. They were trying to make a point.

Julia floated in the void of the Astral Plane, reaching out to the planet with all her senses. Coraolis was at her side, giving her strength and keeping watch. Her first impression of the planet was that it was worse than the original data. The air was too thin. Settlers would need respirators to go outside.

On the plus side, it was rich with easily accessible ore deposits. It might just be worth the trouble to settle. She was delving deeper when she noticed Cor trying to get her attention.

"Pull back," he was saying. "Julia. *Look.*"

Julia drew away from the planet. A Pirr vessel was in high orbit.

They returned to their bodies and hurried to the bridge. Julia gulping down electrolytes on the way. The bridge crew turned as one when they walked in.

Captain Demir stood to meet them. "What is it, Mike? You haven't been gone an hour."

"We detected a Pirr vessel in orbit around Radar. They beat us here." *Again.* Julia struggled to sound professional, but her frustration was too much to hide. "I'm sorry, captain."

"I can't see how it's your fault." Demir squared her shoulders and returned to her seat. "Let's try hailing them, Yves."

"Aye, Captain."

Julia glanced at Cor, who stood close enough for their arms to brush. That was probably a breach of conduct. They'd agreed to keep things completely professional when they were outside their cabin.

Maybe it was a toe over the line, but she was fine with it. She was convinced that every encounter with the Pirr was on a hair trigger. Anything could set off a battle, meaning any moment could be their last.

"They're responding, Captain," Yves reported.

Julia let out a breath.

"On screen," Demir ordered.

A hard-faced Pirr replaced the viewscreen's curtain of stars. Her eyes moved to survey the bridge crew. She lingered over the Mystics with a sneer before she moved on to Captain Demir.

"I am Khiann Xoa. What do you want, humans? You are outside your territory."

"Are you in charge here?" Demir spoke lazily, projecting a calm she likely didn't feel. Julia approved. They didn't need to admit they were intimidated.

"I am. Shall I repeat my question?"

"We are here to scout a new planet and claim it for settlement." Demir stood up and put herself front and center.

"This planet has been claimed."

"I see that. Perhaps we could negotiate." Demir began to pace. Julia was feeling a little restless herself.

"There will be no negotiation. This system belongs to the Pirr." Khiann Xoa drew herself up. "You will leave. Now."

"Are you sure? This is a prime opportunity to make an alliance." Demir's tone was determinedly friendly, but Julia heard the dismissal in the Pirr's voice. This was another dead end.

"Your presence is an infection on this arm of the galaxy. You are a disease, human. We will not allow you to spread."

"All we are doing is working to support our people. We reach out to our galactic neighbors in peace. All we ask is that you do the same." Demir's expression didn't change, but she all but vibrated with tension.

Julia clenched her teeth but managed to keep her thoughts to herself.

"You should have thought of that before you became graverobbers. It does not matter if you were not the human who did it." The Pirr's glare settled on Coraolis. "Some things cannot be balanced out, no matter the penance. Once you desecrate a holy place, that guilt will follow your race for the rest of your days."

The captain lifted her chin, her jaw tightening. "Listen here. Humanity hasn't robbed anyone. We explore, we settle, that's it."

Khiann Xoa made a sound that could have been a laugh, too heavy with contempt to really take off. "Then you lie to yourselves as well. What will you do, human? We are in your way."

The alien spread her hands, inviting an attack.

"Take your time deciding. We will be here."

The call ended. Demir trudged to the captain's chair and dropped into it. She rubbed the bridge of her nose. "I suppose that's it," she murmured. "Bring us about, Holland. We won't let them bait us."

"That was her. That was the Pirr I fought on Amadeus." Coraolis followed Julia into their cabin and shut the door, only to lean against it.

"She wanted us to fight her. This can't go on. Either we keep backing down and look like an easy target to everyone else, or we start a fight and lose our allies." Julia leaned against the wall next to him and stared at the ceiling.

"Maybe if I challenged her again, I could make the terms go our way. If I win, we get this planet," Coraolis moved.

That was possibly the worst idea she'd ever heard. She turned to face him, letting the horror she felt at the idea show on her face. "Don't you even dare. You saw her expression. She looked at us like we were rabid animals, Cor. You don't do pistols at dawn with animals."

"She did before," he protested.

"No. Even if she went for it, you'd have to put something that equals a *planet* on the line. You don't have the authority to do that. I doubt a field leader like her has that either."

"Okay, okay." He walked to the bed and sat on the lower bunk. "It was just an idea."

"I know. I'm sorry if I was harsh."

"You were fine. It just stings a little more when you're right." He looked up with a self-deprecating smile. "You should let me have a turn at that."

"Any time you're ready," she teased.

She tried to shake off her nerves as she moved to sit beside him. They linked their fingers and leaned into each other. Even if they were far from home and on the edge of war, at least she had Coraolis to rely on.

CHAPTER FOURTEEN

The Nexus System was opposite Earth's branch of the Milky Way, far from any other inhabited systems. Its citizens lived on Yuna Station, working at the ore refineries or monitoring the robot-run mines on the rocky planets. Yuna Corp answered to no government. Its laws governed its commerce, and the only way to get ejected from the station was to break the peace.

Dante was familiar with it. He'd been to Yuna a few times as a fugitive, looking for work or fuel for their ship. The Docks had a carnival atmosphere, with beings of every description selling food and entertainment. If it could be sold, it would be found at Yuna.

He'd never heard that you could find *peace* there, yet that was what the Earth delegation was after. Yuna Corp had invited leaders from all over the galaxy to their anniversary celebration. Earth Fleet was there to talk business, but if the Pirr was there, they were going to try and negotiate a truce. If that failed, the humans would seek other allies.

Once they landed, he discovered the other side of Yuna. Their shuttle had a private dock with a well-appointed lounge where they could keep an eye on their ship. A wall panel offered environmental controls so any species could adjust the air mixture, temperature, light, or even the humidity to meet their biological needs.

The default setting for this lounge was fit for humans, as was the furniture. Dante was examining the control panel when the door opened and a human-looking robot entered.

If it hadn't been made of metal, Dante might have mistaken it for a man. Every detail was true to life, down to the robot's eyelashes and fingernails.

"Greetings and welcome to Yuna. Has the lounge met your comfort needs?" The robot smiled, revealing a row of perfect silver teeth.

"We're just fine." Ambassador Gilchrist walked over to shake the robot's hand. "I'm Ambassador Thomas Gilchrist. My companion is Admiral Nanami. Thanks for having us."

The robot looked at the admiral, no doubt taking in the entourage behind him as well.

"The invitation was for three."

Its tone was as polite as before, but there was a finality to its words. There would be no negotiating for more companions. Gilchrist was already nodding. He'd likely hoped to bring more, but even Dante knew they shouldn't test their host.

"Yes, they'll be waiting here. The attendees are me, Admiral Nanami, and Mystic First Class Dante over there."

Dante knew the summons when he heard it. He walked over and nodded to the robot, reluctant to put his hand in the robot's.

"I am not familiar with that honorific. I will add it to my database," the robot answered. "Greetings, MFC Dante. Humans call me Steven. If you are lost or need assistance, you may request me by using that name."

"Good to meet you, Steve." Dante grinned at the robot.

"I am designated Steven." The robot's eyebrows drew down in imitation of a frown.

Gilchrist's hand clamped down on Dante's shoulder, cutting off his response.

"MFC Dante will keep that in mind. Can I assume that your presence means it's time to join the gathering?" Gilchrist glanced at Dante, his face an amiable mask.

The ambassador was too diplomatic to say he didn't trust Dante, but it was easy enough to tell. Dante had one job and that was to watch for trouble from the Astral Plane. The wrong word could set the whole mission askew—and he now knew that included the robots. Dante nodded stiffly. He wouldn't talk to the tin can if that was off limits.

"That is correct, the event is about to begin. Please accompany me to the ballroom."

Steven led them into a corridor as wide as a city street. Dante's feet sank into the rich carpet with each step, and he had the powerful urge to take his shoes off. He walked a little behind Nanami and Gilchrist, listening to the robot chatter about Yuna Station's history, the pride it took in its neutrality.

Dante listened with one ear while he opened his senses. He might not catch much with his attention split, but it was better than not watching at all. He spared only a scrap of his attention to making sure he didn't walk into the others while he stretched out with his mind.

The station was full of life, from the traders and smugglers below to the galactic elite gathering above. He could sense the station's power core, the ships in dock, but he couldn't tell one species from another or read anyone's intentions. He was wasting his energy.

Steven guided them to a lift, then bid them farewell as the doors closed.

"What have you sensed so far, Mike?" Nanami asked as the elevator began moving.

"Nothing useful, sorry to say."

"Keep trying." Gilchrist adjusted his collar, tugged at his cuffs. "I don't want any surprises."

"I'll need to find a quiet place to do that. I don't scan well on my feet."

"Then do it. Admiral, I heard three Yeti clans would be here. Which one do we approach first?"

The lift door opened at the center of a large domed chamber. A tantalizing smell caught Dante's nose, and soft music played just below the volume of the buzzing crowd. Nanami and Gilchrist linked arms and went one way. Following Gilchrist's curt nod, Dante went the other.

There were no dark corners, but an empty bench against the wall looked inviting. Dante claimed it and assumed a relaxed pose with his arms draped across the back of the bench to discourage visitors.

A diminutive robot paused at his bench. It held a large tray overhead with a selection of different foods. Three small banners adorned the tray. Dante wasn't familiar with two of them, but the third was the Earth Fleet flag.

"What's this?" He pointed at the flag.

"This selection of food has been marked as ideal for human, Yeti, and Pirr consumption. The *barefruit* in particular has been popular among the humans tonight, sir."

"Pirr, you said?" Dante took what he assumed was the barefruit, a purple orb that looked like a peeled grape. "Are they here?"

"Yes, they are invited guests. Good evening."

The robot left before Dante got out another question. He popped the fruit in his mouth and wished he'd grabbed more than just one. He hummed a little as he chewed, trying to place what it tasted like. Not strawberries or melon. It called birthday cake to mind, but that was wrong too.

"Do humans usually make mouth noises when they chew?"

The icy tone startled him out of his reverie. He'd been joined by a Pirr female. She wore an ornate mask woven from copper and silver-colored wires. He could see the shape of her face, but the pattern made it difficult to pull the pieces into a whole image. Her dress was plain, though, and looked like it was woven from the roughest wool they could find.

He was intrigued, but a twitch of her lips reminded him that he was staring.

"You're a Pirr."

"An astute observation. You are from Earth. Why aren't you with your masters?"

"No one is my master. I'm a Mystic. My role is to sit here and keep an eye on things." He looked around for another servant robot, hoping for more of that fruit. "Why aren't you with yours?"

"I am in my rightful place. If you are a Mystic, you are the one I am looking for."

He sat a little straighter. He knew he wasn't supposed to be talking to strange aliens, yet she'd started the exchange. Gilchrist might not see it his way, but he'd already gotten tangled in this conversation. Backing out now would be rude and possibly compromise their mission.

"You were looking for me, specifically?" He searched the crowd looking for Gilchrist and Nanami.

"The Mystic, yes. If you seek peace, we will speak to you. There is a private balcony on the floor above. Two hours. Come alone, so you may speak freely."

"I'm not the ambassador, you know. You'll need to talk to him if you want any binding deals."

"If I wished to speak with your ambassador, I would." She walked toward the crowd, which melted away from her like ice from a blowtorch. Two other Pirr appeared, putting themselves in protective positions between the female and the crowd. The party guests closed around her, and she was lost to his sight.

"Absolutely not," Gilchrist hissed.

Nanami glanced at them both, eyes narrowed. She was acting as crowd control, keeping strangers from wandering too close. This conversation needed to be private, but Dante wondered how it looked, the three Earth delegates whispering in a lonely corner.

"You said it yourself. The Pirr are dodging you at every turn. Have you gotten a single other being to talk to you about the Pirr or about an alliance against them?"

"No." Gilchrist pursed his lips. "This is some sort of game. I'm the ranking delegate. If they won't speak with me, they're already playing games."

"Better to talk to me than no one," Dante argued.

"He does have a point." Nanami edged a little closer. "Rumor has it that all Pirr are Mystics. Maybe they respect him more."

Gilchrist rolled his eyes, and Dante didn't blame him. Maybe he'd earned his rank among the Mystics, but his reputation wasn't the healthiest. He wasn't there to throw political weight around. He was there because he was strong and, if pressed, could manage without backup.

"Got it. You'd rather go home empty-handed than give me a shot at this. I might not be a diplomat, but I've handled delicate situations before."

"We've been here for hours, and people will only talk to you about tariffs." Nanami inclined her head toward Dante. "He can listen to what they say, and report back. They just need to understand that this isn't a negotiation. You can't make any deals on Earth's behalf."

"I know that much and already told them that." Dante wanted to smile at the admiral, but Gilchrist's expression was a little too stony. Maybe that meant he was thinking hard, nothing else.

"Very well. You can go, but you will wear an earpiece and leave the moment I tell you to. Don't say one word without my consent, Mike. Do you understand me?"

"Perfectly." Dante reached out and plucked a barefruit from a passing robot. "You can count on me, Ambassador."

"For our sake," Gilchrist muttered, "I certainly hope so."

Dante stepped onto the empty balcony. He checked his earpiece, making sure it was firmly in place.

"Testing," he said.

"You're coming through just fine, Mike." Nanami's voice was as clear as if she were standing next to him.

"Remember. Don't say a word I don't approve first."

"Understood." Maybe if he said it one more time, Gilchrist would believe him.

Dante leaned on the balcony, looking at the wheeling and dealing going on below. He had to guess fifty people were down there. Some were politicians, some were there purely on business. Not one of them would talk to Gilchrist.

Either their ambassador was terrible at his job, or the Pirr were scarier than he thought. Earth Fleet had a lot to offer. They had resource-rich planets, Mystics, power; anything an ally might find valuable. They shouldn't get blown off this easily.

The door opened behind him, and the masked alien stepped through. Her lithe movements told him she was either an excellent dancer or very dangerous in a fight. Hell, maybe it was both.

"Evening. Glad you could make it."

Her gaze swept down his body. Her expression never changed as she looked at his hair, his clothes, his boots. Her attention returned to his head, or maybe it was his throat she was glaring at.

"Your device. You will remove it." She tapped her ear.

"That's a very bad idea," Nanami said into his ear.

"What? This?" His finger brushed the earpiece as he scrambled for a story that would let him keep it.

"Yes. Your paid liars are not worthy of my speech. You will discard the listening device or our meeting is at an end."

"Mystic First Class Dante. You *will not -*" Gilchrist's warning cut off as Dante removed the earpiece. He hadn't *actually* heard anyone say no.

"I guess I don't really have a choice." He turned off the device and shoved it into his pocket. "Now what?"

"Now I will tell you how to make peace with my people before more lives are lost."

Dante's eyebrow twitched. "I thought your people didn't take responsibility for pirates."

"We do not, but we could stop them if we wished. Return the Key to me, human, and I will stop the corsairs from attacking your vessels."

Dante tried to get a read on her the way she had him, but her mask was just as confounding as before.

"Maybe you could start by telling me your name. I'm Dante, Mystic First Class."

Her lips twitched downward. "I am Commander Xoa. Answer my demand, human. Will you return that which is ours?"

"I don't know that I can. What does it do? Why do you need it back?"

"None of that is your concern. It is an artifact from ancient days, and your kind stole it from us."

"From what I hear, it came from an empty planet."

"Tell me, how do humans feel about taking heirlooms from your graveyards, your sacred places? No one lives in them, yet is it acceptable?" Xoa took a step closer. It wasn't an overt threat, but there was something menacing about the way she stared at him.

"No, ma'am, but you tried to kill my friends to get this thing from them. That doesn't exactly call for a reward." He crossed his arms over his chest, trying to look more certain than he felt. Her graveyard analogy bothered him, but so did her murder attempt.

"They trespassed on sacred ground. They got better than they deserved," she hissed. Dante leaned back as she loomed closer. "I am not surprised you would justify the theft. It is the only way you get to keep your treasure."

"I'm not saying that," he protested.

She stepped back and pulled off her mask.

Recognition slapped Dante. This was the Pirr from the broadcast right after Cor and Jack got home. Commander Xoa, she'd called herself. If she didn't run the pirates, she surely held their reins.

"Tell me what it does," he repeated.

"That is none of your concern."

He shrugged and made as if to put the earpiece back in his ear. "Then I guess we have nothing to talk about."

She hissed something in an alien tongue, and the door slammed open. A trio of tall humanoids in concealing armor stepped into the chamber. They carried blunt weapons the length of their arms that glowed an electric blue.

"If you will not be my emissary, you will be the message." She spat, then vanished through the door as the newcomers rushed him.

"Can't we talk about this?" Dante called after her, but she was already gone. He backpedaled, but there was nowhere to go with the balcony ledge at his back. His attackers came at him in slow motion as his thoughts raced.

He jerked back as the leader swung. The very tip of the stave caught Dante across the teeth. White-hot fire rippled through his body, yet his jaw was frozen shut. He couldn't even cry out. He slumped against the railing, attempting to get his muscles to stop acting like gelatin and *move.*

Jump.

The impulse shot through his nervous system like an electric jolt. He shook his head even as he put his hand on the rail.

"You must be crazy," he muttered. "You're the one with wings here, remember?"

A stave came down on the railing inches from his nose. Dante hauled himself to his feet through sheer force of will. Sure, he'd jump. It was much better to go splat on the floor than get beaten to death with glowing ice clubs.

Jump now.

People were shouting below as Dante climbed up on the balcony ledge. A wound in reality rippled in the air below him, wisps of bright green and violet escaping it like smoke.

He didn't jump so much as roll over the railing. One of his attackers caught him with a parting blow, sending another jolt of pain through his midsection, but then he was gone, enveloped in the veil between worlds.

"How?"

He was wheezing, but he could at least manage that much of a question.

Our bond strengthens by the day. The ritual is no longer required.

"That's one silver lining." He looked around, rubbing his arms. The hole into the physical world was shrinking. "Am I going to get trapped here?"

Only if your ship leaves without you. I will guide you, but you must hurry. When your biometric signature is gone, they will assume you are dead and leave.

"We can't have that."

He followed his dragon's urgings and ran. Ribbons of light swirled around him as he passed through the in-between realm. When the light touched him, it felt like a warm ray of sunshine. Still, it was unnerving to see the light passing through him.

He tumbled through the rent in the ground before he registered its presence. One moment he was falling through a tangle of violet and blue, the next he was face-down on cool metal.

"I don't want to leave him any more than you do, but the readings are indisputable. He is dead, Nanami. We need to protect the crewmen we have left."

"And I tell you that I won't believe that man is dead until I see the body. Have you read his file, Ambassador? I won't leave him behind. Not until I'm sure."

"You'll get us all killed."

Dante groaned as every muscle in his body threatened to cramp up. He could feel the loss now; every ounce of energy had been stripped from him, body and mind. Even his heart beat slower, feeling as weak and fragile as a butterfly in slow motion.

"What is that? Mike? How in blue blazes did you get in here?"

Nanami turned him onto his back. The muscles in his back twitched painfully.

"I'm going to guess your talk went poorly. You...Ensign. Go get the Mike's drink. Captain, let's get underway. If they're willing to attack a member of the delegation, there's nothing to gain here."

The crewmen moved to obey in a flurry of activity. Dante lay still as he waited for the electrolyte drink to do its work. His muscles eased, but were still as soft as angel food cake.

Things got blurry. When he opened his eyes in the medical bay, he had a needle in his arm and a few electrodes slapped onto his forehead. The pain was gone, along with his exhaustion. He felt nearly human again.

"Dante." Ambassador Gilchrist sat in the corner, hands folded in his lap. "I'm glad to see you with us again."

"Yeah? You were going to leave me."

"I thought you were dead." Gilchrist came to stand over Dante. He looked a lot more concerned than Dante had imagined. "How do you feel?"

"Like I went ten rounds with a tank. Less tired, though."

"I see. Did you learn anything useful?"

Dante grinned. "I did. We have something she wants."

A smile cracked Gilchrist's somber expression. He fetched his chair and dragged it over. "Now that is good news. Tell me. What is it?"

CHAPTER FIFTEEN

The shuttle dipped away from the E.F.S. *Vaughan* and sliced into Geneva's atmosphere. It was packed with crewmembers on leave, with Julia Ronasuli and Jack Gagnon sitting together at the front of the cabin. They were surrounded by excited chatter. Geneva had gone from a renegade settlement to a legitimate Earth Colony and, from the sound of it, was a favorite place to go.

Julia pressed her hand against the viewscreen as the shuttle slowed for landing. Geneva City had started out with buildings fashioned from spaceship parts. Its cobbled-together beauty had been just one part of what made Geneva feel like home.

Now, years later, those unique buildings made up Old Geneva. The "new city" had sprung up around it as the colony prospered. As soon as Julia stepped out the door, the colony spread out before her, the gleaming white of prefab buildings in concentric circles around the center. Shady trees lined the narrow streets, and the only vehicles in sight were floating barges, pulled by large dog-like creatures with too many legs.

A hand on her shoulder dragged her from her reverie, and a bearhug followed. Ephraim laughed gleefully as he lifted her off her feet.

"Julia! It has been too long."

"I missed you too, Ephraim." She tried for a hug in return, but her arms were pinned to her sides. "How have you been?"

"Everything is wonderful, but we are missing four of our favorite citizens," he chuckled.

He released her and turned to Jack, giving him the same warm welcome. That was when she saw Nada hanging back, shifting her weight from one foot to the other. Julia put an end to that by walking over with her arms out. Nada had all the time in the world to dodge or pull away; instead, she relaxed and returned the hug fiercely.

"I'm glad you could come. We asked for you four specifically. The others could not come?"

"One of us had to stay on Earth, and Cor drew the short straw. Dante's on another mission right now, so you get us."

"At least we're your favorites," Jack cut in, grabbing Nada for a quick embrace. "You're looking good. The city looks like a *city,* now."

"We've been lucky. Our technology has done well, and Nada here has negotiated some very good trade deals for us." Ephraim smiled proudly at Nada. "But we should not stand here all day. What do you want? A tour? Rest? Food?"

Julia heard his emphasis on the word *tour* and saw the way Nada's expression sharpened as she looked at her partner.

"What do you have for food around here?" Jack asked.

"A tour would be great. It's still early for us, going by ship-time."

"Both, then. Come. We have a sledge reserved just for you, our honored guests."

The sledge turned out to be a small floating barge with seats built into it, pulled by one of the creatures that looked like a greyhound mixed with a horse, with big doe eyes and a stubby, wagging tail.

They climbed aboard and although Ephraim took the reins, they seemed to be for show only as he called out a command and the creature began to move. They glided past crewmembers on their way toward town, the creature's tongue happily flapping out the corner of its mouth.

"What is he?" Julia asked

"He's a mammal native to this planet. We found them on the southern tip of the continent. They're smarter than horses, but not sentient. We made sure of that before we put them to work." Ephraim called out another command

and the creature slowed. "We call them Greys, after the man that discovered and trained them."

"Not Tommy Grey?" Jack leaned forward to look at the creature with renewed interest.

"That's him. We can't help but impact the ecology here, but we stay as green as we can. The Greys are better than personal vehicles. When we expand the colony, we'll have electric trains for travel and shipping between settlements."

"He's on all the committees." Nada patted Ephraim's shoulder.

"Not all of them," Ephraim protested, but she just laughed at him. After a moment, he joined in, but some tension rose between them.

Jack didn't seem to notice; he was leaning in closer now, telling Ephraim about a dog he'd had as a boy. Julia sat back and listened while she watched the buildings grow larger.

Their visit was sanctioned by Earth Fleet, and the message she'd received had made it sound urgent. Yet, from the moment they'd landed, they hadn't said a word about why they were there. She was glad to see her friends, but the odd silence and the tension she sensed said this was more serious than she'd thought.

The Grey slowed just before it entered the city, matching the pace of the pedestrians. The outside buildings were prefabricated and decorated with mechanical parts and chunks of metal that recalled the buildings of Old Geneva. Stained glass was very popular. Most of the windows were decorated in abstract patterns. Some had images such as birds or Greys, each of them unique. In a city of identical buildings, the people had done what they could to personalize their homes.

They stopped at a restaurant to pick up meals, then turned onto a quieter street leading away from the center of the city. They took a winding route, eating their hot sandwiches and taking in the sights. Still, Julia noticed how they danced around the subject of their visit and focused on telling stories or reminiscing about the old days when Geneva was first founded.

She didn't miss the way Ephraim kept looking over his shoulder. He seemed to pretend it was to look at her or Jack, but his eyes were aimed at the street behind them. Julia raised her eyebrows. He pretended not to see.

"I think we lost them," she said drily when he looked back one more time. He winced.

"You can never be too sure. Please be patient with us. We'll explain everything when we get where we're going."

She thought that must be soon; she could see the spire of her old house not far ahead. Emotions unexpectedly filled her heart. That had been her first home with Cor. She wished he was with her now.

Ephraim made a sharp right turn and left Old Geneva behind.

"Where are we going?" Jack asked.

They didn't answer. Picking up speed on their way through the streets, Nada took over the 'tour' as she identified different buildings and talked about future plans. Julia tried to relax and pay attention, yet every time Ephraim looked over his shoulder, she had to resist the urge to look back as well.

They left the city and entered the forest. There was no road to speak of; instead, they wound their way between the trees, the Grey following an invisible path without any guidance.

They stopped next to a huge tree covered in a blue hanging moss. The whole affair was larger than most houses Julia had lived in. The Grey padded forward, but before its nose brushed the moss, it parted, revealing a split in the trunk large enough to contain their vehicle.

Once inside, Julia spotted an opening in the ground at the far end. She jumped down and walked over for a closer inspection. A smooth-walled tunnel led down into the earth at a gentle slope, illuminated by a soft white light.

"This is the reason we invited you. It was better to show you right away, before too many New Genevans learned of your presence." Ephraim unharnessed the Grey. It licked his hand and curled up on the ground with a huff.

"Why the secrecy?" she asked.

"A lot of traders come through here. Some of them deal in information, and not all of them are loyal to Earth. We think it best to keep this place a secret, at least for now."

Ephraim led them into the tunnel. At first, she thought the curved walls had been cut from stone, but when she ran her hand over the surface, it felt far too smooth to be cut from natural earth.

"We found this tunnel not long after you left. We haven't been able to identify the substance. It won't chip, and we can't find its power source. We don't even know how old it is. It baffles every instrument we bring down here."

"It feels very old." Julia continued studying the strange material.

"I agree, though Ephraim doesn't feel it as strongly." Nada stopped; they had reached the end of the tunnel. A solid metal door blocked their way. Nada pressed her hand to the sensor plate on the wall. Something heavy shifted inside and the door slid open, revealing the space beyond.

A low-ceilinged room stretched out a dozen meters from the end of the tunnel, the walls lined with instruments and workstations. When Nada stepped inside, the walls came to life with moving images and glyphs.

"What is all this?" Julia asked.

"If you go through that far door, you'll find our archaeology project. There are dozens of buildings under the forest, maybe hundreds of them. This planet was inhabited a long time ago, but something happened to make them leave. They left some devices behind, but not a single skeleton. Assuming they were a species that would leave skeletons," Nada explained.

Ephraim nodded. "The things we found seem to be nothing more than trinkets. They generate light or work as communication devices, but our engineers have been able to study them and make a few breakthroughs in our own technology."

"The most interesting thing about them is their limited use," Nada added. "Only the Enhanced and a handful of engineers can make the artifacts work. I suspect Mystic abilities are required." She picked up a pyramid small enough to fit in the palm of her hand and handed it to Julia. "Hold this for a moment."

Julia accepted the trinket and nearly dropped it when a chill shot up her arm. The pyramid crusted over with a cold blue crystal. It began to grow over her fingers, and Nada plucked it from her hand. The growth turned to dust and she brushed off her hands.

"I'm sorry about that, it usually grows much more slowly. It works for Ingram, but not for Sophie or Kenzie, our other engineers."

"Maybe he's got Mystic potential. Has he ever tested for the talent?" Julia scrubbed her hands together. They still felt prickly and cold.

"He says no, but we don't know how to test for the ability."

"Jack, you went through the testing. Do you think you could test Ingram?"

There was no answer. Julia turned toward her friend. He'd wandered over to one of the walls. He had his hand pressed to one of the images, one that could have been a winged snake or a very abstract dragon.

"Jack?" she repeated.

"What's the Astral Plane like down here?" He was frowning at the wall like it was an especially annoying puzzle. He'd missed the crystal generator entirely. "Let me guess. The walls glow and there's working technology in it."

"How did you know?" Ephraim had gone pale. "Who have you been talking to?"

"No one. I don't know about your gadgets, but these walls, these symbols...this was on Amadeus. A Pirr tried to kill us over a gadget we found there. Did you find anything like a cylinder with gold rings around it?"

"Nothing like that, no. All the technology we found is in this room," Nada answered.

"It was the only technology we found on Amadeus. I'd like to know why the Pirr want it so badly."

Ephraim beamed. "Then it is lucky we called you when we did. We need you to bring us to Earth with the data we've collected. Our team would be glad to look at this device while we are there."

"We also wish to help against the Pirr. They hide behind criminals who murder our kind. We found weapons that may help the Mystics protect themselves."

Nada stepped to the nearest table and picked up a blade shaped like a crescent moon with a grip that spanned the inside curve. When she held it up, the edge glowed silver.

Julia moved to Nada's side to get a closer look. "Is that a weapon?"

"Yes, and it is one that carries over to the Astral Plane. We've never seen anything like it." The light went out, and Nada returned it to the table. "Our engineers believe they can replicate the weapons, but we don't have the resources."

"We want to be able to protect ourselves as well," Ephraim added. "What if they decide to attack the colonies? We're near the outer edge of Earth's territory. We're a prime target."

"We'll get you to Earth," Julia promised. "But first, could you show us around? I want to see this alien city."

Ephraim led the way through the far door and into the ancient world.

Julia was enthralled by the strange images and alien architecture. Jack acted jumpy at first, but he calmed as they walked through the tunnels from one building to the next. Ephraim offered some theories as to what the buildings were, emphasizing that they were only guesses. They hoped to get the writing deciphered on Earth.

After the tour, Julia and Jack helped pack up the devices that would be coming back with them. She held the crescent blade and watched it glow, the edges crackling with tiny silver lightning bolts. She could feel her strength going into the blade, and she soon figured out how to limit the feed, then cut it off altogether.

She felt a little pang when she put the weapon away with the others. She already felt attached to it after holding it for only a few moments. Maybe she could get one of her own, once the engineers made more.

Once they returned to the city, Julia walked the familiar streets with Jack and met with old friends. They set up a public testing event, implying that this was the official reason for their visit.

Ingram was the first of the Old Genevans to come through. Julia watched as the flame-haired man sat down facing Jack, a nervous smile on his face.

"Nada says we need to know if I can do Mystic stuff, and if that's why I can make the gadgets run." He glanced at Julia, who was trying not to hover. "I don't want to be a Mystic, you know. I like my job."

"Don't worry. You don't have to do anything you don't want to." Jack held up his hands palm out. "Put your hands to mine and try to empty your mind."

"You know that gets harder the more you try to do it?" Ingram put his hands against Jack's, but his eyes stayed open.

Jack chuckled. "Just try to relax your mind. Think of a calm ocean or the night sky. Whatever you think of when you're trying to sleep."

"I'll try." Ingram closed his eyes, and Jack bowed his head.

At first, nothing happened. Ingram's nose twitched from time to time, and once he broke contact with Jack to scrub his face with his sleeve. Jack said nothing, just waited for Ingram to settle back into position and clear his mind.

Five minutes passed, then ten. Ingram began to breathe in sync with Jack. Julia found herself doing the same and silently laughed at herself. She wasn't the one being tested!

Another ten minutes passed, yet nothing happened. She began to think their theory was wrong. Then she heard the hum, a soft reverberation between the men's hands. It rose in volume until it filled the room. It tickled her mind, tugging at her to enter the Astral Plane.

Then, it stopped. Jack dropped his hands and smiled at her. Ingram rubbed his eyes and looked around the room, eyebrows furrowed.

"Did I fall asleep? Sorry about that. I guess I'm not one of you after all." He stood. "Should I send in the next guy?"

"I'm sorry to tell you this, but you passed. You almost jumped into the Astral Plane once we got in sync." Jack clapped Ingram on the shoulder. "You could be one of us."

"No thanks. I like being home too much." Ingram nodded to Julia, then shook Jack's hand. "I'll see you two on the flight to Earth."

The rest of the day went by in a blur. They took turns administering the test, which was just as tiring as spending hours in the Astral Plane. They took it better than an ordinary Mystic, but they still only got through two dozen subjects before they had to stop for the day.

It took five days to get through the Old Genevans and the other volunteers. Several people who passed genuinely wanted to become Mystics, so they spent the sixth day helping those people fill out paperwork for the Academy. Most importantly, they confirmed that the devices from the ruins only worked for those with Mystic potential.

Two weeks after their arrival, they were ready to return to Earth. Nada and Ephraim's team got onboard *Vaughan* with the new Mystic students. Julia and Jack didn't challenge the assumption that those returning to Earth were enrolling in the Academy of Mystics. They settled in for the voyage home, secrets weighing heavily on Julia's shoulders.

CHAPTER
SIXTEEN

Barbara McNuggen rejoined Earth Fleet two months after her return to Earth. At first, that meant days of questioning that were just this side of interrogations. She told them everything, from the dragons' blessing to the Mystics' plans. There was no sense in hiding the truth, it would only do harm in the long run.

Her honesty helped her, at least. After only a few months as XO on a Solar System patrol boat, she was transferred to the E.F.S. *Siren* to take the place of its retired captain. After a week on the boat, she wondered if *Siren* should be retired as well. Its engine was in constant need of repair and she never saw an engineer without a tool in their hand.

She grimaced when her ship lurched under her captain's chair again and punched up the line to Engineering on her datapad. A moment later, the Chief Engineer's face appeared on her datapad screen, painted red by a flashing light behind him.

"Captain. How can I help you?"

"What's going on back there, Alan?"

"Coolant valve got stuck. We've got it under control, Cap." He grinned. "Never a dull moment, eh?"

"I prefer my excitement *not* to come from the engine room. At this rate, *Mariana* is going to leave us in the dust."

Barbara glanced at her tactical display. The colony ship *Mariana* was matching their speed, which meant they'd noticed the slowdown. She pressed her lips together. Alan was doing his best. Snapping at him would be counterproductive.

"Doubtful, captain. We're her escort to Geneva. If she leaves us, no telling what the rats will do to her."

His smile was supposed to be reassuring, but it didn't do any such thing. His mention of the rats—*pirates*—reminded her of dangers beyond the engine room. At least their weapons were top of the line. Plus, once they got to Earth, an array of shiny new engine parts awaited her ship.

She swallowed a sigh and stood from her chair. "Noted. Let's keep her in motion, chief. We're out of range for Triple-A service."

"Aye, Aye."

"McNuggen out." She disconnected the call. "Masters, the bridge is yours."

She had half a mind to march to Engineering to inspire some motivation. She thought better of it.

She was used to being a part of everything, having spent so long on a five-person crew where everyone pitched in without getting in the way. If she went to Engineering now, she'd just be in the way. She might even make things worse.

She turned toward the galley. The lunch shift was beginning, and she'd skipped breakfast in favor of a workout. Maybe she'd be calmer about the engine room situation if she had a full belly.

The galley was already halfway occupied, chatter echoing as if a stadium full of people had been crammed into the small space. She grabbed a tray and found a seat at a mostly empty table. Across and down from her, M1C Dawkins and M2C Koenig were lingering over their mashed potatoes, deep in discussion.

No one else was at the table, as usual. If Mystics were present, no one would fill the seats if there were any other options. More than once, Barbara had seen a crewperson walk into the galley, see the only empty seat was by Dawkins, and walk back out.

She didn't know how to combat that. If she ordered people to sit with the Mystics, it would only create more resentment, making everyone uncomfortable and damaging morale. One of her leadership challenges was how to bring the crew closer to their Mystics.

"Good day, Mike. Mack," she greeted, using the casual pronunciation of their ranks. They both looked startled, then Koenig smiled at her.

"Hello, Captain McNuggen. How's your day going?"

"As expected. The way I like it."

Dawkins chuckled. "Same here. If I can go a day without surprises, I call that a good day." He stood, and Koenig followed.

"Don't leave on my account." Barbara gestured at the table. "There's plenty of room."

"We appreciate it, but we've got work to do, and these seats will be needed in a moment. Have a good afternoon, captain."

"Same to you." Barbara turned her focus to her food. It was surprisingly good; she'd missed the simple things like meatloaf and coffee out on the edge of everything. She was just digging into her pudding when she heard a word whispered behind her.

Brainwashed.

She put her fork down and listened, sipping her coffee slowly.

"She spent years with them. They did something to her. She used to see what freaks they were," the hushed voice continued. "Now she's friendly with them?"

"Maybe it's their powers. They forced her to like them." A second voice joined in, slightly louder than the first. "They'll do it to all of us, one at a time."

"It could be easier to explain than that. You've heard of Stockholm Syndrome, right? They kidnapped her, forced her to be their pilot. After a while, she started identifying with them. It's that simple," a third person spoke up.

Barbara clenched her teeth. She set down her coffee cup before she spilled it. She'd heard those whispers before, back at HQ, but she hadn't expected it on board her own ship. She got up and turned around, nailing the gossips with a glance. They were huddled at the end of the table behind her, leaning in close like the conspirators they were.

In a moment's thought, she recalled their names: Hayes, Olsen, and Crewes. She leaned between Hayes and Crewes, putting her hands on the tabletop as she glared directly into Olsen's eyes. Technician Olsen resembled a rabbit in headlights as she looked up to see whose shadow had been cast over her tray.

"I take the morale of my crew very seriously." Barbara knew the smile she currently wore was known for inspiring terror in young crewpersons. She saved it for special occasions. "Do you feel like your captain is compromised, Olsen?"

"N-no, ma'am." Olsen shook her head violently.

"How about you, Technician Hayes? Crewes?"

Their denials echoed Olsen's. They were false, of course. She'd hoped at least one of them would have the spine to say yes. Maybe these insidious rumors would stop if she could confront them directly. Sadly, these three weren't going to give her the chance.

"The Mystics on this boat work as hard as you do, with more risk of exposure to hostile forces. They are as loyal to Earth as you and me. It doesn't take Mystic mind tricks to see that." She straightened, watching how Crewes and Hayes twisted to face her.

"I don't believe in forcing people to believe what I do, but I do believe in maintaining morale. If I hear of the three of you, or anyone else, spreading rumors that denigrate my character or that of other members of my crew, you will regret the day you crossed me. Are we clear?"

They assured her that she was, made of crystal and glass, she was so clear. Her smile deepened, and the three of them blanched.

"Wonderful. I want the three of you to meditate on this while you're helping with clean up after the lunch shift. Report to Mister Reagan. Tell him you're on galley cleanup until further notice."

"Aye, captain," they chorused.

She disposed of her tray's contents and left the galley, maintaining her cold smile while she clenched her teeth. She'd like to go back to her habit of eating in her office, but she knew her presence among the crew was a great benefit. They would follow a captain who cared enough about them to learn their names, see them at work, appreciate who they were as individuals. She wouldn't let a few rumor-mongers deter her.

It wasn't hard to pin down what bothered her most. Even though they were turning her into a victim, the worst was their mentality of Human versus Mystic, Us versus Them. It divided the crew, created animosity where none belonged.

She returned to the bridge, mulling the problem over. She couldn't force anyone to change their minds. She could only set the right example and put down the rumors whenever she could. She'd get her crew's trust. It was just a matter of time.

The ship bucked, throwing Barbara to the deck as the claxons wailed. She wasn't alone; a few of her bridge crew climbed to their feet alongside her.

"Engineering better get their act together," Johnson growled.

"That isn't an Engineering alarm," Barbara said, raising her voice to be heard above the alarm. "That's a proximity alert. Higgins, sound general quarters."

The claxon muted, and a different alarm echoed through the ship. Throughout *Siren,* crewmen hurried to their battle stations, engineers and Mystics included. She hoped Alan and his team were up for this because if they couldn't outmaneuver the pirates, they were in a lot of trouble.

She harnessed into her seat and put the tactical display on the main screen. Three unknown ships closed in on *Siren* and *Mariana.* Coming from different vectors, they seemed most focused on *Siren,* though Barbara was sure they'd take out the more vulnerable colony ship if left exposed.

"Higgins, call *Mariana.* Tell her to stay on course. Take evasive maneuvers as needed, we'll keep them busy."

"Aye, captain."

"Bring us around, Ensign Johnson. We'll take the fight to them."

He acknowledged, his hands flying over the controls. Everyone strapped in as McNuggen gave orders. They'd go after the enemies' engines, then get *Mariana* to safety. The important thing was to keep the civilians safe. If the pirates couldn't' catch the colonists, they couldn't harm them.

Siren hummed as the engines kicked in at full power. They wove between two of the attackers, peppering their hulls with railgun projectiles. Once in close range, Barbara maneuvered them so if the pirates fired, they also risked striking their ally. If they went after *Mariana,* they'd expose their backs to *Siren.* They eventually broke formation to move from the crossfire position, so *Siren* stayed alongside one ship, using them as a shield against the other two.

They were grazed by a laser weapon. Barbara had never seen the like, and she set Masters to analyzing the weapon. The pirate ships were nearly works of art, outfitted with weapons beyond her experience. Yet none of them flew like Johnson, and their captains couldn't outthink McNuggen.

They fought a battle of attrition, wearing away at their enemies, slowing them down and doing damage that was minimal on its own but crippling when compounded. She kept the fingers of her left hand crossed, praying *Siren* would hold together long enough the pirates would give up, and the *Mariana* would get away.

Their concentrated barrage on one of the ships suddenly ripped its hull open. The bridge crew whooped as the ship drew away. Johnson sent the speedier *Siren* spiraling around the ship they were using for a shield, ready to engage the next enemy. All at once, *Siren* groaned, and a shudder ran through her from stem to stern.

The lights went out. Something crashed into them and sent them into a spin sure to carry them into the void, but they stopped so suddenly Barbara was thrown against her harness with gut-wrenching force. Her shoulder popped and she gasped in pain. The emergency lights came on, but the ship's screens and controls remained dark.

"Report." She coughed amid the grinding pain shooting through her shoulder. It was broken, then. She held still as she fumbled for her datapad. "Is everyone alive?"

"Johnson is unconscious, but I see him breathing," Higgins reported. "I'm not feeling great myself, but I'm here."

"Good. See if you can get us up and running. I don't like being blind. Anyone need a medic?" She unsnapped her harness and stood up, looking around. Everyone looked dazed, if they had their eyes open at all. "Who's unhurt? Yates? Get to the medical bay and see who's—"

Another groan shook the ship, followed by the deafening screech of metal cutting into metal. Yates froze with his fingertips pressed to Johnson's throat, poised to follow her order.

"They're boarding us," Barbara murmured. They were cutting through the hull, and without her instruments, she had no way to know where they were coming through.

"Yates, new orders. Find out where they're coming through. Masters, see who you can raise via datapad. We'll need a force to meet the enemy. Nobody steps foot on my ship without my leave, do you hear me?"

Their answering "Aye-aye, *sir!*" was more spirited than she'd hoped. It didn't raise her estimate of victory, but it told her there was still some fight left in her crew.

Barbara leaned against the bulkhead, peering around the corner at the white-hot circle someone was cutting into her ship. They had already breached the outer hull, now they had come to the starboard airlock.

They were leaving the ship spaceworthy. Even the exterior hole wouldn't matter if they kept this airlock shut. Some of her crew viewed it as a good sign. She'd put that idea down as soon as it came up. She didn't believe the pirates intended to be merciful. She saw it as part of a plan to steal her ship.

The piece of hull hit the deck with a loud *clang*. She lifted her weapon. She wouldn't be getting any points for accuracy with her left arm in a sling, but she was going to fight this out with her crew.

"Masks," she called out as gray smoke rolled into the corridor. Everyone sealed their rebreathers. She switched on the private communications link with those in a sealed helmet. "Wait until I give the word, then fire. I don't want one shot going out until we can see their ugly faces."

They didn't have to wait long. Heavy boots clomped on the deck, but she didn't see a single pirate. They were right on the other side of the hole. She could hear them moving.

"My kingdom for a grenade," she murmured.

Someone chuckled in her ear. She ignored it; it was just a nervous reaction.

A hand appeared in the doorway, flicking in and out of sight before she could react. Her mouth opened to give the firing order, but the pirate stayed behind cover. She grit her teeth. Half her fighters were in bad shape, and the other half weren't much better. Their fight was to scare off the pirates. She expected things wouldn't go her way. Their only real hope was to die well.

Something caught her eye; the emergency lights hit it at the right angle, outlining a copper disc floating silently on a cushion of air. It drew close, a set of lights blinking on its surface. They flickered slowly at first, then faster, and it emitted a high-pitched hum that intensified as its lights sped up.

"Take cover," she yelled.

The words were still leaving her mouth when electricity exploded from the disc's surface. A tendril of energy hit Barbara, and the next moment she was on her back with the scent of burned hair in her nostrils. She tried to stand, but her body felt disconnected from her brain. She told her right arm to reach for the gun she'd dropped, but all her hand did was twitch its fingers. Trying to sit up got the same result, as did trying to speak.

Her eyes closed despite her efforts to keep them open. The next thing she knew, she was flipped over, her hands bound behind her back. Her injured shoulder protested, and she knew it would be worse once her head cleared.

She found herself kneeling before a Pirr in a ragged coat, flanked by two filthy gray Yeti. One of them wore an eyepatch and watched her with lips peeled back to reveal sharp teeth. She looked away. If she knew anything about Yeti, you didn't want to keep eye contact with one in bloodlust.

She focused on the Pirr. Rough clothing or not, he had the look of someone who had never worked a day in his life; even his eyebrows were groomed.

"I don't see any peg legs," she croaked, wobbling to her feet. "Some pirates you are."

The Yeti on the left stepped forward and pushed her back down to her knees with a growl. The Pirr held up his hand, and the Yeti backed away.

"You are the captain of this vessel, correct?" the Pirr asked. "I ask because the last captain locked himself in his bridge until we cut him out. It went very poorly for him."

"I am Captain McNuggen, yes. If you're trying to scare me, you'll need to try harder." She glared, letting the pain in her shoulder feed her hostility.

One of the Yeti warbled to the other. It had been a long time since she'd heard their guttural, growling language, but she understood it was saying something about honor and war-leaders. Her head spun too much to follow it well.

"Greetings, Captain McNuggen. I am Hyuen. As we speak, your engine is being dismantled. Your Mystics are being cut out of their chamber. Ten of your crew have been identified as Mystics without training. What do you say to that?"

It sounded like an accusation. Barbara frowned. "I guess that can happen. Not everyone wants to peruse their Mystic talent."

"We will remove them from your care. Human Mystics fetch a high bounty."

"You can take me instead. I'm worth more in ransom than anything you could get for a few Mystics."

The left-hand Yeti's fur rippled in happiness. She scowled at it. She wasn't interested in making a Yeti pirate happy.

"You have impressed my friends with your bravery and honor." Hyuen smirked. "They wish to let you live. What do you think? Would you like to ask for your life?"

She spat at his feet. "Do what you want. Either way, you're still a thief and a murderer, and I won't beg for anything but my crew's lives. Let them go, and I'll do anything. Harm a single one of them, and I will hunt you to the grave and beyond."

"You're right. She is brave...in a foolhardy sort of way," Hyuen mused. "Put her back to sleep, will you? Her threats are amusing, but we have more important things to deal with."

"Don't touch me," Barbara started to say, but there was a pinch at the nape of her neck. A soft darkness enveloped her as she sank to the floor.

Siren's engines were damaged beyond repair, leaving the ship to survive on battery power alone. When Barbara woke, the pirates were gone, along with the Mystics and twelve crewmembers.

Nonessential parts of the ship were sealed off in an attempt to use less power. Higgins got communications online but no one answered their distress calls. *Mariana* was long gone, with no way to know if she escaped or was destroyed.

Siren was dead in the water. If they didn't run out of air, they'd freeze. If they didn't freeze, they'd run out of food and water. Odds of rescue were practically nil. Still, Barbara recorded a distress call and sent it out on repeat. She wouldn't give up without a fight.

CHAPTER SEVENTEEN

E.F.S. *Vaughan* was cozier on the return trip than it had been on the way to Geneva. Low-ranking crewmembers had to share bunks with the new 'students' headed for the Mystic Academy. The Genevans adjusted their sleep schedule so that they slept while their hosts were on duty. That gesture made it easier to share, but Jack still heard complaints about lost privacy and personal space.

Nada and Ephraim shared a cabin with him and Julia. He didn't mind, but it left him with nowhere to work on his manuscript. He could use the commune chamber, he supposed, but he didn't enjoy sitting on the floor. That left him with the galley. He lingered over his datapad long after the dinner shift ended, skimming what he'd written and making notes. It kept him busy until his guests woke up and he could turn in.

"Excuse me, Mystic Gagnon?"

"That's me." Jack gestured at the seat across from him before he locked his datapad. "Is everything okay?"

He crossed his fingers under the table as he asked. The younger Mystic recruits had decided he was the one to go to with their problems. He'd already navigated more roommate problems than he'd ever expected or wanted. He still preferred those over rescuing someone who decided to screw around with their Mystic abilities without any training or oversight.

At least this young man didn't seem panicked. That boded well. His visitor's name came to him as Jack waited for more information, then he realized it probably wasn't coming on its own.

"You're Nico Carter, right? You were on *Doomslayer.*"

"Yes, sir. I worked security, actually. I'm surprised you remember me."

"Not so much from *Doomslayer,* but I heard about you on Geneva. You turned out to be a pretty good hunter if I remember correctly."

Nico shrugged, ducking his head modestly. "I guess so."

"So what can I do for you, Hunter Carter?" He was rewarded with a self-conscious laugh. Jack set his datapad aside to give Carter his full attention.

"Nothing much. I just was wondering about some things." Carter looked around the galley. It was mostly empty. Their only company was a handful of playing cards. "Can I ask you some questions?"

"Yes, of course. Are you having second thoughts?"

"Not really. Unless...well, I was wondering about dragons." Carter's gaze became fixed on a point just above Jack's shoulder. He could almost feel the force of the recruit *not* staring.

"What about them?"

"How did you get yours? Could anyone just suddenly get...attached to one?"

Jack shook his head gently. He was pretty sure *attached* hadn't been the first word that came to mind. At least Carter was tactful.

"No, not just anyone. We entered a pact with the dragons at Ian's World. This was part of the deal." Jack waved one hand around his face. "And it was all voluntary."

"What about on Cavey? I heard that Mystic First Class Dante got possessed there and did a lot of bad things. I heard he wasn't in control." Carter's skin flushed pink.

Jack could understand the young man's curiosity and the worry. It was brave, too, to enter in a new life with new rules, without knowing all the consequences.

"That was different. Dante's a good man, and dragons only have good intentions for mankind— for all life, really." Jack leaned back, folding his hands over his belly as he assessed Nico Carter's expression. "And that was one rogue dragon. We know much more now how to avoid an unpleasant situation like that one."

"If you could end the pact, would you?"

Jack considered how he had entered into the partnership with both eyes open. It had seemed necessary at the time and also final.

"No."

"Because it makes you stronger?" Carter asked, his brow furrowed.

Jack shook his head again. "No. The power is nice, but I wouldn't miss it the way I'd miss my dragon. She's part of me now. We're partners, and I'd be incomplete without her."

"How do you know those are your thoughts and not the dragon's?"

Jack raised his eyebrows. That was a good question, but he wasn't about to say so. He trusted his dragon. She'd done well by him, and he had no reason to doubt her. Yet that didn't sound solid enough for a stranger to trust.

"I'm in her head as much as she's in mine." Not entirely true, but close enough to reassure a new Mystic. "If she was messing with me, I'd know it. We've built trust over the years. Don't worry, we're good."

Carter nodded thoughtfully. His thumb drifted toward his face, and he began to chew on the nail. Jack tried not to be impatient. Then the young Mystic seemed to realize he was chewing on his nails and dropped his hand into his lap, wiping his fingers on his coveralls.

"What if I wanted a dragon?"

Jack chuckled, then regretted it when Carter's face darkened. "I'm sorry, man. I don't really know. Maybe when you're done training, you'll find a dragon who wants a toehold on the physical plane. They approached us. I don't think it's anything that can be forced from our side."

He nodded, but it was hard to tell if it signified agreement, or just that he'd heard and understood. Jack glanced at his datapad, thinking of the work he still had to do, but he didn't want to drive Carter off. The young man still had something to get off his chest, Jack could tell.

"Why do you want a dragon?" Jack asked when he couldn't take the silence any longer.

"I don't...not especially. I'm just thinking tactically. If we've only got four big guns and they're light years away from where the pirates are attacking, what good are they? And the Pirr are threatening all of us, especially colonies on the edge like Geneva."

Jack couldn't argue with that. He hadn't thought much about how those on the border would feel with pirates and hostile aliens so close. The E.F. had patrols out this way, but they couldn't watch every inch of space all the time.

"I understand how you feel. I keep looking for answers too. I'm in no position to suggest strategy to E.F. either. Even Julia isn't, and she used to be an officer. I trust our leaders know what they're doing, and when I get orders, I follow them."

"But you rebelled before. You didn't think they knew better then."

Jack wondered if there'd come a day when he didn't get reminded of that. It was a fair statement, sure, but it was undermining his point.

"We were in a unique situation I hope to never be in again." Jack checked the time. Nada and Ephraim would be getting up any moment. He yawned. "You aren't regretting the decision to enroll, are you? Believe me, the first week can be a little rough; after that, you'll be fine. If you made it into Earth Fleet, you can make it anywhere."

Carter grinned and shook his head. "No, sir. I've just got all these questions bouncing around my skull."

"Sounds to me like you'll do fine at the Academy. They like thinkers." Jack stood and stretched. "But cut out this 'sir' nonsense. I'm not an E.F. officer. It makes me feel like an old man."

"You got it."

"Anything else for me? I'm about to crash."

Carter shook his head no, so Jack grabbed his datapad and said good night. He liked Carter already. His questions weren't comfortable to think about, yet he asked them anyway. He didn't flinch. That was a good sign for a Mystic, one who would contribute to accomplishing whatever mission he was given.

Alarms woke him from a deep sleep. Jack's feet hit the floor before his eyes opened. He fumbled his way into his clothes before he registered the sounds of Julia doing the same. He could blame his sleep-befuddled brain for some of that; he was still letting go of the dream he was having, something to do with dragons and popcorn.

"What's going on?" He fastened the last of his buttons. He knew he wouldn't get an answer, but his filter hadn't woken up yet.

"Don't know. We should be near the wormhole." Julia moved past him to open the door.

Jack frowned and followed her. The wormhole should mean they were home free, or as good as. The mothership would take them into the wormhole, because little ships didn't have the energy to survive the event horizon. Once they were on the other side, they'd be firmly in human territory. That meant they were still on the Geneva side of the wormhole. Probably.

Carter's questions returned as they jogged toward the commune chamber. The alarm's volume tapered off, but half the lights had turned red.

"Tell me this doesn't mean what I think it does." He glanced into the face of a security officer running the opposite way. His eyes were wide, his lips pressed into a thin line. It wasn't the most reassuring expression.

"It's a call to battle stations."

"I said to tell me something else," Jack groaned. It was meant to lighten the mood, but not much of it struck him as funny.

Julia didn't answer.

When they reached the commune chamber, they found Ephraim and Nada clearing crates so the chamber could be used. Jack pitched in, earning a nod of thanks from Ephraim. Once he stepped in, there wasn't much room for Julia.

"I'm going to see what's going on. I'll be back." Julia sprinted up the corridor, headed for the bridge.

Jack nodded, even though she wouldn't see it, and focused on getting the room cleared out. It took a couple minutes, but those moments stretched like warm taffy. The strain in Nada's face was obvious, while Ephraim's was completely blank.

Both of them were enhanced humans, which meant they were volunteers who had been turned into Mystics through technology. Jack wasn't sure if they'd ever seen combat before. He'd been in a few confrontations as a Mystic, but he'd never been in a ship that was getting shot at. He didn't want to break that streak now.

His datapad pinged. He accepted the inbound call and got a glimpse of Julia's face before she turned the camera on the bridge's viewscreen.

A ship like a crystal knife dominated the view, hovering directly between *Vaughan* and the wormhole. Light rippled under its surface and, most concerning, something like giant cannons were pointed their way and glowing with energy. Beyond them, a squad of six more alien vessels hovered in formation.

"Comms has identified these ships as Pirr." Julia's voice came through pitched low.

Ephraim and Nada moved closer, making a sandwich out of Jack so they could see his pad's screen.

"This is an established wormhole," Nada protested. "This goes beyond blocking expansion."

"Not that we're a fan of that either," Ephraim added. Nada rewarded him with a dirty look.

"We have been given five minutes to surrender our Mystics and potential Mystics." Julia's voice dropped into a monotone. "Their tech is hard to read, but I believe they've got a lock on us."

"What do we do?" Nada's voice tremored. She fought to remain calm. Jack admired her for that, since he was still looking for his voice.

"Get in here and shut the door," he told them.

There were things left to move, but they didn't have time. Jack stepped into the commune chamber and sat down cross-legged. After a moment, Nada joined him. Ephraim locked them inside and assumed his position with the others.

Jack took their hands and projected calm. That proved difficult, considering he felt anything but. He took a long, slow breath. His friends imitated him.

"I'm going to get us out of this, but I'll need your help. Share your strength with me."

Nada squeezed his hand more tightly. After a moment, he felt energy trickling into him from her side. It wasn't much, but it was a start.

Ephraim's hand spasmed a few times. He'd done this before, Jack knew, but it was under very different circumstances. Jack counted backward from ten.

Ten.

Even If he didn't get support from Ephraim, Nada was doing fine. He could last a little while with just the two of them. Once Julia knew what he was doing, she'd get back here to help.

Nine.

Speaking of that.

"Julia, I'm going to give the Pirr a little surprise. Can you make sure they move quickly once I do?"

"Yes. I'll talk to them. Stay focused, I'll be there soon."

Eight.

The connection died. Nada's hand was damp with sweat. Jack's palm tingled as he took in the energy she offered.

"What are you going to do?" she asked.

"I'm going to hide us," he said.

Seven.

Ephraim turned red. He looked skeptical. Jack didn't blame him. Cloaking technology hadn't been invented yet, at least not on the human side.

"Explain," he demanded. "Distract me until I can get this link working.

Six.

"I can make us unnoticeable. It's hard when they already know we're here. That's why I need help." Jack squeezed Ephraim's hand a little harder. "Let go of the lock, buddy. I won't take more than you can share."

"That isn't the problem. I'm just not good at this."

"It's true," Nada offered. "He's very slow to open up to people. He isn't being mistrustful on purpose."

"I said it isn't about trust," Ephraim grumbled. "There's no one I trust more than Jack and Julia."

Five.

Jack closed his eyes and bowed his head. Either Ephraim would get it, or he wouldn't. As warmed as Jack was by the declaration of trust, actions were going to carry more weight.

Nada cleared her throat.

"Well, besides Dante and Coraolis," Ephraim said agreeably.

"Even with these circumstances, I could tell you that was the wrong thing to say." Jack forced a laugh. "We'll be fine. Once we vanish from plain sight, we'll move out of their sensor range."

"Then what?" Nada squeezed his hand again. She seemed more relaxed; enough that the trickle of power was turning into an open faucet.

Four.

"That's up to Captain Elliott."

Jack began the mental exercises that would relax him just enough to use his abilities without popping out of his body. The longer he practiced as a Mystic, the easier it was to reach the Astral Plane. Most of the time that was fine with him, but today he had to stay rooted in the physical world.

Three.

"Remind me of how far it is to the next wormhole," Ephraim murmured to Nada.

"Months away," Nada whispered. "That's why Geneva was such a good hiding place."

"I was afraid of that."

Two.

They kept talking, but Jack had sunk into the zone. His dragon felt as close as if she were hugging him from behind, with her tail wrapped around both of them. Her presence was reassuring, especially with the strength she was giving him. Love was mixed in there too, and not the universal love the dragons seemed to hold for everyone. This felt very specific.

Where is this coming from?

Usually she didn't give him anything. Her bond with him was enough to feed his power levels. She never gave him extra. He'd always assumed he had access to all of her reserves if needed. He thought they were his as much as hers.

I am collecting it from you. You plan to hide the human ship, yes? Do it now, before they attack.

One.

Jack nodded, knowing his dragon wouldn't see it. She'd get the emotional gist of it anyway. His hands clenched Ephraim's and Nada's tighter, then he sank into himself.

In the Astral Plane, a rippling cloak of energy rolled over the crystalline mass that was *Vaughan's* representation. An energy field spread out over *Vaughan's* frame at the same time, forcing all mortal eyes to look away.

Or it *tried.* Ironclad minds pushed back against the illusion. They *knew Vaughan* was present.

They wouldn't trust their eyes or give into his trickery without a fight.

He tugged at Nada's power and was rewarded with another surge. He turned his attention on Ephraim and did the same. At first, it felt like pushing on a brick wall, then the brick sagged and became something closer to foam. The barrier tore open, and Jack was flooded with strength.

He grinned. This was *more* than enough. He felt it when *Vaughan* dipped down and away from the wormhole, moving just in time to avoid the enemy's first volley. Then they changed course, and Jack poured more energy into keeping hostile eyes away. He relaxed a hair; he didn't need such an iron grip on his concentration at that point.

"Now we hold until we're out of sensor range." He relaxed his hands and felt his friends do the same, though they didn't pull away.

"How are you doing this?" Ephraim asked.

"My dragon. She taught me a few tricks."

That was met with silence until the door opened and Julia pushed into the small room. She hurried to kneel next to Jack and squeezed his shoulders, feeding her strength into him.

"Are you doing okay? There were a lot of eyes on us back there."

"I'm fine. How long before we're out of range?"

"Ten minutes if they don't follow. Longer if they do." Julia settled back on her heels. "As soon as we're clear, captain's going to call me so you can stop. We might need your powers again in a few hours."

"What for?"

"We picked up a distress signal. It's verified Earth Fleet encryption. Someone's in trouble out there. It sounds like pirates hit them."

"With Pirr in the area? I'm shocked. What's next, Mystics going into the Astral Plane?" Jack tried to keep his tone light, but even he could hear the strain in his voice.

"Are they all right?" Nada asked.

"Not all of them." Julia sounded grim. She patted Jack's shoulder and stood. "We'll be there in a few hours."

As soon as they were clear of the enemy, Jack grabbed some food from the galley, then took a nap. When he returned to the chamber a few hours later, the others were already waiting. He yawned, peering through bloodshot eyes within dark circles as he took his place on the floor. He didn't feel mentally ready for a fight or a retreat, but he knew he had the reserves for either. He just wanted an encounter to go simply for once.

To his surprise, he got his wish. They came upon the E.F.S. *Siren* drifting in the void. Its engine

Dragon Invasion

was dead. By all appearances, the rest of its
systems were about to collapse. Jack and Nada
checked out the Astral Plane, hoping to make
contact with *Siren's* Mystics. Julia and Ephraim
worked together to scan the area.

They found nothing but a feeble battery system
barely maintaining life support. Julia found signs
of life, but only a few conscious minds. They
were almost out of air; a few more hours and it
would have been too late.

The Mystics reported in, and their report
matched the bridge crew's findings. *Vaughan*
docked with *Siren,* then sent a security team in
for a search-and-rescue.

Jack went to the connecting airlock as soon as he
heard the captain's name. Barbara McNuggen
was captain of the *Siren.* No one would confirm
one way or the other, so he waited and watched
as one survivor after another came through the
airlock. Each time it wasn't Barbara, his hopes
sank lower.

He looked to Julia for encouragement, but she'd
banished all emotion from her face. That meant
she was bracing for bad news. He sank even
lower.

The airlock opened, and Ensign Thomas came
through with a pale woman leaning on him. She
was the first to come through on her own feet,
support or not. Thomas helped her over to Jack's
bit of wall, then handed her off without a word.

"Wait, what are we supposed to do with her?" he asked Thomas, but the ensign never looked back.

"Wait for a medic, I guess." Julia moved over to help support the woman, glancing at her nametag. "Hey...Jensen? Is that your name?"

The woman rolled her eyes up to look at Julia, then nodded heavily. "Yes."

"Where's Captain McNuggen? She's a friend of ours."

"She won't leave until everyone else has evacuated."

Jack perked up. "She's alive? She's okay?"

"Alive, yes. Okay? I believe so. She's awake enough to give your security team a hard time." Jensen's lips twitched as if she were too tired to smile, yet a hint of pride made her lift her chin.

"What happened?" Julia asked.

Jensen shook her head. The Mystics waited with her until another medic came and got her. Jack was glad Barbara was alive, though he'd feel better if he saw her with his own eyes.

He finally got his wish. Barbara walked through the airlock with an oxygen mask strapped to her face. The moment she was on board *Vaughan,* she stripped off the mask and tossed it to a med team member hovering over her.

"I just want to sleep for a week," she informed the medic.

He gestured at Jack and the others. "They've been looking for you, captain."

She looked their way, and her hard expression bloomed into a beautiful smile. She hadn't taken two steps their way when Julia intercepted her with a one-arm hug. Jack was there a moment later, eyes glistening at knowing his old friend was safe.

"Are you okay? What happened?" Julia asked.

"Pirates. We gave them a fight, but they took out our engines. They took our Mystics and some of the crew and left us to die." McNuggen scowled. "They said Harris was a Mystic. *Harris.* He's been an engineer for ten years."

"Some people never test. We just found seven potential Mystics on Geneva. All of them had careers in Earth Fleet once upon a time. They didn't get tested until we came along." Jack offered his arm for McNuggen to lean on. She waved him off.

"I'm glad you're all right, Barbara, as much as you can be with a broken shoulder." Julia claimed another gentle hug, and Jack stepped back for a little air. "We missed you."

"Same here," Barbara said roughly. "Now, where's your captain? I've got a report to make before I get off my feet."

"Meeting with people in the medical ward, I think." Julia adjusted her stance to give Barbara a little more support. "Come on, we'll take you there."

"I'm fine." Still, Barbara let them help her. Despite her rough voice, she smiled as she looked at Jack, then Julia. "I can't tell you how good it is to see you two."

"Us, too. Now, let's get you checked out."

Jack got Barbara moving down the hall with Julia supporting her from the other side. She was alive, if not completely whole, although she would be. He was glad of that, but the fate of the other Mystics left a weight like a brick in his stomach. This couldn't go on.

CHAPTER EIGHTEEN

Every mothership in Earth Fleet was armored and outfitted with enough capital-grade weapons and fighter squadrons to defend itself. While they stood alone in the depths of space, they still made for too big a mouthful for any raider to bite off, even the Pirr.

The pirates kept a wide berth around the Geneva wormhole where E.F.F. Mothership *Gemini* waited. They were in position to strike any ship entering or leaving the wormhole but were beyond *Gemini's* reach. The fighters could reach them if they tried, but that would leave the mothership exposed.

Vaughan neared the wormhole under the cloak of Jack's powers, invisible to mothership and pirate alike. They made a long path around the pirates to be safe, adding extra hours to the journey. Jack tried to bear up under the strain, but he wilted before the first hour was up.

Julia organized shifts for the Mystics and trainees to support Jack. Ephraim and Nada sat with him first while she gave the students a crash course in sharing their strength. Their natural defenses would keep them from giving too much. She was grateful to have many times the usual number of Mystics to keep Jack going.

They docked with *Gemini,* floating into the mothership's great hangar bay and sealing themselves to the lock. Only then did Jack release his powers, collapsing. Julia and two of the recruits carried him to his bunk.

Gemini's crew was shocked by *Vaughan's* sudden appearance, but it only took a moment to get sorted and they were on their way.

Barbara was outside the door when Julia left the cabin. She had a datapad clutched in one hand as she paced. Julia paused in the doorway to watch her for a moment, noting the lines forming between Barbara's eyebrows.

"What's wrong?"

The E.F. captain spun on her heel and closed on Julia, holding out the device. Up close, the new lines around her eyes became more obvious, as did the hints of gray in her complexion. She was exhausted and looked it. Julia wondered when she'd last slept.

"Look at this. The damned liars are at it again," she snapped, shoving the datapad at Julia.

Julia accepted it reflexively. That same Pirr was on the screen. Her jaw clenched at the sight of the alien. The ticker across the bottom of the screen named her Pirr spokesperson this time, instead of just 'Commander Xoa.' She was nothing more than a mouthpiece to Julia, one that had tried to kill her partner and best friend.

Barbara pressed play. Julia grimaced at her friend, but the video was already playing.

"The Pirr understand your grief, but we did not order the attack on your civilian colony. We would not stoop so low." Xoa's lips parted in a subtle sneer. "We have heard your demands for the return of your Mystics. I assure you, if we had innocent captives in our hands, we would return them to you unharmed. Look to the marauders in our sky, Earth Fleet. If you cannot find your people among them, then I fear it is too late. Our condolences for your loss."

"Our condolences," Barbara mimicked. "Have you heard such a pile of horse pucky in all your life?"

"Can't say I have." Julia replayed the message, focusing on the Pirr's expression rather than the meaningless words spilling from her mouth. She couldn't get a read on the alien. It wasn't surprising, but she was still disappointed. "I'd like to give *her* some condolences."

Barbara made a disgusted noise, probably in agreement. "Give me your stealth Mystic, a fast ship, and a squad of Marines, and I'll show her *piracy.*"

"I'm there with you." Julia locked the screen and offered the datapad back to Barbara. "Too bad we play by the rules around here."

Her friend's nod was sharp. "I'm going to need this a while yet. I've got a few more reports to write."

"Take all the time you need."

When she was alone, Julia went to the galley with its viewscreens to watch the starfield ease past. It was a soothing sight, and it gave her something to concentrate on rather than worry and grieve. She hadn't known the lost Mystics well, yet they were still her people. She didn't hold much hope of rescuing them, but she'd give their memories the respect they were due. One day, when she had the chance, she'd make sure the Pirr regretted what they'd done.

The voyage to Earth went quickly for Jack. He spent much of his time catching up with Ephraim and teaching some of the students how to game. He sold them on it by saying a sharper imagination would help them in the Astral Plane. That was true, but mostly he wanted a way to pass the time that didn't include dwelling on their enemies.

Earth welcomed them with open arms. New Mystics were rare, so getting as many as seven from a single colony was unheard of. Administrator Miller approached Nada and Ephraim, but the two would not be swayed to remain Mystics. Ephraim was shameless when it came to accepting gifts and dinner invitations from the administrators but, in the end, they were unswayed and left the Academy.

On the first morning back on Earth, Jack walked Ingram to the research facility at the Academy and brought him to Isabel's lab. She was bent over an electronic board with a soldering iron. The board was wired to a dark monitor. Every few seconds Isabel glanced up at the screen, cursed under her breath, then went back to work.

Jack cleared his throat. "Hey, Izzy."

She jumped, and the tip of her iron scored a burnt path over the surface of the green board. She pushed her safety goggles on top of her head as she turned around. Her frown transformed into a brilliant smile the moment she saw Jack.

"You're home! I heard about the pirates. I was so worried. How do you feel? Does extending yourself like that feel any different than using your abilities normally? Tell me everything!" She seized his sleeve to pull him toward his usual seat, then stopped when she noticed his companion.

Ingram smiled. "You must be Isabel. I'm Ingram."

"Hello." Isabel blinked and looked Ingram over, taking note of his lack of uniform or even an ID badge. She looked at Jack. "I'm sorry, but this is a secure area, Jack."

"Don't worry. I have clearance from the Secret Council. Ingram here is from Geneva, and we think the ancient tech they found there might be linked to the doodad from Amadeus." Jack glanced at Ingram. "He's figured out how a few of them work."

"They thought I might be of help with the other artifact you found. I agreed to take a look," Ingram said modestly. "I hope you don't mind."

"Why would I mind?" Isabel smiled, but her voice was half an octave higher and her smile a little harder. "I guess the secret is out, we've hit a wall. I'm out of options unless we just try to turn the thing on from a minimum safe distance. If there *is* a minimum safe distance."

She shook Ingram's hand, then spun around to open her wall safe. A moment later, she had the alien artifact held by the tips of her fingers. Her skin didn't so much as brush any of the parts that moved, and she held it so delicately Jack wondered if she thought it was a bomb.

Ingram whistled low and stepped in with his hands linked behind his back. He leaned in close enough to kiss it, moving his head from one end to the other. He straightened after a minute or so and, when he sucked in a breath, Jack realized the man had been holding it.

Isabel's smile had warmed, but she only had eyes for the artifact and Ingram. "What do you think?" She rotated it in her hands, showing him more of the rings that segmented the rod. "Did you find anything like this on Geneva?"

"Not remotely. I mean, the iconography is identical. The matter they used to craft it...let me guess, it looks like ivory but isn't remotely organic? It isn't stone, plastic, or any other synthetic we know of." He spoke quickly as he went, rattling off observations. He brushed Isabel's hands with his fingertips, and she rotated the device another quarter-turn.

"The iconography? Do you agree this is a language?" she asked.

"Without question. Unfortunately, I have no idea what it says. The boss is taking a big sample of the written language to the linguists at Earth Fleet HQ."

"Nice! All Jack could get was a few snapshots."

"In my defense, I was being chased by a psychotic alien," he countered, but the pair were going over the artifact again and speaking in awed murmurs. Technobabble dominated their conversation such that Jack understood one word in three. He gathered they were talking about scanning it without triggering whatever it had been built for.

At first, he simply leaned against the wall and listened, pretending he could follow their conversation. When it became clear that they were neck deep in their geeky pursuits, he sat in his usual chair with his feet propped up on Izzy's worktable. While she'd normally rip him a new one for even looking at her stuff cross-eyed, much less touching it with his dirty shoes, this time she just rolled her eyes before returning to her conversation.

He ignored it and pulled out his datapad. He had work to do, but it wasn't going to get done in Isabel's lab. He began to read instead, just skimming the surface of the words as he listened to them theorize and propose new ways to test the device. He got to his feet and said goodbye.

Isabel waved absently, but Ingram didn't hear him at all. Jack chuckled as he let himself out. If their enthusiasm was matched by their skill, they'd have the thing cracked before the end of the week.

After a long day of submitting reports on Geneva, Jack caught up to his friends at Coraolis and Julia's apartment. Nada and Ephraim were there, along with Ingram and Carter. Everyone but Ingram was sitting at the table, playing a game with spaceships on a board covered in stars.

Curious, Jack helped himself to a plate of nachos and leaned against the counter next to the engineer. Julia whispered with Ephraim, clearly plotting something, while Coraolis and Isabel did the same. Jack cleared his throat, and Nada looked up with a smile.

"We'll be done in a round or so. The bad guys are winning," she said with a wicked smile.

"I told you, we're not evil. We're just more organized than you," Dante claimed, and was met by laughter all around the table.

"Take your time. I'll just eat all the nachos while you strategize." Jack grinned and nudged Ingram. "How did it go today?"

The engineer brightened. "Very well. The linguists are puzzling out the language. They think it may not be a true language in itself. They think it might be more conceptual than that." He pulled out a datapad and pulled up an image.

Jack bent his head to look at the picture. Ingram had zoomed in on two arches. Their lines crossed at one extreme, with another line slashing between them. It could have been anything, especially with the squiggly lines radiating from the half-circles.

"This could be a sun here and another there. But only one is radiant, see? So perhaps the other is the moon." Ingram shrugged and scrolled to the next image. "This is a dragon, of course."

"Yeah, they had these everywhere on Amadeus." Jack only glanced at the screen, then looked again when something caught his eye. "Any idea what any of it means?"

Ingram shook his head and swiped to another picture. "Doctor Nielsen—he is one of our linguists—thinks that this first line is religious in nature. You see that every block of glyphs begins with the same line, exactly. Something so ingrained must have spiritual significance, or so he says."

"What do you think?" Jack accepted the datapad when Ingram handed it over and zoomed in to look at the glyphs more carefully.

"I'm withholding judgment, but it's interesting. It could also be a statement that such-and-such is a law. It could also be the name of an ancient king. Who knows? We may never translate this fully."

"I do love a mystery," Jack mused. "Dragons must have been part of their culture from early on, don't you think? If humans had encountered dragons from the beginning of our civilization, maybe we'd have dragons all over our buildings too."

Ingram chuckled. "That could be. I will keep you updated as we learn more. I may be staying on Earth longer than I thought."

"Any progress with the artifact?" Jack glanced over at the table where Nada was now whispering with Coraolis.

"None. We are trying to borrow some instruments from Yale, but they want to know what we are doing that we need their most delicate instruments. We are negotiating payment that doesn't involve letting them look at the toy."

"What if they don't let you have it? Will you call Harvard?"

Ingram chuckled. "Perhaps. I wish to take it apart, to be honest. That is the best way to know what a thing does, but Isabel won't allow it."

"I'm not sure I'm wild about the idea either." Jack's eyes slid over to Isabel. She was covering her mouth with her hands, as if to hide a smile—or a frown.

"I'm not pushing for it. Maybe when all our other options are exhausted, she'll reconsider."

Dante whooped suddenly, and Coraolis groaned, while Julia and Ephraim broke into laughter.

"Sounds like the game is over." Ingram stowed his device. "I will send you copies of the pictures later, if you like. For now, let's have some fun, eh?"

CHAPTER NINETEEN

One week after he came back to Earth, Jack returned to the *Vaughan*. He shared a bunk with Dante, while Coraolis and Julia took the one next door. Their friends from Geneva continued their work on Earth while the Evolved prepared for a fight.

Jack played the latest newscast on his datapad. He left the sound off this time; the haunted look on the boy's face was bad enough. The ticker at the bottom of the screen summed up what Jack already knew.

Five days before, a squad of pirates had descended on more innocents. The remote and defenseless Iris Colony were mostly farmers. There was no strategic value or an abundancy of resources there, yet the pirates had swooped in, using heavy cannons to destroy the farms and take pot-shots at fleeing colonists. The fields caught fire and, with no one to protect the farmsteads, everything turned to ash in a matter of hours.

Jack's grip tightened on his datapad. It was senseless. People had died, and all he could see was cruelty for its own sake. It had taken two days for the colonists to send a call for help. The rescue ships came, but that wasn't all Earth Fleet was going to do.

The Pirr had to be behind the attack. No one else had the motivation. Few others had the means.

They had no proof, but Earth wasn't taking it on the chin anymore. They were going on the offensive with the four most powerful Mystics in Earth Fleet's arsenal.

He stopped the video and set the datapad on his bunk. He'd watched it enough times; it would only sour his mood to do it again. He left the device behind and set out to find Julia.

He found her in the commune chamber, lying on her back and staring at the ceiling. Jack tapped on the door frame. She welcomed him with a smile and a wave, so he entered and sat on the floor facing her.

"Don't get up for my sake," he said when she sat up. "You look comfortable down there."

"No, if I lay down any longer, I'll fall asleep." She tucked her legs beneath her, then looked into his face, her eyes sharpening. "You watched it again, didn't you? Give yourself a break, Jack."

"I couldn't stop thinking about it. Those people...they didn't deserve that. I can't imagine it *benefited* anyone." Jack rubbed his face, trying to banish the pictures of the burned-out farm. It was about as effective as the last time he'd tried, which was to say not at all.

"I know. They did it to put us off-balance. They wanted to upset us so we'd do something stupid, and it worked."

"What do you mean 'stupid?' We need to defend our people and get justice for the ones it's too late to defend. What's stupid about it?"

Julia's head jerked back; not much, but he knew he'd surprised her.

"As soon as we open fire on a Pirr vessel, it's full-on war. We become the galactic bully. There are other ways to handle this."

"What, for instance? Do nothing and lose a war of attrition?" He was on the edge of shouting, his temper unraveling more with each word. "Let innocent people get hurt?"

"No." She squared her jaw but spoke quietly, making him strain to hear. "We go after the pirates, we get proof of who they're working for. *Then* our cause becomes legitimate. *Then* we go after the Pirr."

"If they don't believe they're the aggressors already, they won't believe any proof we show either. People see what they want. If they need us to be the villains, then we will be."

"I know."

"You *know?*" he asked, incredulous.

"Yes. Strategically, this is a bad idea, but I was the first one to sign up for the mission. I know there will be consequences for this, and we're not going to like them. We could lose allies. Neutral governments might side with the Pirr just to turn a profit."

"We aren't going to lose the Yeti to a bribe," Jack objected.

"Not the Yeti tribes that made the pact with us, no, but there are plenty of tribes that have nothing to do with us, and others that dislike humans on principle."

He shook his head. That didn't feel right; the Pirr had been picking at Earth Fleet for a long time. They'd taken lives and destroyed ships, sometimes for *fun*. No intelligent being would think Earth was the villain. *Would they?*

"I think it's obvious who started this."

She shrugged one shoulder. "I know. And it is. The problem is that this is an official military action. Win or lose, we're attacking based on the blockade, and that the Pirr opened fire on the Vaughan. Will a court recognize those as acts of war?"

"Don't let Captain Crabapple hear you talk like that," he huffed.

"Cranston knows this the same as I do. He's no fool. But don't worry about me. I came in here to blow off steam and complaining about this is part of that steam. We're doing our best, you know? Earth, I mean. I just think this is the wrong move."

"We're taking the chaotic path instead of the lawful one. That doesn't make us wrong," he replied.

"I didn't say *we* were wrong. Earth Fleet would have held out if the government weren't so desperate to do something decisive."

He sighed dramatically. "God save us from election years."

She was surprised into a laugh, and he joined her. The sound of shared humor ate some holes in his bad mood and let some sunlight in. It didn't matter how good an idea the offensive was, anyway. They were going, and the four of them were masters of the Astral Plane. They'd win their battles. They hoped their Earth Fleet counterparts could do the same.

"Well if you came in here looking for an argument, I'm glad I could oblige." She was rewarded with another short burst of laughter. She smiled as she stood and stretched.

"I was hoping you'd make me feel better."

"Next time let me know that from the get-go." She leaned in to ruffle his hair. "Don't worry, Jack. Whether this is a good idea or not, we're going to win this. It's about time things swing in our favor."

"I really hope so," he agreed.

By the time Julia left Jack in the commune chamber, he'd cheered up and gone to stretch his virtual legs in the Astral Plane. Julia, on the other hand, started to feel antsy. She decided to head for the bridge to see what was going on.

Captain McNuggen had transferred to *Vaughan* in time for this mission. The former captain had been promoted and moved to another assignment. Julia couldn't blame Barbara for wanting a piece of this mission; revenge was a powerful motivator. She knew that herself.

She was glad to have a Mystic-friendly captain too. The ships were too small for animosity, too few people for bad feelings or prejudice. Julia had responded to the rare situation by befriending most of the bridge crew. It wasn't the same as being in the captain's chair, yet the nostalgia was nice just the same.

When she stepped onto the bridge, Ensign Taryn flashed her a nervous smile then turned back to the Helm station.

McNuggen stood over Ensign Valentino at Comms. She was frowning. Julia didn't like it when her friend frowned. It usually meant trouble. She reminded herself to address Barbara by her rank while on the bridge, then moved closer, hoping for a look at Valentino's screen.

"How far?" the captain asked.

Valentino, already pale by nature, currently had a complexion best described as *ghostly*. He shook his head. "We could be there in two hours if we diverted course now, captain."

Barbara glared at the screen. Julia shivered as she remembered the bad old days, when her friend held Mystics in contempt. This expression was a lot more hostile, but the flavor was the same.

"Can I intrude, captain? What's going on?"

Barbara looked surprised. She hadn't noticed Julia's arrival on the bridge, and that *wasn't* normal.

"We've intercepted a distress signal," Barbara said.

Julia raised her eyebrows. *That* was why their beloved captain was spitting nails? She peered at the Comms screen again. Relatively speaking, they were close to the source of the signal. Odds were no one else could respond in time.

"The signal is alien in origin. It will take us off our assigned path." Barbara moved to give Julia a better look. She traced a line on the stellar map from *Vaughan* to a blinking dot that approximated the source of the beacon.

"The Presley Nebula is here, Mike." Valentino pointed out the obstacles, and the captain stepped back. Valentino visibly relaxed.

Barbara scowled. "We have an eleven-second stretch that we've identified as the galactic SOS code. Everything else is garbled."

"Gee, that doesn't sound like a trap," Julia observed, a sarcastic edge to her voice.

"You see our problem," McNuggen said.

Julia nodded. They were supposed to be taking the offensive, not waltzing into a trap. Yet unless they could prove it was a trap, they were honor-bound to help.

"Taryn, update our heading to follow the distress signal...but don't go directly through the nebula. Keep your eyes peeled." Barbara went to her station and sat. Thunderclouds still hovered around her eyes. "Ronasuli, gather your team and stand by in the commune. I want the four of you to tell us what's in front of us—pull the curtain aside, as it may be—and show me if we're in for a rescue or a fight."

"Understood."

In the material plane, *Vaughan* soared above asteroids that ranged in size from softballs to the Earth's moon. The warship had to dodge the occasional space rock when it escaped the field, but their sensors gave them enough warning. That was an everyday threat, and one the bridge crew had dealt with a hundred times. They were far more concerned with those they were out to rescue.

In the Astral Plane, Julia and the Evolved stood on the ship's hull, alert for trouble. Julia's senses stretched ahead, seeking the source of the beacon.

"I'm not feeling great about these rocks," Jack muttered to Dante.

"We'll be fine. Taryn isn't going to steer us into an asteroid, I promise," Dante answered. "We could put money on it, you know."

"Yeah, that sounds like a great idea. Either you get money or you don't have to pay out. Very clever," Jack mock-complained. He still sounded off-center to Julia, but she didn't say anything. Maybe this mission would let him burn off some aggression.

"I thought it was."

There was a long pause, and she began to worry that Jack was going to lose his temper. Then he chuckled, and as weak as the sound was, Julia knew he'd be all right.

"Yeah, sure. Just take your scams elsewhere," he parried.

Julia tuned them out and stretched her senses even further. Her Mystic abilities told her about the makeup of the asteroids, but she brushed the information aside. She was looking for the unique composite of alloys and fabricated materials that could only be a spaceship.

A curious pressure brushed against her will, pushing against her seeking mind. She countered gently, confirming her presence. It was alien, but for a moment their contact was mild. She wanted to show that she meant them no harm. They were safe with her. It gave way at her push, soft as a down pillow. She smiled. *That's right. I won't hurt you.*

It lunged so quickly that she missed the transition from confusion to aggression. Icy tendrils whipped her mind, lashing themselves around her sense of self. Something in its façade gave way, and she could sense the abyssal hunger that lurked beneath its surface.

"Oh."

The word escaped Julia's lips in a burst of air. It sounded like she'd been punched in the gut. It felt much worse. Her knees buckled. Dante grabbed her arm to help her stay upright. Coraolis was there a breath later, but she'd already ripped away from the grasping mind.

"What was that?" Coraolis asked.

She grabbed his shoulder hard enough to leave a handprint if they'd been in the flesh. His expression changed the moment their eyes met, and his concerned smile drained away.

"A Wyrm." She pulled all the way into herself, keeping her mind away from the things before them. "It's tearing their ship apart."

She didn't need to read her friends to know their reaction. Not long ago, it had taken dozens of Mystics to fight off the Wyrm swarm at Cavey. They'd had support from dragons and, even then, she'd almost died.

Julia didn't remember much of the fight. Most of her memories of that battle were disjointed. She did remember one thing, and that was their overwhelming hunger. If they were after living people...

"Don't they only exist in the Astral Plane? What could they do to a ship?" Coraolis wondered.

"It must have found a way through. Cor, let Barbara know. Dante, we'll take point. Jack, I need you to stay with *Vaughan.* I don't want to leave the ship unguarded if there are more of those things." She rattled off the instructions, forgetting for the moment that Coraolis and Dante were senior to her, and even Jack technically outranked her.

"Yes, ma'am." Jack snapped off a salute and vanished from sight. Coraolis curled his hands into fists, then released them again. He didn't look happy, but he didn't argue.

"Be careful," he told them.

"We will."

Julia stepped off *Vaughan's* hull and darted forward, homing in on the Wyrm's presence, Dante at her side. As they traveled, they drifted apart. It would be too easy to target them with one attack if they stuck together.

Soon, they found it. Something had torn a messy hole in reality, with strips of solid ether waving around the edges. The curve of a ship's belly showed through the opening against a backdrop of a field of stars. A strip of the hull had been peeled away.

They drew closer for a better look at the ship and the threat. A Wyrm screamed by the hole and dove at the ship. It tore another strip of hull away like paper.

"How do we fight it if it's over there? Can we go through from here?"

The moment the words left her lips, she was wracked with dismay and panic. If her dragon chose to speak, it would be screaming in her ear. As it was, her heart nearly stopped.

"Okay, I get it! It's a bad idea," she snapped, pushing back. Her dragon persisted for a moment, driving its point home, then stopped. She sent a wave of irritation in its direction. "What if we close the rift?"

"I need to be physically inside the rift to do that. If you and the others distract the Wyrm, I'll take a spacewalk."

Julia stood at Captain McNuggen's side as *Vaughan* drew near the ship in distress. She gripped the back of the captain's chair as the viewscreen switched from a tactical display of the area to a live image of the damaged ship and the attacking Wyrm.

Wyrms had been a terrible sight in the Astral Plane. In the physical world, it was a nightmare come to life. Black scales covered its sinuous body, and its ragged wings had more in common with a spider's web than anything meant to fly.

It made a leisurely circuit around the ship, jaws agape in a reptilian grin before it dipped closer to rip away another shred of the ship.

"It's playing with them." Julia narrowed her eyes at the beast. She could sense its malicious glee, even without actively using her powers.

"Shuttle One is away," Valentino announced.

Julia felt a flutter of worry. Dante and Jack were on that shuttle. She dismissed any thoughts of them, though, and focused on her own role. She moved to the empty jump seat and strapped herself in.

"Wait. That's a Pirr vessel," McNuggen breathed.

"Are you sure?" Julia asked.

"I'm sure. I recognize the design, but I don't see any weapons. It must be a civilian ship."

"Or they have a weapon design we don't recognize," Valentino said.

"Do I turn us around, captain?" Taryn was already reaching for the controls but stopped short of taking action.

The bridge crew fell silent, the only sound was from their workstations. Julia's attention snapped to the captain. Barbara seemed hypnotized by the viewscreen, where the Wyrm was taking another lap around the Pirr vessel.

"Continue with our mission." Barbara's voice was flat. "Escher, lock on the Wyrm and fire on my order. Taryn, I want to pass by that ship so close the Pirr could shave their chins on our hull. We draw them off, and we keep it away from that hole."

Everyone responded with an 'aye,' but Julia could tell the weight on their shoulders. She felt the same. They had to deal with the Wyrm before it did more damage. They had to seal the hole into the Astral Plane.

Her feelings about the Pirr weren't so clear-cut. *Vaughan* had been on its way to start a war with the Pirr, after all. As much as she disapproved of that plan, she believed the Wyrms were the greater enemy. Julia was glad the decision to help the Pirr wasn't hers to make.

Dante held very still as Technician Wyss went over his EVA suit, double-checking the seals.

The HUD lit up when Dante lifted his chin. It showed his oxygen supply and his vitals, which included a heart rate that was a lot higher than normal. He tried to calm himself, and his oxygen went down a tick.

Anyone who flew with Earth Fleet had to have a basic knowledge of EVA suits, just to meet basic safety regulations. He'd been trained on how to get into a spacesuit quickly enough to survive. He'd passed his EVA practical exam with flying colors, but that had been with his trainers close by, ready to save his ass if something went wrong.

This was his first spacewalk where he didn't have that safety net, not to mention the Wyrm hanging around outside.

He was completely on his own.

Wyss pronounced him ready, and Dante took one last look at Jack. His friend was deep in a trance, hiding them all from detection. They'd already wished each other luck, so he walked into the airlock and cycled it closed.

Outside the shuttle, he was bathed in a rancid orange light mottled with neon blue that spilled from the rift. This close, he could sense the difference between this rift and the one he'd made at Cavey. The one he'd made had been a surgical cut. Whatever made this hole was to his ritual what a claw hammer was to a scalpel.

He peered into the gap as he gathered himself, trying for a glimpse of Coraolis. Plan B was to lure the Wyrm into the Astral Plane with Cor's lightning and fight it there. Dante couldn't see him. Maybe that was for the best. He saluted the hole anyway, figuring Cor could see him, and pushed off from the shuttle's hull. He was surrounded in blazing orange and blue light that closed around him as he left the physical world behind.

Vaughan wove through the asteroid field at high speed, keeping ahead of the Wyrm through luck and Taryn's quick reflexes as much as anything Julia could do. She kept her eyes squeezed shut, focusing on the ravenous thing threatening to bite them in half.

Triumph. It reared back, ready to attack. Julia gathered her strength and *shoved* with her mind. The Wyrm flinched. As planned, a rogue asteroid slammed into its side. They gained another ship length, and Julia slumped into her seat. She had five minutes, tops, before she'd have to do that again.

"Shuttle One reports, Mystic First Class Dante is away," Valentino announced, and the room erupted in cheers.

Julia smiled tiredly, but she wasn't ready to celebrate. Plan B was looking less feasible every moment. Her strength waned, and Jack would be exhausted from cloaking the shuttle. She didn't know where Dante would come out when the rift was sealed. That left Coraolis. As strong as he was, she wasn't sure he could take on a Wyrm by himself.

"Come on, Dante," she whispered. "We're counting on you."

CHAPTER TWENTY

Khiann sat in her quarters, her ears quivering as she watched the captured human transmission for the third time. A motley collection of gunships swept low over a field, crisscrossing it with lasers and blowing the shelters into a thousand flaming pieces. Humans sprinted for nearby woods with small ones in their arms.

The video ended there, but she could draw her own conclusions. She ignored the well-coifed human talking into the camera. They were blaming the Pirr; she wasn't surprised. The problem was that Khiann recognized the pirate fleet, and *she* blamed the Pirr as well.

They'd made a liar of her. She hissed under her breath. They'd murdered civilians with no strategic value. It hadn't been done on her order, but those pirates were entirely under her government's command. She'd been handed a script. She'd read it, as the face of the Pirr, and hadn't questioned it.

She paused the recording and switched back to the message from the High Commander. He looked earnest enough, but there was such glee in his eyes, he might as well have been dancing.

"Message received, Commander Khiann. You spoke well and from the heart. None here question your integrity." He bowed his head slightly. "If the pirates went a step further than their orders, their only crime is enthusiasm for our cause. If they were given an order to do so, which *I* did not give them, they executed their orders with admirable efficiency."

She glared at his smug expression.

"If you challenge the honesty of your superiors, that would be a conversation best had here on *Hoi.* I look forward to your next report."

There was a crack as her grip tensed. The screen shattered, and the device died in her hands, broken pieces jabbing into her palms. She flung it aside and started to pluck out the broken pieces, snarling at every sting and bead of blood.

He was too far away for her to give the answer he deserved. She knew what he'd say if she protested. Humans were without honor and, therefore, she didn't need to treat them with such. She looked at the wreckage of her screen.

She disagreed.

Khiann stood on the command deck, working on her strategies while her crew flew the ship to the border. There were reports of activity they needed to address. If the humans thought to cross *Hoi's* borders, she would teach them better, and she would do it by following her code of honor.

"Commander Xoa, I have a distress signal from the science vessel *Blessed Discovery*, no flag. An encrypted message accompanies the signal." Communications Officer Yelx twisted in his seat to look at her. "Will you take it here or in your quarters?"

Khiann masked her surprise. Any Pirr message should have a designation and be coded appropriately. Only an emergency would excuse the lack of encryption, especially this close to the border. That told her they were desperate for assistance and didn't care about where it came from. They risked much by marrying that unmasked signal to an encrypted message, but that was a concern for the homeworld.

"Play it," she ordered.

A holographic screen appeared above Yelx's station. The image was distorted, but the person on the screen was still identifiable as Pirr. The communication officer's hands flew over the controls, bringing the image and sound into tolerance.

The Pirr stepped back, revealing the midnight blue robes of a scientist. Blood stained his chest, and one arm hung uselessly at his side.

"I am Uil Ixar of *Blessed Discovery*. Two hours ago, we executed our mission. The experiment was a failure. The command deck has been destroyed, many of my people are trapped in their quarters or dead..." He squared his shoulders; the only sign of the pain he was in was a twitch of his left ear. "The charge breached the Astral Plane. The secondary charge had no effect once inserted through the breach. We were preparing another trial when...a Wyrm passed through..."

He was cut off by a metallic screech. He paled visibly. When he spoke again, his words nearly stumbled over themselves in the haste to get out: "It is tearing our ship apart, piece by piece. Project Resurgence is a failure. I request assistance for my crew and staff. The Wyrm is vicious! Mindless! Once it has finished with us, it will be drawn to more civilized worlds. Our coordinates are linked to the distress call."

The message ended abruptly. Khiann brought up the local starmap, and calculated the distance to the *Blessed Discovery*. Four hours. Another search told her that the *Endless* was the only Pirr warship with any hope of arriving in time.

"Set a course for those coordinates and proceed with all speed," she ordered.

"Yes, commander."

Khiann allowed herself a small smile. This mission couldn't come with better timing. This was her chance to do good for her people without getting tangled in questions of honor. This simple rescue mission was all she could have asked for.

Four hours later, Khiann reconsidered the definition of '*simple.*' *Blessed Discovery* was adrift, an alarming number of holes torn into its side. Orange light streamed from a hole in reality, not far from the ship.

The Wyrm was nowhere in sight.

"Hail them."

"Yes, Commander Xoa," Yelx responded. After a moment, he looked over. "They do not answer."

"Keep trying. Hux, scan the area. We must find that Wyrm—"

"Commander, proximity alert!" Hux exclaimed.

"Take evasive action. Use the asteroids for cover!" She assumed it was the Wyrm. The creatures were strong in the Astral Plane, but she had no measure of what this one could do here.

A sleek, gray shape covered the screen. As it passed *Endless*, it turned, revealing the tell-tale markings of an Earth Fleet vessel. The Wyrm followed with its fangs inches from the ship's thrusters. Neither seemed to notice Khiann's ship.

Everyone was silent, their hands hovering over their controls. Khiann took in the broken Pirr vessel, the Wyrm, the humans leading it away from the *Blessed Discovery*. Hairs rose up on the back of her neck. Were they *helping?*

"Five plat says they get caught in the next pass," Hux called out.

Yelx grinned. "I'll take that bet."

"Silence!" Khiann snapped, and they subsided. "What is happening with that breach?"

It seemed smaller than it had been a moment before. The stream of colors dimmed, then faded away, as the hole stitched itself up from within.

"I can't make any sense of these readings," Yelx confessed. "Still no response from *Blessed Discovery*."

"Keep recording. We'll bring it to the scientists back home."

Khiann left the command station and walked up to the screen. The human vessel was just a point of light now, careening along the border of the asteroid field just ahead of the Wyrm. They were gaining; either they had picked up speed or the Wyrm was flagging.

"Get everything you can," she ordered Hux.

"Yes, commander. Should I fire on the humans?"

"And be the ones to start the war? Do you hate your own hide so much, Weapons Specialist Hux?"

"No, commander. I—"

"It's gone." Yelx cut him off. "The rift has closed."

She looked at the screen just in time to see the last tuft of light vanish. A moment later, the Wyrm's scales turned black, then broke away in a trail of ash. The rest of its body followed.

"The humans are signaling us."

Yelx's words jarred her from her thoughts. The human ship was still far enough away that it could have been just another star. It was coming around, but not nearly as fast as it had been running from the Wyrm.

"Open channel." She returned to her post and stood with chin held high. The screen switched to a human woman in Earth Fleet clothing. By the metal pieces on her collar, Khiann identified her as a captain. Her equal, in position only. The female's eyes widened when they lit on Khiann, no doubt recognizing her from her liar's broadcast.

"Pirr vessel, this is Captain Barbara McNuggen of the E.F.S. *Vaughan.* We came here with the intent of helping a ship in distress."

"You are very close to our borders for a peacekeeping mission, Captain McNuggen." Khiann brought up her starmap. "Much farther, and you would be in our territory."

"Earth Fleet doesn't ignore a cry for help, no matter where it comes from, or who gives it." McNuggen's expression didn't change.

"Surely there are beings everywhere in your debt."

McNuggen pursed her lips, tempering her answer. Humans were so transparent.

"We'll leave this area in peace, once we collect our people. Will you allow that?" she asked.

An alert appeared on Khiann's screen. She frowned as she scanned it. This was impossible.

"I must ask you to wait for our answer, captain. Stand by."

She cut off the call, ignoring McNuggen's protests as she brought up the security alert and read it again. An unknown signal was going off in the depths of her ship. Their security measures had blocked it the moment it was detected, but the source continued.

"Yelx, we have a breach. Make sure Security Specialist Ayo is notified. If there's an intruder, I want them brought here. Not to the nearest airlock."

"Yes, commander."

Dante hit the floor hard, and his helmet rang with the impact. He winced as he rolled to the side and levered himself up. Then he frowned. If he was on a ship, it sure wasn't *Vaughan* or the shuttle. He shook his head, trying to clear it, and when he looked up the HUD informed him that his oxygen tank was at fifteen percent. The surrounding atmosphere was breathable, with a little more nitrogen than usual, but he wouldn't choke on it.

He'd done it. He grinned. He'd made it inside the hole in reality and wove it shut. The place where it had been would be nearly impossible to find unless you knew where to look. It was a win, unless he accounted for popping back into the world in an alien place.

It must be the ship they were rescuing. He switched on his communicator.

"Hey, *Vaughan,* this is Mystic First Class Dante. I survived if you can believe it. I think I'm on the space wreck, if you could come and pick me up." He tried the door, and it opened easily. He stepped through, entering an empty hallway lined by plain metal doors. "Tell me you guys made it too, huh?"

There was no answer. He frowned. He felt like he'd only been gone minutes, but his HUD told him otherwise. He'd used six hours of air, but he couldn't be sure why. Maybe time moved faster inside the rifts, or maybe what he did cost him more oxygen than expected. At least he hadn't smothered and wasn't stuck in that in-between place.

The corridor curved gently around as he walked. He wanted to take off his heavy suit, but he didn't know enough about his environment. It could have a virus infecting everyone on board, or a fungus that would take over his brain. There were too many bad scenarios for him to take that gamble.

Vaughan still hadn't answered. He tried to figure out how to amp up the signal, but either that wasn't an option or he wasn't savvy enough— probably the latter. Plus, he was exhausted. His mind wasn't working clearly.

There were electronic panels on the corridor walls, but he had no intent of pushing random buttons. He lingered at one anyway, trying to make sense of the vaguely familiar writing, when a pack of Pirr jogged around the corner.

Dante stepped back, putting up his hands to shield himself. Thankfully, they didn't open fire. They did close in, however.

He backpedaled, looking for a direction to run, but he was encased in fifty pounds of spacesuit. They weren't. The Pirr were on him, binding his hands behind his back and his ankles together. They then dragged him through the halls, their bony hands digging into his armpits. They held him face down with his head so low all he could see was Pirr boots and polished deck.

Dante explored his options, but he was in no state to be creative. He was already going quietly, thanks to his slow reactions. He could let that continue until he knew where he was and who he was dealing with. He was physically overpowered, he couldn't do much about that. If he could leave his body and seek out the others, maybe they could find him.

It was a flimsy hope, though it was better than none. He closed his eyes and relaxed, giving in to the mindset that would carry him into the Astral Plane. Something hit him hard enough to dent his helmet.

"If this body is vacated, it will be sent out the airlock with no suit," one of the Pirr said in heavily-accented English. "You will stay and speak to commander."

Dante looked at the dent in his helmet. The impression was almost deep enough to poke him in the eye. He nodded, then realized they wouldn't see it. The HUD was gone as well.

"Got it," he answered, guessing they couldn't hear him.

Xoa watched the security detail dump the human on the ground, then pry off his helmet. She recognized his facial markings at once. He wasn't the Mystic she'd dueled, but he must be closely related. His face was flushed pink, and it took him a moment to stop gasping.

"What are you doing on my ship, human?" she demanded.

It took him a moment to focus on her. He said something colloquial she couldn't understand, then tried to rise. The detail stepped in, raising their staves to beat him down.

"Stop. Untie him," she ordered.

To their credit, her people didn't hesitate. They removed his restraints and took him out of his spacesuit. The coveralls underneath were soaked with sweat. The human tolerated this with a wary look in his eye.

"Now you may stand, and answer my question." She folded her arms.

He stood up with a clumsiness that spoke of numb limbs from cut off circulation. "So, we meet again. I'm still not giving you anything you want."

Her crew hissed. Khiann raised her hand, and they stopped. It was natural for him to be defensive, but at the moment, her people were in his debt, even if she was the only one who knew it.

"Very well. I will tell you my guess, and you will say if I am correct or not. Surely that will do you no harm." She smiled, showing a hint of her teeth in the human way. Perhaps that would put him at ease. "You are in this place because of a distress call. You are one of the humans Captain McNuggen wishes to collect before she leaves. Am I correct?"

He raised an eyebrow and looked at the Pirr surrounding him. They held their staves up, ready to attack and looking angry at his disrespect.

"Yes."

"When you saw my ship here, you saw the opportunity to damage my people, as you believe we have done to yours."

He snorted. "No."

She frowned. "Then explain, and perhaps I will return you to your people. We are not openly enemies. *Yet.*"

"I was inside the breach. When it closed, it kicked me out."

She smiled. That had the ring of truth. "Did you close it?"

He didn't answer, but she had already deduced the answer. While his strange connection to the dragons was repugnant to her, he had at least used his dark powers for the good of all. He had gone into the hole in the world alone, with no help, and not knowing what would become of him afterward. In doing so, he had saved civilians he had no reason to help. In fact, he had every right to despise the Pirr after the cowardly attack on the colony.

"Very well. We will call your ship. You will be returned to your people. Then you will leave this place, so I may rescue mine."

"How do I know you won't shoot the *Vaughan* as soon as it gets in range?"

"Because I say I will not." She heard her people muttering, but ignored them. Yes, he was questioning her honor, but he believed her people had murdered civilians—and he was right. It was time to make amends and prevent further dishonor.

"Call the human vessel," she ordered Yelx.

He obeyed, and the human captain reappeared. "McNuggen here."

"Captain, one of your Mystics found his way onto my ship. I have every intention of returning him with a few conditions."

Captain McNuggen staggered at the shock of seeing Dante at Khiann's side. She regained composure quickly. "Dante. Are you okay? Are they treating you well?"

"So far, so good. I wouldn't mind coming home, though."

McNuggen nodded, wrinkles forming on her forehead; that seemed to be a sign of deep thought among humans. Khiann gave her the courtesy of waiting until she was finished.

"I'll listen, but I'm not in a position to negotiate on Earth Fleet's behalf. What do you want?"

Khiann's smile deepened. "Understood. First, I ask that you leave this place in peace. Second, carry this message back to your masters. In light of your actions, I declare you an honorable people, and you will be treated as such. My leaders will contact yours to negotiate a lasting peace."

The captain hesitated.

Khiann respected her mistrust, but also noted the sudden look of hope, however fleeting. She understood. If the humans had come to her talking of peace, it would be dismissed as a trick. But she could not argue the humans had acted honorably. They had done a great service for the Pirr when they could have turned their backs. Khiann couldn't let that go unrewarded. When one's actions are honorable, they are treated with honor until they prove they don't deserve it.

"What about the pirates?" McNuggen crossed her arms.

Khiann wished she could tell the truth, but that would only muddy the waters. "Together, we will remove the threat of piracy from the galaxy," she promised.

McNuggen raised her eyebrows, but she nodded. "I accept. We'll send a shuttle for Dante. As soon as he's safely aboard, we will depart. Earth Fleet will expect to hear from your leaders."

"We are agreed." Khiann turned to Dante, who looked like he'd been hit too hard in the head. "You will be escorted to our hangar with your belongings. You are my guest and will be treated as such."

He nodded slowly, still suspicious, but she could see him beginning to believe. She accompanied him to the hangar with a security escort whose main purpose was to carry Dante's gear. He was silent on the walk and took his spacesuit without a word.

When the shuttle from *Vaughan* docked, he turned and looked at Khiann. "Are you serious about this peace?"

"I am. Very much so."

"I thought you considered us graverobbers."

She grimaced. The memory of her failure still rankled. "Your people took a valuable artifact from my people. We will ask for it back as part of the negotiations."

"Can you tell me what it does?"

"No, I cannot." She set her jaw. Many legends surrounded the Key, but only their priests knew the whole truth. Even if she knew the Key's secrets, she could never speak of them to an outsider.

"Was it the reason the dragon watched that planet? To keep your people away from it?" he pressed.

"You would have to ask the dragon."

The shuttle door opened, and a ramp lowered to the deck.

"I guess that's my ride. It was nice seeing you again, since you didn't try to kill me this time."

She held up her hands in the sign of peace. "I swore I would not harm you, and I will not. Safe travels, Mystic First Class Dante."

"Same to you, Khiann. Peace out."

He jogged across the deck and entered the shuttle while she was still puzzling over his strange farewell. By the time the shuttle came to life and rotated while hovering to angle toward space, she decided it was some sort of colloquialism.

"Peace out," she murmured to herself, as the shuttle vanished from sight.

CHAPTER TWENTY-ONE

Peace came so suddenly no one believed it at first. Ambassadors from Earth Fleet met with the Pirr—this time, on equal ground. The human ambassador returned with a treaty that would keep peace with the Pirr for one year. In that time, they and the Pirr would 'work together' to drive the pirates out of business.

After that, both sides agreed they would meet to negotiate a more lasting peace. Both had something the other wanted. It was just a matter of what they were willing to give up to get it.

Coraolis dreaded war. He was an explorer and a teacher, not a soldier, so he was elated by the peace talks. Julia didn't say so, but he witnessed her relief, too, when the treaty was announced.

Now, he had a new role to play; host and peacemaker. He and Julia had received orders the Pirr were sending a pair of representatives to study with human Mystics. Dante and Jack were on their way to *Hoi,* the Pirr homeworld, to do the same. On Earth, Coraolis and Julia were to show the aliens around and make them comfortable.

When the Pirr ship arrived, it approached casually, slowing and lowering itself on a cushion of air. It touched down so lightly not even nearby birds were disturbed. It was curiously built, with an exterior that might have been hewn from solid crystal. The vessel was roughly the same size as an E.F. shuttle, but it had traveled to the Solar System without a mothership or runabout to get it through the wormholes.

Coraolis was fascinated, but he wasn't about to run up to a strange ship. He'd ask for a tour after he became more familiar with their 'exchange students.'

Two figures in black robes stepped off the ship, adjusting their wide hoods to keep their faces in shadow. The ramp retracted into the Pirr vessel as they walked away from it.

He strode to meet them, trying not to stare at their strange ship. The robes concealed most of their physical features, but the aliens were tall by human standards. He was glad he'd gotten a dossier on them both. The male had a square jaw and was named Honia. The female had a scar on her chin and was called Rry. Those were family names, but he'd been told that using first names would be akin to French kissing an HR rep at a job interview.

"Hello there. I'm Mystic First Class Coraolis. This is my partner, M1C Ronasuli. We're your hosts and tour guides for the next six months." He held out his hand to shake.

Rry looked at his hand, then at her counterpart. Honia laced his fingers together.

Julia stepped forward, her own hands at her sides. "We don't know much of your culture, and I'm guessing you don't know ours. Why don't we start with a tour of the Academy, and we can get to know each other?"

Rry's lip curled, but Honia was quick to answer.

"Very well. Let the learning begin."

The trip to the Academy was filled with long silences, punctuated by failed attempts to get a conversation going. The Pirr showed little interest in the electric train, nor the hydroelectric plant they passed on the way to the city. They didn't offer insight into what they used for power on Hoi.

Coraolis was used to running into brick walls when it came to difficult people, but this surprised him. He thought they were here to learn from each other. He tried to put it down to galactic space lag and culture shock. He still had to counsel himself to be patient.

Once at the Academy, they started with the nature trails, then headed into campus to show them the buildings. Julia took the lead; she'd taken to teaching, and her pride in the Academy was infectious.

"That's the Landon Center, where we have academic courses that aren't directly related to Mystics. We get professors from local universities to teach electives like comparative literature or computer programming."

Rry made a humming noise Coraolis was starting to associate with disapproval. She was looking at a group of students sitting in a circle. Two of them were talking animatedly, while the other three ate ice cream cones.

Honia saw them too. "What is that?" he demanded. "Is it food?"

"Junk food, yes. You can't live off it." Julia pointed over at the café. "You can get it in there if you've got student credits."

"How do I obtain these student credits?"

Julia blinked. "For now, I can buy you ice cream if you want it. We will get you your own IDs and meal cards as special ambassadors to the Academy, even though you are still considered students."

"I'll take care of that tomorrow," Coraolis promised.

Julia led them into the nearby café. She ignored the students' stares, and Coraolis followed her lead. The Pirr returned the stares measure for measure, and the human students usually looked away first.

They reached the ice cream counter before it proceeded beyond staring contests. Honia stepped to the front, pressing his hands to the glass as he inspected the options. "Explain this," he snapped at the young man behind the counter.

"You want me to explain ice cream?" The young man looked at Coraolis with an expression that said he wasn't paid enough for this.

Coraolis smiled reassuringly. "It's a frozen dessert we eat for pleasure. Each of these tubs has a different flavor. I'd suggest vanilla for your first time."

Rry hissed. "Vanilla is a term used by humans to denote things that are not interesting or bland. We do not require bland food."

"Okay then. There's strawberry there, or chocolate." He went through each flavor, doing his best to describe them to his guests. He got stuck on coffee until Julia went across the café to get a cup for them to try. They finally settled on fudge ripple for Honia and bubblegum for Rry. Coraolis got a scoop of vanilla.

"We've got game night tonight," Julia reminded him.

"Without Jack and Dante?" he asked, surprised.

"Yes, Isabel wants to try running, and I thought we could show these two some of our culture." She nudged him. "She's bringing her buffalo dip. I couldn't say no."

That sold him. He was about to say so when he saw Honia open his jaws wide and start to take a massive bite out of his ice cream cone.

"Slow down, you'll get brain freeze!"

Rry shook her head, letting the hood fall back from her face. A streak of blue ice cream had smeared on the tip of her nose.

"Brain freeze? You eat foods that do this?"

Honia had paused, but at Rry's question, he went ahead and bit off half his ice cream, cone and all.

"If humans can withstand it, so can I," he declared, while Julia winced in sympathy. Not to be outdone, Rry did the same with her cone. A moment later they were clutching their faces, which were contorted with pain.

"We can't really. That's why I warned you," Coraolis sighed. "It'll pass."

The Pirrs' groans were his only answer, but as he promised, after a few moments they'd recovered. Rry rubbed the bridge of her nose.

"You do that for pleasure?" Honia demanded.

"We don't eat it too fast. It's a guilty pleasure if you take it slowly." Coraolis nibbled at his ice cream slowly. "Like this."

Honia narrowed his eyes at Coraolis and his vanilla cone, then said something to Rry in their own language. She answered him, her voice just as harsh as when she'd spoken English. After a moment, they moved as one, both jamming the rest of their cones into their mouths.

Coraolis's eyes watered in sympathy, but this time, the Pirr seemed to shrug off the pain.

"Your pleasure foods are indeed a pleasant surprise," Honia admitted. "They are sweet and soft, yet they carry a trial of fortitude. Well done."

Julia covered her mouth with both hands, leaving Coraolis to answer. He inclined his head politely. "While I can't take credit myself, I thank you on behalf of the human race and the dairy state."

Their tour of campus devolved into a tour of the small restaurants and cafes on campus. After a while, Coraolis marveled at the amount of food a Pirr could put away. They tried burritos and hot dogs and dismissed them both as 'vanilla.' Pizza was met with approval, as were jalapeno poppers.

Coraolis worried about the state of their stomachs when they finally slowed down and agreed to observe a class. Julia led the way across campus to where her students were waiting.

"This class isn't required, but my students like to put in extra time to keep up with the nats, er, natural born Mystics." She gestured at the metal plating on her own face. "I like to give them every advantage. Being a Mystic is difficult enough. Coming into it as an adult is a challenge unique to itself."

She pulled the classroom door open and tried to wave the Pirr inside. Ten students were waiting. Their chatter stopped the moment they saw Julia and her companions.

"Hey, Instructor Ronasuli," one called out. "Are those the aliens?"

"Cool," someone else chimed in.

"Are these your students?" Honia asked; his voice had the same angry quality it had when Cor had offered him a taste of his vanilla cone.

"Yes. They're Enhanced, like me."

"Enhanced. They were not born with the gift? It was given to them?" Rry asked. "How long has this been going on?"

"A while." Julia stared back at the Pirr. "Why?"

"This is an abomination. You have the gift or you do not. Mortals do not *choose,*" Honia hissed. He strode into the classroom, and the students fell back. "You have stolen the dragon's fire for yourselves. You will all burn."

"Okay, that's enough," Julia snapped. "We're calling off class for today. You two, please understand that while we are your hosts, we are not your doormats. I demand respect for my students and myself."

"So do I," Coraolis added, even though he wasn't sure how wise it was to aggravate intergalactic ambassadors.

"You are representing your people and your culture. You can believe whatever you like, but believe me, if you try to shame me or my students for bettering ourselves, for becoming more *ourselves* than we ever were before, you'll be on the first flight back to Pirr."

The Pirr stared at Julia, their expressions devoid of emotion. Rry said something to Honia in stiff, formal tones. He protested for a moment, but Rry repeated herself. The tone was the same, at least, and Coraolis recognized the syllables the second time around.

When she was finished, Honia bowed low enough to kiss the ground. "I have wronged our hosts. I deeply apologize for my disrespect. If you wish to call for my death, Rry will assist me."

"How about you just apologize and don't do it again," Julia suggested. "I don't need you to bow like that."

"Very well. I will learn in silence. I will save my conclusions for my reports." Honia straightened. He had an angry glint in his eye, but that mostly seemed to be for Rry.

"Have you anything else to show us?" Rry asked.

"Let's find a private place where you can ask whatever questions you can think of," Coraolis said. "Julia, we can meet you at home at six?"

"If you're sure?" she glanced at the Pirr, questions in her eyes.

She was right to be doubtful. They were already proving to be more difficult guests than expected, but at least they backed down when Julia returned fire. He'd just keep that in mind if they acted up again. In the meantime, he wanted to get Julia some time away from the Pirr.

"Go on. We'll be fine," he assured her.

Fine wasn't the word he'd have chosen later but, after a while, the Pirr got the sense of what was appropriate to say to a student and what was not. Demanding to know if they were born Mystics or Enhanced was over the line. Asking if their ancestors had also been Mystics was not only rude, but their motivations were transparent.

Eventually, they subsided and showed some interest in the school itself. He gave them a brief history as they circled campus. They nodded and stopped asking questions when they learned the research center was off-limits. They moved on to interrogate him about the library.

He was tired of answering questions by the time he took them home. He had to wonder just how he was going to get through the next six months. Isabel and Julia were already there, throwing together the last of the refreshments.

Coraolis escorted them to the kitchen table, where books and dice were already laid out. Isabel came over to shake hands, but they ignored her hand the way they had Cor's.

"This is Isabel. She's a technician in the research center," he said.

"A technician? You are not a Mystic?" Honia asked, then held up his hands in peace. "I only seek to understand your role."

"Nope, I'm a mad scientist," Isabel said. She noticed they weren't taking her hand and hid her own in her pockets. "I'd love to get you in my workspace sometime. You're the equivalent of Mystics, right? I'd kill to get some measurements."

Julia cleared her throat. "It's really a shame they don't have security clearance."

"Hey, a girl can dream," Isabel retorted, but the smile never left her face.

"I would know more of these measurements," Rry said, looking at the couch as if she were trying to decide to sit or not. She narrowed her eyes at Isabel. "Why do you have to kill to take a measurement?"

"Sorry! I don't need to kill anyone." Isabel suppressed a chuckle. "Mostly, does your brain work the way a human Mystic's does? Where does your power come from?" she asked. "I need to get someone with medical training on my team. For now I'm working on it from a mechanical perspective."

"Our abilities were granted to us by the ancient Pact," Honia told her. "The lost ones took a piece of their light and imbued the Pirr with it. We were their most loyal servants and their greatest warriors."

"And then I think, I really need a xenoanthropologist," Isabel sighed. "That's a fascinating story. Maybe you could record your myths for me too?"

"Myths?" Rry began to rise from the couch just as she had settled onto it. Honia, seated beside her, tugged her back down and muttered something in her ear. She nodded and crossed her arms. There was no mistaking her offended glare.

"Oh, God, I'm so sorry," Isabel said, her hands flying to her mouth. "My big dumb mouth. I completely respect your beliefs, I'm sorry. I just get in the academic zone and...how about we get some food, and then we can play?"

Rry still looked sour, but Honia perked up at the mention of food. He stood and followed Isabel to the counter where he loaded a pair of plates. He put one in front of Rry, then sat down with his own, having taken a generous helping of pizza and a small dab of buffalo dip. He scooped one bite of dip onto a chip, then shoved the whole thing into his mouth. He froze, then began to chew more rapidly. He put the rest of the dip on a single chip, then made that disappear as well.

Honia then dumped the slices of pizza on the table and went back for more dip. Coraolis followed him, determined to get some for himself before it was gone. Rry tried it for herself and followed Honia's example.

It took a while to get everyone back at the table and settled. Isabel was flattered by their reaction and seemed quite relaxed by the time she handed out the premade character sheets.

"So...this is the game I told you about. You take on a role and pretend to be a hero gathering treasure and defeating monsters." Coraolis grabbed a selection of dice and put them in front of each of the aliens.

Rry looked skeptical. "I *pretend* to be a hero?"

"Regardless of whether you're one in real life, this is a different type of hero," Isabel explained. "Your sheet has numbers that show how good you are at things. For instance, Honia's paladin is very strong, but not very nimble. That's your seventeen strength and ten in dexterity."

"Understood. Higher numbers are better?" Honia asked.

"Yes."

"But this number is low. Taco? No. That is a number at the end. What is this?" Honia poked at his sheet. At least he wasn't expressing every question as a demand anymore.

"Actually, that and your armor class are the things you want to be low. I'll walk you through it when you get to your first combat. So basically, the four of you are in the employ of Lord Veritus, a wealthy nobleman."

"We are not. I do not know this Lord Veritus," Rry snapped, sounding offended yet again.

"This is pretend. I'm not talking about you, I'm talking about your characters." Isabel looked at Coraolis in a plea for help. Coraolis ran a hand through his hair.

"When you say pretend, you mean we lie." Rry sneered at Isabel, who seemed taken aback.

"Think of it as a meditative exercise," Julia suggested.

"No. We will eat the food, but we will not participate in the lies." Rry shoved a pizza slice into her mouth and chewed it viciously. "Go on. Lie, humans. We will observe."

Isabel hesitated, but Julia and Cor told her to go ahead. Coraolis was glad the Pirr were the ones to come up with the suggestion. He was known as a patient man, but even he was feeling ragged by that time. It was strange, having an audience when they played, but eventually, he forgot about the extra eyes on him as he got lost in Isabel's story.

By the time midnight rolled around, they had rescued the king from certain death and brought much honor to their liege lord. They were on their way back to their home when Isabel noticed the time and excused herself. She had to get up early for work.

Rry requested bed as well, and Julia offered to show her the spare room. The Pirr would be staying overnight with them and, in the morning, they would move into their dorm rooms. Honia stayed behind, looking over his character sheet curiously.

"What did you think?" Coraolis asked while gathering dice and stowing them in his bag.

"It was interesting. You create a reality by consensus and narrate events there by your words. It is not true, but you all know this. It doesn't have the taint of a lie." Honia held up his sheet. "I would like to keep this."

"It's all yours. Do you think you'd want to play?"

Honia's ears twitched. "Perhaps. I can see the value as a mental exercise, and it seemed pleasurable. The buffalo dip was wonderful. I would like to have this again."

"Maybe next time, then." Coraolis stood and started to gather the dishes. "I'm going to clean up, so if you want to go to bed, Julia can show you where it is."

Honia stood, but he didn't leave the room. Instead, he joined Coraolis in gathering dirty dishes. He didn't say much, but he asked questions while Coraolis loaded the dishwasher.

"Do you normally do this at home?" Coraolis asked when they finished.

"I clean my own quarters, but we eat communally. Hired servants cook and clean up for us. Your school campus seemed to have a similar setup."

"Well, we don't refer to them as 'servants,' but I see what you mean." Coraolis put in the soap and closed the dishwasher door. "You seem to have some pretty strong feelings about Mystics."

"The gift is central to our culture. Everyone has it, if not all to the same degree. It is our sacred charge." Honia scowled. "Your approach lacks faith."

"I guess it does, at that. We like to know how things work."

"As do we, but we have the guidance of a greater power. Perhaps that is why our technology outstrips your own." Honia sounded thoughtful more than hostile, so Coraolis tried to take his words as they were meant. "Yet, your culinary arts surpass understanding. It may only be that our efforts have advanced in different directions."

Coraolis couldn't help but laugh. "You may just be right about that," he agreed. "Now let me show you the guest room, and we can start again tomorrow."

"That is acceptable." Honia dipped his head in the slightest of bows and allowed Coraolis to show him his room.

CHAPTER TWENTY-TWO

Dante and Jack waited outside the hangar on the E.F.S. Mothership *Pisces*, their bags on the floor next to them. The clock was ticking down to their rendezvous with the Pirr. They'd been waiting on the mothership for three days. Most of the trip out had been spent on a crash-course in diplomacy.

"Nervous?" Jack asked.

Dante nodded. He was still surprised he'd been chosen for this mission, blank slate or not, but the Secret Council had decided that he had a connection with Khiann Xoa. She'd only tried to kill him fifty percent of the time, so maybe they were on to something.

"We'll have a week to get over it, once the Pirr pick us up. Maybe our pilot can give us a few clues on how to act. I get the idea they're all hung up on honor, but that doesn't tell me what their code entails." Dante shifted his weight from one foot to the other. "They got mad when I implied that Xoa might not keep her word."

"That seems obvious, though. There are probably all kinds of minefields we need to avoid that we wouldn't even think of. Like are they going to be mortally offended that I brought them a cheese box?"

"That does sound like a risk. Maybe we'd better eat it before we arrive on Pirr, just to be safe."

Jack grinned. "Do you know what my mom would do to me if I showed up at someone's house without a gift? I'd rather risk the Pirr's wrath."

"You've got a point—" Dante was cut off when the warning siren sounded. He went to the window that overlooked the hangar. A vessel no bigger than an Earth Fleet shuttle landed at the center of the bay. It was bathed in flashing red lights indicating the hangar wasn't pressurized. The Pirr vessel wasn't compatible with the usual airlocks, so they had to partially open the atmospheric shield to let the Pirr fly in.

When the pressure stabilized the red light flashed green, then returned to the usual white light. The Pirr ship didn't react, not even to open a door and let the pilot out.

"Gentlemen. Let's get you on board and on your way."

Captain Fisher had entered the room while they watched the ship land. She took them through the airlock, then escorted them to the ship. There was still no sign of the Pirr within. As the minutes passed, Dante's nerves ratcheted a few notches.

"Okay, is this weird, or is it just me?" he asked, after standing around awkwardly for far too long.

The hatch on the side of the ship hissed, then slid to the side, melding with the rest of the cabin. A short ramp extended from the new opening to the deck.

"Welcome, humans. Please come aboard." The voice came from somewhere near the nose of the ship. It didn't sound exactly like Commander Xoa, but the accent was the same.

Captain Fisher stepped forward. "Welcome, *Night Thorn.* I apologize for not knowing your name, pilot, but you are welcome aboard if you need refreshment or just want to stretch your legs."

"Thank you for your offer of hospitality. It will not be necessary. I am required to convey the humans to *Hoi* with all haste."

Fisher looked to Dante, eyebrows raised. "You're the diplomat here," she said.

"Do you want to come on board?" he offered.

"The passenger limit is two humans. Please do not exceed that number," *Night Thorn* announced.

"I guess we better not push it. Good luck, gentlemen." Captain Fisher shook their hands. "See you in six months."

They grabbed their bags and boarded the Pirr ship. The access hatch took them directly into a small cabin area with a pair of low, comfortable-looking chairs with harnesses. Dante peered into the room beyond. There was no one in sight.

A door slid aside, revealing a compartment for their luggage. Dante put his bag in, followed by Jack's, and the door slid shut again. When they turned away, the door to the outside had closed.

Jack took out his datapad and held it up, recording the room. "First humans on a Pirr ship, and there's no one to greet us. What's your first reaction, M1C Dante?"

"I was already on a Pirr ship once, so let's say, second time in history."

Dante went to the door at the front of the cabin and it slid away as he approached. He stepped into the cockpit, or so he assumed, but the seat was empty. It reminded him of a barber's chair with a few dozen extra buttons and switches. Three screens hung in the air in front of the seat. Two of them closed when he approached, but the third stayed.

"Is that *Pisces?*" Jack was right behind him, still recording. "Did we just take off without knowing it?"

Dante leaned in for a closer look. The ship went on shrinking as he did, making it hard to read the markings, but now they could see the wormhole.

"Who's piloting this thing?" Dante asked out loud. "Where are you?"

Night Thorn spoke, her voice projecting from every angle. "I am."

"Are you the ship?" Dante looked for the Pirr behind the curtain.

"That is correct. My instructions are to rendezvous with two human Mystics at your mothership, then convey you to *Hoi.* A pilot is not necessary for such a simple transport mission."

"Okay." Dante tried to find the next words to say. He'd expected a lot more formality, for one thing. Either this was a giant slight from the aliens, or they were trying to impress the humans with their technology. "I guess I expected a live person."

"If you wish to speak with someone, you may talk to me. I am fluent in English and Pirr, and have studied many human topics of interest." *Night Thorn's* voice sounded a little wounded at first, but by the end of the sentence, she sounded almost hopeful.

This had to be artificial intelligence. More than that, it was an AI with feelings that could be hurt. That was unheard of.

"I'd be honored," Jack spoke up. "We'd be the first humans to have a real conversation with an alien AI. What do you want to talk about?"

At *Night Thorn's* suggestion, they went to the cabin and the guest seats that had been installed just for them. *Thorn* wanted to talk about movies first, then they moved on to musicals. Dante joined in when he could, but mostly he was too off-balance to participate. Jack, on the other hand, was all too happy to talk about his culture.

Dante felt the same wonder, but his stomach had settled down by his knees. This had to be a power play by the Pirr. They were more advanced, and they wanted the humans to know it.

The feeling persisted as *Night Thorn* showed them the facilities, and provided them with a dinner that was close enough to beef and broccoli to fool someone who'd never had takeout. All through the meal and the trip to *Hoi,* the ship was ready to talk about anything at all, as if she were starving for conversation.

By the time they landed, Dante realized that even if the trip was a ploy, the ship herself was lonely. That became clearer at the end of the trip when *Night Thorn* said goodbye and asked them to come and see her if they had time.

Khiann Xoa awaited them when they disembarked. She was out of uniform and wore a loose red toga with a collection of pins to hold it together. She had a long-handled sword on her back, like something out of a fantasy story.

"Greetings, humans. Welcome to *Hoi.*"

"Thank you. That's quite a ship you've got." Jack affixed a smile to his face and offered his hand. Khiann looked at it for a moment, then took it.

"I ordered it to keep you comfortable and entertained. Did it do so?"

"Yes, she was very knowledgeable about our culture. I've never seen anything like it." Dante shook hands as well, then hefted his bag. "It honestly felt like talking to a person sometimes."

"Then it followed my instructions well. If you will come with me, I will show you your quarters."

"That's a nice dress," Jack offered. "Is that your planet-side uniform?"

From the way she stiffened, Dante knew that had been a misstep. He looked over at Jack, who'd seen it too. "I'm sorry, I assumed...I just think it is nice. I didn't mean anything by it."

"Thank you for the compliment, but this is not a uniform. It is simply appropriate dress for a civilian ambassador when greeting dignitaries from another planet."

"Civilian ambassador?" Jack repeated.

"Yes. I am to accompany you in your first days and help you become acquainted with our culture. I am here to answer questions in our exchange of information. I have been authorized to answer any question you might ask."

"Any question?" Dante wasn't sure he believed that. There would be lines—like the one around the artifact they'd found on Amadeus. "This seems like a strange job for a space fleet captain."

"It would be, yes. My path has changed since we last met. You may call me Khiann. Your version of my title is inaccurate, at best."

"I see." They lapsed into silence as she led them through the strangely silent compound. Not a single motor or Pirr-made sound intruded upon the serenity. Even the wildlife tempered their calls and cries. Dante looked for a question to break the weight of silence.

"Can you tell us about your Mystics?"

"We are known as Exalted. All are born with the gift. Those who have it strongly enough are trained for military or government service."

Khiann led them past a building that overlooked the landing zone. It could almost have been a human building—there was only so much one could do with plain walls—but the proportions seemed off.

"Could you do something else, if you wanted to?"

"I had other choices, yes."

"What about everyone else?" Dante asked. "Do they have a choice?"

"There are always choices, but all who are born owe a debt to the society that raised and protected them. We must repay that debt and more in our lifetime or be remembered in shame. The Exalted have a higher calling, but there is always work for the gifted."

"And the ungifted?"

"They become wards of the Temple and are cared for all of their life."

"So, you isolate anyone who isn't born the right way?" Jack had his datapad out. Dante shook his head at him, but Jack ignored it. "That seems a little harsh."

"They are honored in their own way."

Jack frowned, clearly suspicious. "I'd like to meet one of these Temple wards..."

"What about the artifact from Amadeus?" Dante interrupted. "You wanted it so badly you tried to kill me. Why?"

"That was my mission. I no longer wish to harm you, if that is your concern." Khiann stopped walking and turned to face them. "Your people are gentler than mine. Your desire for peace is a weakness, yet your Mystics are stronger. This should not be, but it is."

"Do you just mean the Evolved? The ones who've bonded with dragons?"

Khiann's lip curled back before she smoothed her expression. "No."

"You don't like dragons, do you?" Dante had been watching her closely, and her reaction had happened the moment he mentioned dragons.

"No. We do not *like* dragons. They have been an obstacle to my people through our recorded history. We do not have the strength to confront them."

"That Amadeus dragon was keeping you from the gadget we found." Jack grinned. "Then we came along and talked it into letting us land."

"Yes. That is what happened."

She turned her back and started walking again, her long strides forcing the humans to jog if they wanted to keep up.

"We don't know your ways." Dante was glad he'd started exercising again, but it was still hard to keep up with her. "If we ask something offensive, it's because we don't know."

"The planet you call Amadeus was my first great failure. The second is why I am your host, rather than doing more important tasks."

"What was the other one?" Jack asked.

"I prevented a war."

The Mystics glanced at each other. When Jack and Dante locked eyes, he thought he felt some of Jack's confusion, but it was faint. They didn't have the same bond that Coraolis and Julia did. Dante decided to change the subject, but only by a little.

"Tell us about the artifact. You told me you weren't allowed to before, but you just said you got permission to answer our questions."

"Within my own discretion, yes." She slowed her steps, allowing the Mystics to draw nearer.

Dante wondered again where everyone was, and if he should be worried. Earth didn't expect them back for six months, help would be a long time coming if they needed it. "Why did you try to kill me for your artifact? It wasn't even yours. That city was empty for longer than humans have been in space. At least. It couldn't be yours." Jack hadn't even broken a sweat, Dante noticed. He was used to running every day.

"It is a sacred treasure of my people. We have been waiting for thousands of years to get it back from *Ixhoi* only to have humans defile the planet and take our treasure from us."

"It's sacred? As in, it has religious significance? Why didn't you just say so?" Jack asked.

"Would it have made a difference if I did?"

"Yes! We make a point of honoring others' beliefs. If you'd said it belonged to your religion and *asked* for it, Cor and I would have handed it over right then and there. There'd be no need for pirates or whatever else you've got up your sleeve."

Khiann stopped to stare at Jack, her face working in a way that made it look as if she were on the verge of either tears or a fit of rage. She produced a small square object and slapped it into Jack's hand.

"This is the key to your rooms. It will guide you."

She began walking away.

"Wait! What did we say?" Dante jogged after her and put a hand on her arm.

She stopped to look at him. "You are trusting fools, you and the rest of your race. You let dragons into your souls, and you would...you have the comprehension of an infant! I cannot believe you got off your own planet without assistance."

Dante stepped back, surprised. Before he could say anything to smooth this over, she spun on her heel and walked away, vanishing into a nearby building.

"I think we made her mad," Jack observed. "Did I miss something?"

Dante shook his head, just as confused as his partner. "No idea. But, as long as we're unsupervised, what do you say we do some exploring?"

Jack grinned. "Buddy, you just read my mind."

CHAPTER TWENTY-THREE

The Pirr settlement consisted of clusters of buildings separated by fields or stands of forest. Jack and Dante chose to go in the opposite direction of the landing field, but soon their steps were pulled a different way. Their dragons whispered to them, but not so much in words.

Jack had a strong feeling of *déjà vu*. The shape of the buildings seemed familiar, but it took the first building with glyphs on it to be sure. The structures resembled those on Amadeus and Geneva. That confirmed the Pirr's claim on the artifact, he supposed, but Khiann's reactions worried him. She should want the treasure back. But when they said they'd support giving it to her, she called them idiots.

"What do you think? Did she get kicked out of the alien navy for making those promises?" Dante asked.

"Seems reasonable. She said something about a title, so I'm guessing they stripped her of her rank, but they could only go so far. She's probably a noble or something like it." Jack held up his datapad, recording each of the buildings as they passed. "Too bad we can't get someone to translate these runes."

"Right now, that's the least of my worries." Dante stopped and grabbed Jack's arm. "Do you hear that?"

Voices. Jack pulled Dante against the wall, then focused. His will covered them both, rendering them invisible. It had proven to be useful more than once, but Jack still didn't understand where it came from, and why the other Mystics didn't have the same ability. Maybe Isabel would eventually find that answer for him.

Two Pirr in military black turned the corner. Their faces were masks of discipline, and their voices were devoid of emotion. Jack tensed when their eyes passed over him and Dante, but neither of the soldiers reacted. He didn't release his death grip on Dante's jacket until the pair vanished from sight and hearing.

"Okay, so not everyone has disappeared," he murmured. "We'll have to be careful."

They kept going in the same direction, but now they paused every dozen steps to listen. Jack cast his senses out, trying to detect their presence, but the effort felt clumsy. He didn't want to warn any Pirr in the area, so he stopped, and went back to following the dragons' guidance.

Their path took them through a dense forest with trees that were as smooth as green twigs and nearly as thin. A winged creature swooped by his head. He ducked, covering himself with his arms. When it didn't come back, he and Dante stood to move on, watching the air above as much as the forest around them.

"How much farther?" Jack asked his dragon out loud.

Dante put a finger to his lips and shook his head. "I think we're close."

Jack paused to listen and realized Dante was right. What he had taken for wind in the trees sounded more like music. There was humming, too, with dozens of voices in harmony. The voices broke into song. Jack couldn't understand the words, but the reverent tone was unmistakable.

Both Mystics crouched low as the forest thinned, urged on by their dragons and their own curiosity. A break in the trees provided them a glimpse of a stone tower rising above the treetops. As they came closer, Jack took in the beautifully intricate carvings on the walls, as if all were created from one solid piece.

They neared the grounds surrounding the tower but didn't break through the treeline. Instead, they crept around the perimeter, following the sound of the voices. Neither Mystic spoke. They were trespassing on a ritual they knew nothing about, but they did know the Pirr were prickly. They couldn't afford to get caught.

The back of the tower came into sight, and they stopped. A balcony jutted out over the courtyard.

An elaborately-dressed Pirr male stood on a dais. Hundreds of aliens were gathered in the courtyard below, their gazes fixed on the robed figure as he chanted. They hummed in time to his words. When he paused, they knelt on the ground in unison.

The priest—he had to be a priest—stepped back. A pair of acolytes appeared from within the tower, dragging a man in Mystic robes between them. He didn't fight but seemed so dazed he couldn't quite get walking right. The priest spoke, exhorting the crowd about something Jack couldn't follow.

"That's Dawkins." Jack knew the man. He'd thought the guy was dead, shot out an airlock or something by the pirates. Instead, he was on the Pirr homeworld, being strapped into a device like a giant sextant.

The priest shouted again. Dark smoke rose from the floor of the balcony, meeting in an arch above Dawkins's head. Instead of rising further, the smoke came together to create a dark cloud over the balcony. Its shape bulged and stretched, growing wings in one place and a long, sinuous tail in another. Claws and a mouth bristling with fangs came into being.

"What does that remind you of?" Dante breathed.

"A Wyrm...no. A dragon. It's kind of both." He looked at Dante. "They're going to kill him."

He was on his feet before he finished speaking, but Dante slammed into him. "Hide us. *Hide us!*" Dante nearly screamed into his ear, and Jack realized they were tumbling into open ground and in plain sight.

He pulled his cloak over them, but when he tried to move again, Dante dragged him up and pushed him against a tree. The thin stems were as strong as steel and held him up against Dante's weight.

The worshipers looked their way. The priest barked orders, and a handful of acolytes who'd been mingling with the crowd rushed toward them. Dante tightened his grip on Jack's shirt. Jack tried to move one more time, but Dante wouldn't allow it.

"We have to stop them," Jack hissed.

"We can't! They'll kill us too. I'm sorry, Jack. We need to find out what they're up to and warn Earth."

The acolytes drew near, and the men fell silent. Jack was tempted to shout at them, give their presence away. He wanted to fight. But Dante was right, as much as he hated it.

The device holding Dawkins lit up, crackling with energy that made the man's skin seem as thin as paper, revealing the shadow of his skeleton underneath. Energy exploded up into the dragon shape, and they swirled together to form a whirlwind made of light and darkness.

Jack's dragon weighed on him. He could sense the danger the whirlwind posed and the intent behind the ritual. It was a weapon, but there was a deeper intent behind its creation. This wasn't just an attack.

He shook his head, trying to clear it, and pulled Dante to his feet. "Come on. We need to warn Earth."

"How are we doing that?"

"First, we'll try *Night Thorn.* She likes me. Maybe she'll boost my signal if I ask nicely. If that doesn't work, I don't know. We'll figure something out."

Far away, on the other side of the galaxy, Julia rolled onto her back and groaned. At first, she thought her alarm was going off, but it was too dark and felt far too early. Then she realized her datapad was blaring its 'urgent message' alarm, and so was Cor's. She sat up and opened the message.

Jack's face filled the screen. "This is M1C Jack Gagnon. This is an emergency message, and I hope it gets to you in time. The Pirr are sending an energy strike toward Earth. I don't know exactly what they're doing, but you need to be alert. And the Pirr on Earth. You need to see what they're up to." He gasped for breath; he must be running. "Move quickly and be safe. Gagnon out."

The screen went dark. Julia looked at Cor. He'd sat up during the message, and he looked extraordinarily pale in the light of her datapad. They didn't need to speak. She set the message to forward while Cor dressed at record speed, and she did the same.

"Where are they?" she asked Coraolis.

"They got a suite in Brinkman Hall." He frowned, then shook his head. "They won't be there."

Julia nodded. If the Pirr were up to something, their student ambassadors were either sacrifices or they were a part of the puzzle. She'd bet on them being complicit. In the week since they'd arrived, they'd asked too many questions about the wrong things. Looking back on it now, she should have known the moment they got too interested in the research facility and Isabel.

"The research facility," she said.

"I'm calling them now." Cor dialed as they rushed out the door, then sprinted down the stairs rather than wait for the elevator. "No answer."

"Campus security isn't answering either. Keep trying."

They burst out the door of their building and sprinted down the street, across to the wall around the campus forest. Julia went straight to the barrier, then turned to look at Cor.

"What are you doing?" he asked. He was already out of breath.

"Give me a boost. You can go around to the gate and get some help."

He hesitated, but instead of arguing, he cupped his hands. She backed up and made a run at him, jumping at the last second to plant her foot in his hands. He lifted her up and she grabbed the top of the wall, then vaulted over it.

"Julia?"

She landed in a crouch on the other side. "I'm fine. Get help!" she shouted then took off.

Despite the darkness, she'd been running in those woods for years. Once she hit a path, she put on more speed. She zipped past a pair of students canoodling on a bench and shouted to them, but didn't stop to see if they understood, or if they would follow.

She set a ground-eating pace and, before long, she reached the open ground of the quad. The streetlamps that ordinarily lit the grounds at night were out, and all of the buildings were dark. Her heart leaped to her throat. She poured on speed, heading straight for the research center.

Julia slowed when she reached its door. Glass crunched beneath her feet. She got low and crept into the building. Someone was shouting up ahead, near a flicker of blue light she couldn't identify.

Her instincts said charge, but she didn't have a weapon, and she was probably outnumbered. She needed to do this the smart way.

She followed the sounds of fighting, which brought her closer to the blue light. Isabel was collapsed on the floor, cradling a broken arm. Ingram was up and swinging a fire extinguisher like a club, but Honia ducked and wove around his attacks as gracefully as a dancer.

Rry was at the safe in the back, trying to break in. The hairs rose on Julia's neck, and she charged. She grabbed a needle nose pliers from a counter as she passed it and flung it at the back of the Pirr spy's head.

It hit dead-center, but all it did was make the alien angry. She whirled around and met Julia's attack. Rry telegraphed every punch, making it easier to dodge, yet she also took every one of Julia's strikes like they were nothing.

"This is a fine way to repay our hospitality! Don't you have any manners on *Hoi?*" Julia huffed, dodging another punch. That time she wasn't quite fast enough. Rry's fist clipped her jaw, sending her spinning.

She landed on the floor but pushed herself up just before Rry's boot came down where her head had been. The Pirr was slowing, but so was Julia, and Ingram was losing his fight. Pretty soon it would be two on one, and she didn't care for those odds.

"Julia!" Coraolis charged into the building, followed by two security guards. One of them tasered Honia from behind. The Pirr went down, twitching. The guard used zip-ties to bind the Pirr's hands, while Ingram turned his fire extinguisher on Rry. He pulled the trigger and white foam hit the alien in the face.

She screeched—it was hard to say if in outrage or pain—and clawed at her eyes as a hand reached between Julia and Ingram and hit her with the other taser. Rry went down, and Julia let herself gulp several breaths of air.

Julia was on the verge of sitting on the floor when she felt the approaching attack. Energy and darkness twisted together, and it was coming directly toward the Academy.

"It's coming," she breathed. She dropped to the floor and let go of her body, leaving the Pirr to the security guards and Ingram. She left her body and soared into the Astral Plane, rising up to meet the threat as it approached.

She sensed it better from there. The attack ripped through the Kuiper belt, narrowly missing Pluto before it screamed toward the inner planets. It left tiny shards of glass and rock in its wake, and she could see that nothing physical would stop it or slow it down.

Coraolis appeared at her side. He grabbed her hand, sharing his strength with hers. Their wills pushed against the cyclone, trying to change its course or unravel its power, but the best they could do was impede it some, as if standing on the seashore trying to hold back the tide.

She pushed harder, squeezing Cor's hand hard enough to cut off circulation. She hardly noticed when the hand came down on her other shoulder. She didn't react at all until Honora shouted in her ear.

"Instructor! We got your message!"

Julia looked back. Her students formed a half-circle behind her. Beyond them, she saw instructors and students from all over the Academy. They'd all come at her summons, no questions asked. Despite the situation, Julia smiled.

"What do we do?" Honora repeated.

"Feed your strength to Coraolis!" she said, turning to address everyone. "Slow it down, get it under your control!"

"Is that possible?" Coraolis asked, sweating.

"Do the best you can. I need a little time." She squeezed his hand and let go as the first of her students put their hand on Cor's shoulder, then another. The power of almost every Mystic at the Academy flowed into Cor, and he wove it into a shield against the energy attack.

Julia darted away, leaving the others on defense. She thought she could sense the attack slowing, but not by much. Not enough to stop it from touching down on Earth.

Coraolis's strength was flagging. Which said a lot, considering all the power feeding into him. It meant all of them were running low. No matter how hard he pushed, no matter what tricks he used to divert the attack, it was implacable.

He needed Julia's strength. He had no idea where she'd gone, and he didn't have the strength to spare to seek her. Something told him to leave her alone, anyway. She knew what she was doing. She *must.*

Then, he spied her, and his concentration fizzled. Coraolis scrambled to put his defense back in order as Julia soared above them all, her hands outstretched toward the ridiculous sparring ball. Her students called it Thunder Ball.

He frowned. What was she doing with it now?

"Oh," someone breathed in his ear.

He glanced at the source of the voice. Julia's prize student, Honora, hovered nearby. She was grinning. It looked like hope.

"What?" he demanded, a little too harshly, but she didn't seem to hear him. Rather, she *whooped* as Julia dove, sending the sphere ahead of her until it crashed into the side of the attack.

The whirlwind writhed, trying to tear itself away. Within moments, it was contained inside the globe. Streaks of blue light and sooty black swirled together, pressing against the inside wall, yet it didn't budge.

"Thunder Ball absorbs all the energy you throw at it. If you touch it, it sucks you in, and only Julia can let you out," Honora breathed. "It's brilliant!"

Julia left the sphere where it was and returned to Coraolis. She was pale and exhausted-looking, but he'd never seen her look so proud. Behind her, the attack raged in its prison, but only kept feeding the power that imprisoned it.

"Thank you, *Thorn.*" Jack hoped his transmission went through. He was sure that was their only shot. Any minute, the Pirr would close in on them, and she'd have no choice but to open her doors for her masters.

When it opened, Dante was there, ready to fight his way out. He didn't want to be taken prisoner, not on Hoi.

Khiann stood at the foot of the ramp, her hands clasped in front of her. She wasn't touching the sword on her back, and there was no sign of any others...yet.

"I'd really rather not get in a swordfight," he told her. Too bad he probably didn't have a choice. He'd just feel better about it if he had a sword of his own.

"I don't believe in genocide."

"What?" Jack peered over Dante's shoulder. "Is she stopping us?"

"I am not. I am here to tell you that while my faith is strong, I don't believe that the Reckoning requires the sacrifice of an entire race. We have behaved dishonorably. I have done what I must to alleviate some of the damage."

"What are you talking about?" Dante asked.

She shook her head. "No time to explain. It is simple. You fooled me into joining you on the Astral Plane, and you struck me down. I do not know what happened after that, but you somehow hijacked my ship."

Jack whistled. "You're going to...lie for us?"

She shook her head. "It is what I would like you to do so that I do not have to lie."

"You could come with us," Dante suggested.

"I cannot." Khiann stepped onto the ramp and took Dante's hand, sliding something onto his forefinger. It was a gleaming blue band that could have been carved from a sapphire, but he could see traces of the circuitry within.

"Night Thorn," Khiann called.

"Yes, Commander Xoa?" the ship responded promptly. "I have assisted the humans, as ordered."

"You will assist them further. You are Dante's ship now, *Thorn.* Keep them safe, and follow their commands."

"What about you?" The ship sounded so forlorn it hurt Dante's heart a little.

"I will be fine. If you stay here with me, you will be grounded for a very long time." Khiann stepped back. "I'll be waiting for you on the Astral Plane."

"Wait," Jack said, as their door started to slide shut. "Khiann, if you meet us on the Astral Plane, we'll tell you all our state secrets!"

She smiled and nodded. "Peace out."

It was easy enough to overpower someone who didn't want to win. She still put up a fight, but her heart wasn't in it, and that let Dante knock her out of the Astral Plane hard enough to render her unconscious on the other side. When he came out of the trance, *Night Thorn* informed them that they had already left the system and were running dark. She would have them on Earth in a week.

Dante dropped into his guest chair and settled in. The trip back felt infinitely longer than the journey to *Hoi,* but at least he had a strange friendship with a spaceship to build. He'd be home soon enough.

CHAPTER
TWENTY-FOUR

"Alzarak the Red flaps his wings, sending most of you flying back in a gale force wind. But Coraolis, thanks to the bonus from your magic sword..."

"Leviathan's Fang," Coraolis supplied.

"Right," Jack agreed. "Leviathan's Fang gives you the extra strength you need to stand against the mighty wind. It's your turn. What do you do?"

"I think he's panicking. He's probably flapping his wings to try and fly away. I'm going to charge right up the middle and finish him off."

"Are you sure? You see smoke coming out of his nostrils. The air around him is starting to distort with heat," Jack warned.

Coraolis grinned at Jack. They'd been playing long enough to know when Jack was bluffing. He shook the twenty-sided die in his hand.

"Is the princess still back there?" he asked.

"Yes."

"Will she still die of a curse if he lives through the night?"

"Yes, if you care about that sort of thing," Jack scoffed.

"Then I'm going for it." Coraolis rolled, and his die bounced across the table. Everyone went silent, watching it ricochet off a rulebook then an empty nacho bowl, until it came to a stop in front of Jack's screen. The number twenty faced up.

"Yes! A natural twenty," Dante said.

Coraolis grinned and grabbed his dice to roll damage. Jack looked at the total and groaned.

"Okay, Hector the Mighty charges straight at the evil dragon. In one mighty blow, he separates its head from his shoulders. There is a bold shout, as if all the gods in existence are cheering your victory. Congratulations, you have saved the kingdom."

The room erupted in cheers. Dante and Julia high-fived Coraolis in turn. Even Jack was grinning; Dante knew he didn't *really* want to kill off their characters. He just liked to present a challenge.

When the celebrations died down, they picked up their drinks and moved to the living room. There was a mess to pick up, but they were still basking in their victory while Jack enjoyed the feeling of a story well told.

"So how much experience was that worth?" Dante asked.

"All the XP. You now have all the XP there is to be had in this world," Jack teased. "But if you really want to know, I'll add it up and message you tomorrow."

"We need to decide what to do with the loot, anyway," Julia pointed out. "I guess we'll have to meet again next week."

"I've got no more epic stories right now. You guys can take your loot and buy castles or start your own temples or something, but I have nothing else for you."

"What about non-epic adventures? We could jump ahead fifty years and play our own grandchildren," Coraolis suggested. "That could be fun."

Jack chuckled and nodded. "Sure, just give me a little time to put something together. Hey, Julia, no electronics at my table please."

"This is my living room," she pointed out, but she put her datapad away. "I wanted to see if there was anything new about the negotiations. It looks like our prisoners are being sent back home."

"Good for them. Honia needs to learn moderation for his junk food consumption and he isn't going to learn it here," Coraolis quipped. "Really, I'm not surprised. It's a relatively small concession, but it'll help them feel better about the loss."

"I don't know. It doesn't seem like they take failure well," Dante mused. "I heard Khiann was involved in the negotiations, but I never see her on the broadcasts anymore."

He hadn't heard from her since they escaped Hoi, but he hoped she was all right. She'd committed treason in the name of doing the right thing. He couldn't imagine the bravery it took to do that.

"They don't trust her to play along with their scheming." Jack took a long drink of his beer. "She was surprisingly decent."

"She was," Dante agreed. "Have we heard anything from the probes?"

"The ones watching the black hole? Nope," Coraolis shook his head. "It's been quiet since we chucked in the Pirr artifact."

"I sure hope a black hole would be enough to destroy it." Jack shuddered a little. "If they weren't going to tell us what it did, it was best that no one have it."

"We couldn't find out the hard way." Coraolis draped his arm across the back of the couch, and Julia leaned into his side.

Dante sat back in his chair, feeling content. Thanks to Jack's determination, Dante was back in the fold, trusted by his friends again. If his smile was a little dopey, he didn't mind, not even when Cor noticed and called him out on it.

"What's going on with you?" he asked, smiling.

Dante shook his head. "Nothing really. I'm just happy to be here with my friends."

"I'll drink to that." Jack raised his glass.

The most powerful Mystics in the galaxy saluted each other and drank as one. Beneath the surface, their four bonded dragons rested in the place between the physical world and the Astral Plane. Their humans would face more challenges in the future but, for now, it was enough to take pride in their hard-fought respite from annihilation.

Humanity would live to see another day.

The End

If you like this book, please leave a review. This is a new series, so the only way I can decide whether to commit more time to it is by getting feedback from you, the readers. Your opinion matters to me. Continue or not? I have only so much time to craft new stories. Help me invest that time wisely. Plus, reviews buoy my spirits and stoke the fires of creativity.

Don't stop now! Keep turning the pages as there's a little more insight and such from the authors.

Author Notes – Valerie Emerson

Written February 19, 2019

Thank you for reading. If you've made it this far, I hope that means you enjoyed the story. Writing the Mystically Engineered series has been a wonderful learning experience for me. I've been making up stories and writing them down for most of my life, and it's all culminated in this project.

The Pirr have surrendered and peace has returned to the galaxy. The Mystics have found an unexpected friend among the enemy and worked through their conflicts. As an avid gamer myself, I enjoyed turning the Mystics into gamers themselves as a way to rebuild their friendships. Many of my own friendships as well as my relationship with my boyfriend were started at the gaming table.

But peace is only temporary, and soon the Mystics will have to face a new threat as more is revealed, including the dragons' history and their connection to the Wyrms. Coraolis, Dante, Julia, and Jack have more adventures coming in Book 3. I've got some exciting developments in store, so I hope you'll join me for it.

A few months ago I teamed up with Craig Martelle on this series. It was a leap of faith for both of us. He'd only seen my short stories, and this has been my first organized foray into writing novels. I feel very fortunate that he took a chance on me, and I'm glad I put myself forward, or else this never would have happened.

Author Notes - Craig Martelle

Written February 19, 2019

You are still reading! Thank you so much. It doesn't get any better than that.

Again a monster thank you to Valerie for her work in making this story come to life. We have been working on this project for a few months now and I'm becoming far more friendly with the characters.

I feel like I should buy them a beer or something, or maybe run a roleplaying game for them. I've game-mastered a few adventures and played in even more. I prefer game mastering, because I get more into the story. It's funny. As a player when I should become fully embroiled, I usually feel like I'm on the outside looking in. I see it from a Marine officer's perspective conducting a tactical battle, planning the strategic support – supplies and support.

Maybe that's me ruining a good game, but I do enjoy the company of other players. Valerie will be going to GaryCon just like me in a couple weeks. I owe her breakfast (at least one) in the delightful Grand Geneva in Lake Geneva, Wisconsin. I don't think we're in any games together, but we'll be there, doing some glad handing and showing the series flag.

I have signed up for two 77 Worlds games, a Traveller game, a Metamorphosis Alpha game, and a Top Secret game. I'll mill about and talk to people outside of game time. It will be an exhausting four days, but I won't miss it for anything.

That's it for now. I'm off to keep writing and working with my co-authors to bring these incredible stories to you.

Peace, fellow humans.

Craig Martelle's other books (listed by series)

- **Terry Henry Walton Chronicles** (co-written with Michael Anderle) – a post-apocalyptic paranormal adventure

- **Gateway to the Universe** (co-written with Justin Sloan & Michael Anderle) – this book transitions the characters from the Terry Henry Walton Chronicles to The Bad Company

- **The Bad Company** (co-written with Michael Anderle) – a military science fiction space opera

- **End Times Alaska** (also available in audio) – a Permuted Press publication – a post-apocalyptic survivalist adventure

- **The Free Trader** – a Young Adult Science Fiction Action Adventure

- **Cygnus Space Opera** – A Young Adult Space Opera (set in the Free Trader universe)

- **Darklanding** (co-written with Scott Moon) – a Space Western

- **Judge, Jury, & Executioner** – a space opera adventure legal thriller

- **Rick Banik** – Spy & Terrorism Action Adventure

- **Become a Successful Indie Author** – a non-fiction work

- **Metamorphosis Alpha** – stories from the world's first science fiction RPG

- **The Expanding Universe** – science fiction anthologies

- **Shadow Vanguard** – a Tom Dublin series

- **Enemy of my Enemy** (co-written with Tim Marquitz) – A galactic alien military space opera

- **Superdreadnought** (co-written with Tim Marquitz) – an AI military space opera

- **Metal Legion** (co-written with Caleb Wachter) – a galactic military sci-fi with mechs

- **End Days** (co-written with E.E. Isherwood) – a post-apocalyptic adventure

- **Mystically Engineered** (co-written with Valerie Emerson) – dragons in space

- **Monster Case Files** (co-written with Kathryn Hearst) – a young-adult cozy mystery series (coming Mar 2019)

If you liked the story, please write a short review for me on Amazon. I greatly appreciate any kind words, even one or two sentences go a long way. The number of reviews an ebook receives greatly improves how well an ebook does on Amazon.

If you liked this story, you might like some of my other books. You can join my mailing list by dropping by my website **www.craigmartelle.com** where you'll always be the first to hear when I put my books on sale. Or if you have any comments, shoot me a note at craig@craigmartelle.com. I am always happy to hear from people who've read my work. I try to answer every email I receive.

Amazon   -
www.amazon.com/author/craigmartelle

BookBub   -
https://www.bookbub.com/authors/craig-
martelle

Facebook   -
www.facebook.com/authorcraigmartelle

My web page – www.craigmartelle.com

Made in the USA
Columbia, SC
21 July 2022

63805620R00200